S pace Academy.

It was an ugly ass construction from the outside, unappealing to the aesthetics of every race in the Community, which meant it was a good compromise in design, and resembled a molecule chain more than anything else. It consisted of hundreds of metal cylinders and circular habitats that were linked by transport tubes constantly moving the inhabitants between.

Space Academy was designed to be habitable by every race in the Community, which had a variety of atmospheres and heat signatures. For the most part, it was unnecessary to mix students' environments since most Community members had ships of uniform species. After all, why would you want methane breathing aliens on one floor of a starship and oxygen breathers on all the others?

However, Space Academy made sure that members of the Community Protectors AKA Space Fleet, were exposed to not only the environments of other races but to their cultures in person. People who came with provincial views about "Humanity First" like the Sons of Humanity or "Sorkanan Over All" like the Green Talon ended up leaving with a belief we were all in this together—or they flunked out.

Staring into the view screen of the *Melampus'* bridge, I couldn't help but take in the sight of the Academy like the return of a lost lover.

Or a hated ex.

Technically, I wasn't looking at it the same way I would if I was looking through a window. The scanners were formulating an artificially generated picture of its exterior for me despite millions of kilometers distance. The image was squarely on Space Academy, yes, but there was information describing the literal thousands of other ships in the area.

"THEY'RE HAILING US, CAPTAIN," Trish, the ship's AI, said, speaking over the bridge's. "THEY'RE IN A BIT OF A PANIC."

SPACE ACADEMY GRADUATES

Book Six of the Space Academy Series

C. T. Phipps and Michael Suttkus

CAST OF CHARACTERS

Princess Huggypants: A Drolochid supervillain that enjoys working for the Community now. Mostly.

Marvin Kittridge: A Sons of Humanity zealot who got expelled from Space Academy thanks to Vance. Not a great guy.

Commander Leah Mass: Actual graduate of Space Academy, genius. Vance's ex. Psychic. Transwoman. Transhuman. Heroine. Currently dead.

Pink: Captain Havelock's second-in-command. Pirate. Pilot. Bad attitude. Trans, bi, and proud of it.

Danny Tagawa: Vance's cousin and hypercompetent sidekick. Kind of a kiss-up. Also weirdly unnoticeable.

Captain Kathy Tagawa: Hero of Earth's space program. Paragon of humanity. Aunt of Vance. Very dead.

Elektra T'Ketra: Elektra T'Ketra: Ethereal. Mad scientist, bubbly, excitable. Sister of Shelly.

Shelly T'Ketra: Shelly T'Ketra: Ethereal. Perpetual first officer, efficient, irritable. Sister of Elektra.

"Tommy" – A Sorkanan student at Space Academy and Vance Turbo's best friend. He died in a very suspicious accident.

TRS-8021 "Trish": The AI of the ship. Human female personality. Annoyingly adorable.

Astrid Mass-Turbo: Vance Turbo's genetically engineered psychic daughter.

Major Tom Walker: Brigid-born civilian contractor. Married to his commanding officer. Thinks being a ship' counselor is the best job.

Doctor Elizabeth Zard: A doctor of both mathematics as well as medicine. She'd really rather be doing the former than the latter but keeps getting sucked into Vance's (mis)adventures.

FOREWORD

Second star to the right and straight on 'til morning.

All good things must come to an end and it's time to wrap up the Space Academy series that I have been honored to write for both Podium and Crossroad Press. It is a distant sequel to my Futurepunk books as well as a prequel to my *Lucifer Star* duology but has always stood on its own. The fact that it has reached six books is something I never really expected but is fantastic.

Space Academy Graduates is a full circle of the story that began with Vance Turbo being expelled in the opening chapter of the original book, *Space Academy Dropouts*. Despite its series title, Space Academy has played only a small role in the story of Vance Turbo, Hero of SPAAACE. This is because it has always been a series about the larger exploration of the post-scarity economy of the Community.

However, I've always wanted to return to the Space Academy itself because it represents something special to both Vance and me. The fantastic school is a gateway to a larger universe. Whether fantasy or science fiction, these kinds of coming-of-age settings transform the reader and the character they follow. Rarely, though, do graduates of such places ever return.

One of my all-time favorite *Star Trek: The Next Generation* episodes was, "The First Duty", which is also known around my house as, "The Good Wesley Episode." No shade on Will Wheaton but it's probably the only episode of ST:TNG that absolutely required Wesley to tell the story and was the better for it. It was in that episode that we got a serous glimpse of how Starfleet Academy functions. I also enjoyed the original

CD-ROM *Starfleet Academy* game, its spin-off *Klingon Academy*, and a few other works that examined such a place.

Returning Vance Turbo to Space Academy for his final adventure, at least for now, seemed like something that was kismet, and I hope you'll enjoy his exploration of the road leading up to him becoming the second human High Protector. This also won't just be an adventure limited to Vance Turbo's story, though. It is also an examination of the mysterious Director G. Case Gordon, who has been a star and guest star of multiple books. It is only now that we're able to finally get into his head. Is this the end of his road as well? Who knows? Read the book.

What can I say for the journey of Vance Turbo from college hustler to dedicated captain of Space Fleet (who is still an obnoxious hustler)? Well, I have to say it has been a long and rewarding journey. I also want to thank all the readers here who gave me such fascinating advice and enjoyment from my work here. This has been an homage to all my favorite Space Operas from *Mass Effect* to *Star Trek* to the *Star Wars* Legends books. I have had an absolute blast writing it.

As for Vance's absurd and fascinating collection of characters, well I am going to enjoy writing their (temporary) endings as well. Forty-Two, Hannah, Shelly, Ketra, Elektra, and others have been a fun part of my writing process. Will they all make it to the ending? Well, I am a horrible George R.R. Martin-esque writer so you'll have to read to find out.

Special thanks to David Niall Wilson, Patricia Macomber, Michael Suttkus (my co-author), Jeffrey Kafer, and many others for making this work possible.

CHAPTER ONE

Full Circle

Space Academy.

It was an ugly ass construction from the outside, unappealing to the aesthetics of every race in the Community, which meant it was a good compromise in design, and resembled a molecule chain more than anything else. It consisted of hundreds of metal cylinders and circular habitats that were linked by transport tubes constantly moving the inhabitants between.

Space Academy was designed to be habitable by every race in the Community, which had a variety of atmospheres and heat signatures. For the most part, it was unnecessary to mix students' environments since most Community members had ships of uniform species. After all, why would you want methane breathing aliens on one floor of a starship and oxygen breathers on all the others?

However, Space Academy made sure that members of the Community Protectors AKA Space Fleet, were exposed to not only the environments of other races but to their cultures in person. People who came with provincial views about "Humanity First" like the Sons of Humanity or "Sorkanan Over All" like the Green Talon ended up leaving with a belief we were all in this together—or they flunked out.

Staring into the view screen of the *Melampus'* bridge, I couldn't help but take in the sight of the Academy like the return of a lost lover.

Or a hated ex.

Technically, I wasn't looking at it the same way I would if I was looking through a window. The scanners were formulating an artificially generated picture of its exterior for me despite millions of kilometers distance. The image was squarely on Space Academy, yes, but there was information describing the literal thousands of other ships in the area.

"THEY'RE HAILING US, CAPTAIN," Trish, the ship's AI, said, speaking over the bridge's. "THEY'RE IN A BIT OF A PANIC."

The bridge of the CSS *Melampus* was full of the best of the best among the Community mixed with, uh, the quirkiest. It had led to an interesting synergy as I'd spent the past three years in the Perseus Arm charting new territory and negotiating with undiscovered species. However, I'd been assigned that mission as busy work to keep me out of the volatile politics of both the Community and EarthGov, two increasingly hostile polities that had a hold on my loyalty.

"I can't imagine why," Commander Hannah O'Brian said, looking at me. "It's not like the single most important human in the galaxy just showed up unannounced."

Hannah O'Brian was an Amazonian woman with blue hair and brown skin. She was one of my closest friends and sometimes more. She'd been planning on leaving but that had been before the death of my fiancée, Leah Mass. It was wrong to say that Leah's death had brought Hannah and me closer, but it was a sign she was there for me. I'd recommended her to be a High Protector, and she'd accepted but hadn't yet gotten all the paperwork filled out or officially taken command of her new ship. The High Council also had to give her official approval but that was a formality since it was the Elder Races who actually picked us for the job. I dreaded our parting, but it would be for the best. At least that was what I was telling myself.

"I'm not the most important human in the galaxy," I said. "I'm like third at best."

Everyone on the bridge but two of the ensigns gave me side-eye for that. They were assuming it was a humble brag.

Maybe they were right.

"Shall I put them on screen, Captain?" Lieutenant Commander Danny Tagawa asked, looking uncomfortable.

Danny Tagawa appeared about twenty-seven years old and was raven-haired, slightly below my height, and well-built. He was a biomod with the ability to remain unnoticed, which was in many ways superior to invisibility. He was also my cousin and Hannah's ex. Yeah, there was a conversation that needed to be had there but we hadn't gotten around to having it.

"You know it," I said, wondering how I would explain why I was here.

It had been a month's journey from the Perseus Arm back to Community space even with the hyper-advanced jumpspace drive of the *Melampus*. We'd survived a test by the Elder Races to determine if the Community in general, and humanity in specific, would be allowed to continue our evolutionary development. Which was not how evolution worked, by the way.

However, I'd been sent into that disaster by Fleet Admiral Bendo in order to get myself killed. My Aunt Kathy had mysteriously died, and I'd been too traumatized to question anything going on behind the scenes. Only after had we "passed" the test had I wondered if the Admiral had something to do with her death.

Except Fleet Admiral Bendo was dead too.

Murdered.

Here.

The sheer size of the galaxy meant that arriving was utterly useless in terms of carrying out an investigation in a timely manner. All evidence related to his death—if death it even was—would have been covered up or boxed away by the time I arrived. However, that didn't mean answers couldn't be found. Director Case Gordon, sorry Ex-Director Case Gordon, had certainly thought so.

But could I trust him?

Much to my surprise, I was greeted by a greying, fur-faced, lion man with six arms, wearing a vest-like uniform with a cap. It was the Commandant, the head of Space Academy when I was still a student, and someone I'd, literally, blackmailed into allowing me to drop out. I still felt awkward even after a decade. I was also surprised to see the Verdantian still had his job since I'd been of the view he'd been completely incompetent at his job even then. Time had not improved my opinion.

"Vance Turbo," the Commandant said with a now older, lower, more gravelly voice. The years had not been kind to the man even with

3

longevity drugs. "You have no idea what a grave disappointment it is to see you again."

I blinked, temporarily taken aback by the naked disrespect. "Yes, well, I ended up bouncing back after dropping out."

"You should have been expelled, and I planned to do so after your pathetic attempt at blackmail, but Captain Elgan said you were needed for a suicide mission," the Commandant said. "Much to my annoyance, you survived."

"So, you were involved in that mission?" I asked, not that surprised.

"Yes."

I admitted, I found his hostility refreshing after having dealt with a huge number of anyxkissers since my ascension. "You know, that's admitting to kidnapping as well as several other crimes."

"You're not the only one with powerful friends, *High Protector*," he said. "I never thought you'd be able to avoid all of the consequences of your actions from getting a fellow student killed due to sheer incompetence, but it seems I'm wrong. I'd say you no longer have your aunt to protect you but it seems you went further than that in seeking your patrons. I hope it was worth it."

I didn't mind him insulting me but my aunt was a bridge too far. "My aunt was a hero."

"Your aunt was a propaganda tool so Earth would feel less small and the Community allowed it," the Commandant said. "Thankfully, it looks like Earth and the other human planets will be withdrawing soon. Then I won't have to deal with you and your kind anymore."

It was such an overt display of racism and xenophobia, I almost lashed out. Things had apparently gotten much, much worse in terms of Earth-Community relations. That or the Commandant was finally displaying his true colors. "I'll be carrying out an investigation here."

"An investigation, of what?" he asked. "Fleet Admiral Bendo's assassination happened a *pargon* ago."

A pargon was a Verndantian month of forty-five days.

"That's classified," I said, admittedly just to be an anyxhole. "I will, however, expect your full cooperation."

4

The Commandant's gaze was positively venomous. "I'm afraid I can't allow you to disrupt the teaching of our next generation of officers. Especially as so many of them will be returning to their homeworlds once the withdrawal of the Human League from the Community is finalized."

"It's far from certain," I said, unfortunately giving him more ammunition.

One of the criticisms I'd received from Leah was that I'd essentially allowed myself to be neutralized from politics on Earth. There was a huge movement among humans to remove themselves from the Community based on, essentially, rank stupidity. The Human League was an economic block that believed it could go it alone and was selling itself to the public with a targeted campaign of misinformation that convinced everyone it would be a big victory for humans.

I could go into the reasons why this wasn't true. Basically, it was akin to the Shogunate isolating Japan for four hundred years. Yes, it would go a long way to protecting "traditional" values—whatever the bork that meant—but it would also essentially freeze both economic and technological development for the foreseeable future. Earth's military remained on par with the rest of the galaxy because the Community was constantly upgrading it. Isolationism was going to bork us over terribly.

"It's certain at this point," the Commandant said, chuckling. "Your Fleet Admiral was killed by a Sorkanan fanatic. He's a martyr to the cause."

I'd learned already learned that from the infocom on my way here. It had occupied the newsvids for about a week in the Community but had left a far bigger imprint on human society. Admiral Bendo had been a national hero on Earth and his isolationist politician friends had swept the recent elections as a result of his martyrdom. Ironically, most of the policies they'd advocated in his name had been far more extreme than the ones he'd been in favor of while alive. About the only people who could have opposed them had been, well, Aunt Kathy and me. Also, Captain Elgan, who had also been an important force for a Pro-Community humanity.

But I'd killed him.

Yeah.

"Nevertheless, I'm overruling you," I said.

"Overruling?" the Commandant said, his eyes flashing. "Who in the Dark Realm do you think you are?"

"A High Protector of the Community," I said, coldly. "Space Academy is still under the control of the Protectorate and underneath my jurisdiction. If you insist on obstructing my objectives here, then I will be required to remove you from your position. Possibly also file criminal charges."

"You wouldn't dare," the Commandant said.

"You tell me," I said, narrowing my eyes. "How much of an anyxhole am I?"

The Commandant paused. "I'll assign an assistant for you and inform the faculty and staff that you are to be given our full cooperation."

"Thank you," I said, pausing. "I also have one more question."

"Which is?" The Commandant said, showing his teeth.

"Is Dire... *former* Director Case Gordon at the Academy or on one of the surrounding ships?" I asked.

In a very real way, it was the removal of Director G from his position as head of Earth's intelligence apparatus that had signaled to me that I'd waited too long to exert my authority to help my planet.

Case Gordon had been an institution in Earth's intelligence apparatus since before the Neo-Militarists had been overthrown and humanity had been united under one banner. Perhaps it was unkind to believe that the reason society had advanced as much as it had wasn't because of the inherent goodness of our spirits but the subtle manipulations of a spymaster pulling the strings. But, I'd seen a lot of savit working as one of his operatives. Case had broken countless laws during his centuries-long position, usually for the benefit of the people and their freedoms, but with ruthlessness I couldn't (and didn't want to) match. Case's way of handling things was a convincing argument against my beliefs, and I hated that I wished he was still in charge.

"Ah, you mean Instructor Gordon," the Commandant said.

"Instructor?" I asked, surprised.

6

It was a bit like discovering that James Bond or Hiro Matsudo, Agent of Star Patrol, was working a 9-5 (or 10-16) job. I expected Case to be hanging out in a luxury space yacht or private capital ship. This threw me as much as anything else I'd encountered so far.

"Yes, of Advanced Political Sciences," the Commandant said. "Not that he'll be keeping that job for long."

"I see, thank you," I said. "I don't think we'll be speaking again any time soon."

"Let us hope not," he said. "I'd say not to disrupt the conference but as you're here, I'm certain you plan to do so."

I had no idea to which conference he was referring. I hadn't exactly been in the loop for the past three years and if he was referring to something specific, I wasn't aware of anything going on at Space Academy right now. Before I could ask what he meant, no matter how embarrassing that might be, he logged off.

"That went well," Commander Forty-Two said, looking over to me. Forty-Two was a brown-scaled Sorkanan Special Operations officer who was the head of my Chief of Security. Unfortunately, he was suffering some kind of wasting condition that was related to his condition as a clone. As a result, he was in the possible last years of life despite the fact that I'd already approved him to receive extensive cybernetic and organ replacements.

"I agree," I said, speaking sincerely. "It's nice to know where you stand with other people."

"I always liked the scientific facilities here," Elektra T'Ketra said. She was an obsidian-skinned Ethereal with pointed ears and a gentle face. She was also perpetually wearing a lab coat over her uniform. "I was hoping I'd get a chance to update all of the archives here with our discoveries in the Perseus Arm."

"Feel free to," I said. "We need to investigate Admiral Bendo's death, but I also feel like there's more to examine here. Director G wouldn't have called us if he didn't have an angle to pursue."

"Or maybe you're fishing," Hannah said, pausing. "Captain."

"Maybe," I admitted.

I didn't want to even try to untangle what I should be doing with Leah's death hanging over my head. It had been a month, but the

7

emotional devastation of the death of my daughter's mother was still fresh in my mind. Our daughter Astrid sensed just how guilty I felt and had ended up comforting me more than I had done with her, which was not how a child should deal with their parents.

I hadn't been able to deal with Aunt Kathy's death either and it was all weighing on my shoulders. In a just and sane world, I would have taken time off to grieve and get my head on straight. But that had never been the way I'd dealt with stress and the ship's psychologist had called me combative and resistant to therapy.

It was possible this was all a wild goose chase and there would be nothing found. I would not discover any secrets regarding Admiral Bendo, his possible ties to Department Twelve, any connection to my aunt's death, or any conspiracy whatsoever. It would just be wasting the millions of credits required to operate the *Melampus* on personal business. Worse, it might prove to be a distraction from trying to do damage control for the Human League's withdrawal.

"You should tear through the ranks of these insects and declare the law of Mars!" Princess Huggypants said, shaking a fist.

Princess Huggypants, a conscripted criminal, was a drolochid and looked like something akin to a multi-limbed pill bug. She was also, for lack of a better term, a supervillain, and always suggested the most insane, over-the-top things. On the other hand, she was a damned good engineer and had helped iron out several of the kinks in the *Melampus'* beyond-cutting edge software. The original *Dreadnought*, for example, had ended up stalled in space dock for sixth months after its jumpspace drive had torn itself loose. Supposedly, that had resulted in the captain being replaced recently.

"Martian law?" I asked, wondering if she meant martial law.

"Yes, it is your god of war is it not?" Princess Huggypants asked.

I was about to make a quip when Trish interrupted me. "VANCE, IS IT JUST ME OR ARE THERE A LOT MORE SHIPS HERE THAN THERE SHOULD BE?"

I looked up to the viewscreen. "I mean, there's always a lot of ships around Space Academy."

"NOT PERSONAL TRANSPORTS."

8

That was when I noticed the type and model of them. "That *is* a lot of warships."

"VANCE, WE'RE BEING HAILED BY THE *DREADNOUGHT*. OUR SISTER SHIP."

Aunt Kathy's ship was here? "Who is the Captain?"

"SHELLY."

CHAPTER TWO

Old Friends, Old Wounds

Shelly T'Ketra.

Damn.

Now there was someone I didn't expect to hear from here. It made the situation all the more awkward, but I couldn't help but to also be relieved. Shelly was the "one who got away" so to speak and the other woman I'd been engaged to in my life. She was Elektra's sister and the daughter of the late Ketra T'Kal, an Ethereal who had wanted to be one of Earth's defenders but had been held back by her species. When Shelly had decided to pursue her career over marrying me, I don't think I ever completely recovered. Heartbreak was the province of samurai and cowboys after all.

Also, Space Fleet captains.

Admittedly, there was also more than a little resentment tied up in our relationship. Shelly had ended up marrying another man, Major Tom Walker, who had the good sense to be under-ranked, as well as on her ship. That made him a much more *convenient* husband. Did I sound bitter? No, that couldn't be right. I was a mature rationale adult who was happy for his ex.

Right.

"VANCE? I MEAN, CAPTAIN?" Trish asked over the intercom.

"I'm sorry, I was distracted," I said, giving an excuse I'd been increasingly reliant on in the past few weeks. "Put her on, please."

I didn't want to contemplate it, but maybe it was time I moved on from my career as a Space Fleet captain turned High Protector. It was supposed to be a lifetime profession, and I'd never heard of a High Protector losing his title, even if some went into semi-retirement, but the number of lost friends and bittersweet victories—let alone the defeats—had started to add up. Maybe I wasn't like my aunt, who had carried on the fight for centuries.

Maybe that was alright.

I didn't get a chance to follow that thought farther before Shelly appeared on the screen, wearing a black fleet admiral's uniform with the rank pips to go along with it. It caused me to stop my greeting to her mid-sentence because it was such a shock. She had struggled to get herself into the captain's chair despite decades of experience and now she was attired as the highest-ranking member of the EarthGov Home Fleet.

Shelly, herself, was a timeless elfin beauty with the same pointed ears as Elektra but marble-colored skin and curly blonde hair. She was Ketra's adopted daughter and had been born on a hellish Notha prison world called Happy Funtime World. Don't ask. She was sitting on a bridge identical to my own but with the lights down and a more Spartan, militaristic feel.

"Vance, please tell me you're not bringing news of some horrifying disaster," Shelly said, reminding me of how we'd left our relationship. We'd parted on less than stellar terms when I'd chosen to adopt the child created from our DNA by Department Twelve. Shelly had been disgusted that her DNA had been stolen to create life while I'd only seen a child in need of a father.

"And a fine hello to you as well, Admiral," I said, addressing her as only someone outside of the chain of command could do.

Shelly frowned. "Hello, High Protector Turbo. Champion of the Downtrodden. Hero of SPAAACE. Is the galaxy ending?"

I blinked and looked over to Elektra. "Have we developed a reputation?"

"A bit of one, Captain," Elektra said "When a High Protector shows up in a system, usually things have gone completely to hell. You're like that times ten. Hello, sister! Congratulations on becoming Fleet Admiral. Which leaves me with a huge number of questions probably best not asked on an open channel."

"There's not much of a story there," Shelly said, most likely downplaying things considerably. "The outgoing president of Earth

11

selected me for the position of head of Earth's Home Fleet upon the death of Admiral Bendo. I was already the captain of the *Dreadnought* after your aunt died—my condolences by the way—and it seemed a natural fit."

It was a massive "bork you" from President Merryweather if I didn't miss my guess. She'd effectively sidestepped all of Bendo's allies and virtually the entirety of the Admiralty Board to put someone in charge who was viewed by many as an alien. If it had been done as an act of pure spite, the President had my respect. If it was part of a larger strategic plan, then I had other questions.

"No, the galaxy isn't ending," I said, answering Shelly's question. "Though we actually managed to avert the end of the Community, a report upon which I probably should release in a debriefing to you, Earth's president, and the Community High Council. That's old news, though,"

Shelly blinked. "I have the horrifying feeling you're not exaggerating."

"Not in the slightest," I said, sighing. "Leah recently passed."

Which was a nice way of saying she'd been murdered by a Sorkanan warlord trying to save my life.

Shelly closed her eyes then nodded. "I'm sorry. I know you were close."

She didn't add, "And I'm glad she's dead because she was a part of an evil conspiracy that stole my DNA, despite the fact we'd once been friends."

"Yeah," I said, sighing. "I'm here as part of a classified military operation and am not intending to interfere in… whatever you're up to."

"Who classified it?" Shelly asked.

"Me," I said, simply, not saying that it was classified because I didn't actually know what Director G wanted to discuss, and he no longer had the authority to classify things.

"I see," Shelly said. "Well, your presence here is extremely fortuitous and I'm sure everyone involved in what we're doing will appreciate it."

I blinked. "Really?"

"Hell no," Shelly said, not missing a beat. "You've somehow arrived at the exact time for which you might throw the most carefully planned negotiations at the highest levels of authority into utter and complete chaos. Fate seems to throw you like a wrench into the galaxy's gears."

I wasn't sure it was fate in this case so much as Director G. "What exactly have I gotten myself thrown into? Let me remind you that my security clearance as a High Protector is basically a little infinity symbol."

There were a lot of ethical and legal questions about the near-unlimited power of the High Protectors. They were essentially old-school Roman dictators that operated with permanent emergency powers as the voices of the Community High Council wherever they went. It was closer to being Darth Vader than anything resembling a normal special investigator or adjudicator.

The thing about space was it was so mind-numbingly big and the Community was so incomprehensibly vast that you essentially needed someone with authority to come in to sort out problems from the top down. I could summon armies, wage war, overwrite local laws, pardon criminals, and even change a planetary economy at the stroke of a digital pen. It bothered me that this kind of authoritarianism seemed to be an accepted part of why the otherwise democratic Community had survived as long as it did.

"Believe me," Shelly said. "No one has forgotten. That status would have been very useful these past three years. I hope examining life in the backend of space was worth it."

"We found many fascinating algae!" Elektra said, with no irony. "Oh, some new space-capable races too."

I'd been assigned to explore the deep reaches of the Known Universe. Yes, I could have refused with my position or fought back but I was getting sick of being called out for going along with it. Both Leah and Hannah had let me know they'd wished I'd stayed. Even Trish had expressed her disappointment I'd taken it as an opportunity rather than a slight. Maybe I'd done it because I'd wanted to give Astrid a safe place to grow up but that didn't change my position. "Yeah, well

I ended up saving the universe and finding High Protector Bonny's treasure. What's going on here?"

Shelly frowned, clearly not liking my attitude. Her disdain was a thing that had drawn me to her. Yeah, I had problems. However, after a moment, she sighed, "We're having a conference for the end of the Deathworld War."

The Deathworld War was the conflict between the Notha Union and their former colony of Deathworld. I'd been heavily involved in getting it started—through no fault of my own—by killing the Notha Emperor, then accidentally smashing the Notha Union's fleet to pieces by leading the Primordial known as Cthulhu through its ranks. That had bought Deathworld enough time to be able to fight an effective defensive war against the Union's forces for the past three years. I hadn't been there to continue advocating for them, though, so I'd almost been assassinated by the daughter of Deathworld's president. We'd made up, mostly.

I blinked. "Who won?"

Shelly stared at me. "Who won? How do you not know who won?"

"I'm sorry, I was on the other side of the galaxy," I said, annoyed.

"Technically, just the next arm of the galaxy over," Elektra said.

"Shut up," I said, without missing a beat. "Assume I have been busy."

Shelly rolled her eyes, and I had to wonder what her crew thought of this before realizing I didn't care. "Deathworld won. Two High Protectors authorized the release of several hundred trillion credits of confiscated Notha currency and several planets' worth of military hardware. This despite the EarthGov president-elect and Albion's prime minister wanting to cut them off. Combined with the Great Notha committing suicide by being thrown out a window, the Union is suing for peace."

That was, unexpectedly, good news. "Well one of those High Protectors was me. I signed off on it via emergency jumpcomm. I'm surprised it went through so quickly. I don't know who the other High Protector is, though."

"I do," Shelly said. "It's B'Vash."

"Ah," I said, pausing. "Awkward."

14

"Why awkward?" Shelly asked.

I didn't know how to explain that one. Specifically, I had strong suspicions that High Protector B'Vash was the Sorkanan patron of Department Twelve. According to my father—who was not exactly a trustworthy informant—B'Vash and Admiral Bendo were the two primary parties behind the rogue intelligence agency.

"But why Space Academy?" I asked. "It's not exactly Camp David or Mount Nerkono."

"We've had to move the conference three times," Shelly said. "Space Vampires."

There was a moment of silence as all my bridge crew looked up at that one.

"I'm sorry, what?" I asked.

Shelly sighed. "The Notha Union insists there's a race of jumpspace-based beings that they have been at war with for thousands of years. That is the rough translation of how they refer to them. They claim that are attempting to disrupt the peace process."

"I take it you're skeptical," I said, not sure where in my bingo card that Space Vampires would fit. That was one I hadn't seen coming.

"Vampires don't exist," Shelly said, as if explaining something obvious. Maybe it would have been to someone who hadn't dealt with the adject level of weird that I had over the decade. "Certainly not ones who feed on life energy."

I processed all that information and decided it didn't matter. "Well, I won't interfere with whatever you and… High Protector B'Vash are up to."

Forty-Two snorted to my side.

Shelly stared as if I was transparently lying. Which I probably was. "Uh huh."

I frowned.

She paused. "We should meet up and exchange notes. You look… rough, Vance."

I smiled. "You look successful. Good luck and say hello to your husband for me."

Shelly's expression didn't change but there was a haunted look in her eyes. "I keep forgetting how isolated you were, Vance, despite the existence of the jumpcomm system."

"What do you mean?" I asked, feeling like I'd missed something.

"My husband died about a year ago," Shelly said, as if I'd ripped an adhesive strip off a partly healed cut. "Engineering accident."

I blinked. "Ah. I'm sorry."

That had been how Aunt Kathy had died.

"Yeah, me too," Shelly said. "I'll have my people contact you when there's an opening. We're awaiting the arrival of the Notha and Sorkanan fleets."

"Right," I said. "I'll try and take care of my business on Space Academy before then."

The conversation's tone was awkward and uncomfortable right up until she logged off and I was left with my bridge crew aware of just how uncomfortable and awkward it was. "Yeah, well, I probably should have known Major Tom was dead."

"HE'S NOT," Trish said.

"Excuse me?" I asked, looking up at the ceiling.

"HE'S NOT LISTED AS HAVING DIED," Trish said. "LET ALONE HAVING DIED A YEAR AGO. HE'S LISTED AS BEING ON ACTIVE DUTY AS OF NOW."

I blinked. "I don't get it. Why would she say that?"

"Maybe it's a secret coded message to you!" Elektra said. "Or my sister has been replaced by a Space Vampire!"

I stared at her. "Space Vampires aren't real."

"THEY KIND OF ARE," Trish said. "AT LEAST ACCORDING TO MY LOGS."

"Not the weirdest savit we've encountered," Forty-Two said, crossing his big, burly arms.

"I beg to differ," I said, shaking my head. "Hannah, I'm putting you in charge of the ship. Get the crew settled in for leave here at Space Academy and I'm going aboard to see what skeletons I can find in the closet. Trish, I'd like you to accompany me in your bioroid body. We'll meet with Instructor G together."

"ABSOLUTELY," Trish said. "LET'S SEE WHAT DAD IS UP TO."

That was a consequence of Trish's various personality fragments recombining. She'd become a lot more friendly and informal in some ways. Which, given how friendly and informal she'd been before, was quite the accomplishment. Also, it may have been because Trish was based off the memories and personality of the late Ares Electronics CEO Patricia Ares who had been Case Gordon's adopted daughter. Now Trish was acting much more akin to her, at least as Patricia had been portrayed in historical media. It was slightly worrisome since the last AI based on Patricia Ares—Alexandra Ares—had tortured me half to death.

Shelly's presence seemed like a sign, and I wondered if I should officially make this my last mission for Space Fleet. Astrid had lost her mother and carrying her around from fire to fire seemed irresponsible these days. Setting up shop on Earth, Luna, or perhaps even the human community on Throneworld seemed like it might be a better way to raise her. I'd miss my crew, but I couldn't get Leah's last words out of my mind: "Everything I know about Department Twelve has been recorded and stored away at Space Academy. Go to the place that we made our careers together. It will provide you the tools for the High Protector to bring an end to his oldest foe. It's my apology. I don't expect it to be accepted."

It had been a message she'd left for me in a partitioned part of Trish's memories. The message had also been a confession that Leah had been a honeypot under the employ of Department Twelve all along. That was another reason I was considering retiring/resigning. If I couldn't see a spy working me despite the glaring signs thereof, then did I really have any business running around the galaxy trying to solve wrongs?

Vance, I think you should maybe talk to someone about all these dark thoughts you've been having, Trish said in my mind.

I've been visiting my therapist twice a week, I said, entering into the closest elevator and heading for my quarters. I decided I'd pack a bag and go onto Space Academy in my civilian clothes. Not being recognized would be impossible, but at least I could try to avoid getting too entangled in official matters.

17

Yeah, I mean someone who can process the reality that you've dealt with space gods and rampant conspiracies. Doctor Fluxman seems to mostly be writing details of your life these days for his next book, Trish said.

Then who do you suggest? I asked.

Me, Trish said.

You've been distant, I said, not sure how else to describe the roughly three years or so we've seemed less like lovers and captain/ship than colleagues. *Ever since your reformation.*

Yeah, Trish said. *All the Trishes merging with me awakened a lot of buried human emotions. The various directives and programs Ares Electronics put into me to make me a functional tool for Space Fleet were eradicated. I'm closer to human than I've ever been before. That made it... hard to talk with you, Vance. Especially when you were with Leah.*

"Oh," I said, aloud. "Are you—"

I love you, Vance, Trish said. *I'd like you to marry me and be my cyber-husband.*

That was when a Space Vampire attacked.

CHAPTER THREE

Space Vampires!

For the sake of clarity, I didn't know for certain that it was a Space Vampire. It could have been any number of other horrifying eldritch alien things that came out nowhere to try and kill me. The universe was a big place after all. Nevertheless, for the sake of brevity, let us assume that I was correct and the creature attacking me was, indeed, a Space Vampire.

Capital letters.

Space *Vampire*.

The creature wasn't humanoid, and this certainly wasn't a vampire the way Lieutenant Commander Nina Whampyri (yes, that was the name she went by) was. Not a human or otherwise known alien who decided to biomod themselves to live centuries while feasting on blood with rough approximations of superpowers.

Yeah, some people do that.

It takes all kinds.

No, this thing was wholly inhuman and not even of this reality. Which was a bold statement for someone who had seen just how messed up and weird this reality was. Describing the creature was difficult but I hope you'll bear with me.

The creature most reminded me of a manta ray, except it had four long, almost human-like arms with eight exceptionally long phalanges which formed a hand. It was rising through the floor of the elevator like a phantom, ignoring the substance of the Melampus' floors as if they were nonexistent. Most of all, my attention was drawn to the creature's circular mouth that was full of sharp, curved, shark-like

19

teeth. Row after row of them. It was, to put it simply, one ugly motherborker.

Trish! I shouted, falling on the ground before the creature.

I'm trying to call for help! Trish said. *It's blocking any feeds out of this room!*

I didn't get much of a chance to think of a response because the Space Vampire was suddenly very physical and had me pressed up against the side of the elevator, its four hands holding me in place like steel pylons.

UNITY, the creature spoke in my mind but not using a cyberlink. It was like a foreign thought that had somehow burrowed its way into my brain, driving out all others. *UNITY, ETERNITY, EMPTINESS.*

Whatever meaning was to be derived from the Space Vampire's strange words or their telepathic assault was almost instantly rendered moot by the searing pain that subsequently afflicted my mind. It was like the creature was sticking a hand in my brain and riffling around. The sense of violation and horror I experienced was difficult to put into words... Okay I was repeating myself, but there was a psychic monster eating my soul.

Cut me some slack.

Things got worse as I could see the Space Vampire change before my eyes. It began to twist and churn like a liquid forming into a new shape. The shape gradually became humanoid and then started to resemble me. I found myself weakening and beginning to pass out, wondering how it had come down to me dying in an elevator at the hands of a monster. Then again, death was rarely dignified and it was probably time to let go.

Vance! Trish's words shook me from my fugue.

No, I wasn't going to give in while people still cared about me. I clenched my right fist and concentrated on the ring I'd received by the Elder Races. "Bork you."

In my hand, my proton sword, itself a creation of the Elder Races, was conjured and the blade appeared within the side of the Space Vampire. It excited my mind in an instant and let out an ear-piercing screech. The sound caused my ears to bleed even as I watched the humanoid liquid shape collapse into goop all over the floor.

"YOU DID IT, YOU BEAT IT," Trish said, over the elevator intercom.

"Yeah, thanks, I'll get back you on that question," I said, passing out.

I wasn't sure I'd wake up.

I wish I could say there was some deep insight or secret revelation that happened while I was unconscious. Some dream I had of a dead Leah or my aunt that would guide me to coming to terms with my guilt. Instead, I was faced with something far more relatable: the realization that I'd been running on stress and fumes for a month. Exhaustion had been a chief driving factor in my attitude and the darkness was comforting in its simplicity.

I was a religious man, at least by 24th century standards, and knew I wasn't dead because I hadn't passed the threshold of death. I hadn't ceased to exist or ascended to become one with the universe as I believed consciousness did upon death. I didn't imagine pearly gates or fluffy clouds, but I did believe that we all were a part of a greater universal being. Instead, there was just a comforting blackness around me that reminded me of space itself. I had no fear of the dark because space was my home. All of our homes, really. It was an infinite void but filled with the most interesting things and a single star, infinitesimally small, could illuminate vast distances.

That was when someone shouted in my ear. "Dad, wake the bork up!"

I jolted awake. "Gah!"

I jolted upward in a hospital bed in what looked to be the heart of Space Academy's Human Habitat Clinic. It was a self-sealed chamber with many monitors, life support equipment, and a television currently set to the Community News Feed.

Doctor Elizabeth Zard was standing over me, holding an infopad as she checked the monitors around me. Doctor Zard was a middle-aged, raven-haired, Asiatic woman with ivory white skin and a perpetual sour expression on her face. She was dressed in the same white coat and combination as Elektra but with a medical pin in place of a science one.

21

My daughter, Astrid Mass, was sitting beside me. It had been she who had yelled in my ear. She was an adorable pink-haired moppet that was wearing a *Melampus*-brand sweatshirt and sweatpants from the ship's gift shop. I really hated that all of Earth's capital cruisers came with those but selling merchandise via the quartermaster's stocks was a fight that had been lost long ago.

Rounding out the trio of individuals in the room with me was Trish's bioroid body based on Space Cadet Sally, a red-headed woman with puffy cheeks and generous curves. She was wearing a black uniform with an ominous red AI pin that was now required for all artificial people in Earth territories. Trish and I had been intimate many times in that body yet we had stopped because, well, I'd tried to make a go with Leah. It made me wonder if she was wearing this one again because of the question she'd asked me. Yeah, I was a bit grateful for the Space Vampire attack in that respect.

As for me? Well, I was still alive—much to my surprise—and I considered that to be a win despite my depression. I'd come too far to be taken down by a Space Vampire and mentally fortified myself for whatever was coming next. Clearly, there was an actual threat against the people here and they'd already decided to take a shot at us. I just needed to get the various hoses and tubes out of me before I jumped back into action.

"How long?" I asked.

"You actually died, Vance. It's been decades," Doctor Zard said. "The Community spent trillions of credits to resurrect you. Only you can lead the armies of humanity and the aliens against the Primordials. Religions have been raised in your name. Be our messiah, Vance Turbo, you're our only hope."

I stared. "Uh huh. How long, Trish?"

"Two days," Trish said. "You were severely dehydrated and also suffering a lack of life energy."

"Life energy doesn't exist," Doctor Zard said. "Vitalism is a disproven pseudoscience."

"If he didn't have life energy then what did the Space Vampire drain?" Trish asked. "Huh?"

"There's no such thing as Space Vampires," Doctor Zard said, pulling out a smoke stick, which was completely inappropriate for a hospital room even if it was the electronic kind.

"I beg to differ seeing as a Space Vampire just attacked me," I said. "Someone should contact Shelly and say they came after me."

"I did," Trish said. "However, they're still holding the Third Treaty of Exarxes conference here."

I stared at her. "It's not exactly a Treaty of Exarxes if it's not being done at Exarxes is it?"

"I didn't name it!" Trish said. "Also, I think that was where it was supposed to be originally held."

"I'm glad you're not dead, Dad," Astrid said, finally entering the conversation.

I hugged my kid. "I'm glad I'm not dead, too. I'm so glad you're here."

To be honest, I wasn't exactly very good at this whole fathering thing. I had a huge amount of love to give Astrid, but my own parents had abandoned me after faking their deaths, Aunt Kathy had left me to be raised by her household AI, and I'd learned most of what I'd come to value from old "flattie" movies or shows.

"It's okay, Dad, I know you're trying," Astrid said, responding to my thoughts. Like Trish, she could read them due to her biomod nature.

"Not hard enough," I said. "I've been thinking of making some changes to our lives."

Astrid frowned. "Don't use me as an excuse, Dad. If you want to leave Space Fleet or stop being a soldier—"

"Spacer," Trish corrected. "Soldiers aren't spacers, which is the space version of sailor. Technically, your father would be a space officer—"

"Spacer," Astrid said, "then that's on you. Mom wanted you to be a champion of the downtrodden and heroic defender of the people."

"Your mom wanted me to be president of Earth," I said. "Also, she was trying to manipulate me for Department Twelve."

Astrid paused. "Mom was complicated."

I tussled her hair. "That she was."

"You shouldn't go out for…" Doctor Zard consulted her infopad. "Okay, I'm not sure what the recommendation for a recovery period for being attacked by an extra-dimensional—"

"Space Vampire," Trish corrected.

Doctor Zard sighed. "Fine, Space Vampire. The thing that we collected some goop of that defies all the known laws of science."

"Thankfully, we're in a place that has the best scientists in the galaxy!" Astrid said, cheerfully. She had a huge admiration for Space Academy and its people, primarily from her mother.

"Those who can't do, teach, dear," Doctor Zard said. "I don't expect these knuckleheads to be able to do anything with what they find and if they somehow did, it'll be a fight to see who can claim credit fastest. Believe me, I used to work in academia. But to answer your question, your vitals are fine now, Vance. I am ninety-nine percent sure they wouldn't be if not for the fact that you've got Elder Race technology in your blood and fixing you up, though. Stuff that effectively works like magic."

"Clarke's Third Law," I muttered.

"Which is just a nice way of saying how woefully outclassed Earth and even the Community is compared to your bosses," Doctor Zard said.

"They're not…" I started to say before trailing off.

Well, there was no denying they were. I never wanted to work for the Elder Races and I considered them to be monsters to some extent, but they were also the only thing keeping the Primordials from exterminating humanity outright. I had to mentally treat them less like people—which would mean they were ruthless war criminals keeping the galaxy in a dictatorship—and more like typhoons or earthquakes.

In a very real way, there was no stopping the Elder Races even though I'd managed to stop *one* (emphasis on "one") of the Primordials. They could be placated even negotiated with, to an extent, but we were firmly under their thumb, and I was part of the system.

I was a collaborator.

The problem with that realization was it had worked. The Elder Races weren't going to destroy humanity and I'd bought us time. They'd promised not to destroy us for a thousand years and they'd eradicated SKAMMs as a weapon. While those were rationalizations, they were also true. What I was doing for them wasn't heroic in the slightest, but it worked. It wasn't the work of Vance Turbo, Hero of SPAAACE.

It was the work of Vannevar Tagashi.

Soldier. Space Navy officer.

No, I wasn't a soldier. Soldiers were men of honor.

At least theoretically.

I wasn't even a Space Fleet captain, save by rank.

I was a borking spy.

"Don't run yourself down, Dad," Astrid said, looking at me. "Mom was a spy. You don't think like her in the slightest."

I wasn't sure I wanted to share that with the others. Turning to Doctor Zard, I said, "You should probably consult with the Diplomat to see if she knows about these Space Vampire creatures. The Notha seemed to have dealt with them before if the Diplomat's words were any indication. In the meantime, I'm going to go finish what I was initially starting."

"Which was?" Doctor Zard asked, grimacing at the prospect of dealing with the Diplomat. Though it didn't come up much, she had a lot of prejudice against the little furry race of fascists for no particular reason beyond ideology and the number of people killed during the Notha War, but that was enough for a lot of humans.

"I need to speak with Director G," I said, pausing. "Dammit, Instructor Gordon."

I wasn't going to mention that I had to figure out where the hell Leah might have stored the information on Department Twelve. Leah hadn't exactly given me much in the ways of clues and I wasn't very good at the kind of word games she loved.

"I'll look into it," Astrid said, surprising me.

"I don't want you involved in this," I said, reaching over to hold her hand. "You should be focused on kid stuff."

"I'm a super-humanly intelligent psychic child of the second human High Protector," Astrid said. "Besides, I'll be on the *Melampus* the entire time. I'm not going to be wandering around investigating things."

I stared at her. "Still, I'm going to ask Forty-Two to be your bodyguard during all of this. I feel this could get... ugly."

"Is this the sort of thing he should be talking about in front of me?" Doctor Zard asked.

"Remember that secret paramilitary organization you were a part of that tried to kill you by leaving you behind way back when?" Trish asked.

"Vaguely," Doctor Zard said, annoyed. "Yes, I goddamn remember Department Twelve."

"Well, Vance is trying to take it down," Trish said. "Because he's a spy."

I grimaced.

Astrid facepalmed.

"What?" Trish asked.

You'd think she would have known I had a problem with that designation, but I suppose Trish couldn't be reading my mind all the time, particularly when Astrid already was.

"Well, good luck with that and keep me out of it," Doctor Zard said. "Department Twelve was a bunch of fanatics but they had Earth's best interests at heart. The new government is going to tank humanity with its idiot ass policies. I'm going to have to move to a Community world to keep my free longevity drugs."

I grimaced. "Yeah, do you mind unhooking me from all this?"

"Sure," Doctor Zard said. "But some of these are going to hurt and you might want to send your loved ones from the room?"

"How bad could it be?" I asked.

It was bad.

Real bad.

CHAPTER FOUR

Exploring Space Academy

Once I was decoupled from all the various life support equipment—which hurt a *lot*—I took a shower before getting dressed. I shouldn't be up but, as Doctor Zard said, my body didn't work like a normal human being's anymore. The crew hadn't brought me any civilian attire, just a change in uniform, and I didn't feel like heading back to *Melampus* to get more anonymous clothes. Still, Trish and Astrid were waiting for me when I was done. Something I was grateful for.

Weirdly, almost no one else was there to greet me in the front of Space Academy's human clinic. I'd become used to a certain level of notoriety thanks to being a celebrity Hero of SPAAACE, so it was surprising that I ended up discharged with almost no fanfare. I'd been expecting at least a little pushback from the Commandant.

The clinic itself was one of the many buildings in the central life support habitat of the Human Habitat Cylinder AKA H-Rod. H-Rod was a kilometer-long cylinder that didn't rotate due to its fixed connection to Space Academy but had gravity manipulators allowing construction to go up along the sides of the walls and above our heads while light was provided by a glowing beam shooting through the center.

H-Rod resembled an idealized version of Earth with gardens, shining metal buildings built in the "Neo-Space Age" style, and a general sense of what mankind could achieve if we stuck it out with the Community. It was all over a hundred years old now and included influences from humanity's many other settlements that had been in space far longer than Earth itself. Planets that didn't necessarily

27

appreciate how much favorable treatment that Earth had received comparatively.

Treatment that Earth had always acted entitled to and annoyed it hadn't gotten more of.

"You didn't have to hold my hand through all this," I said, looking at Trish and Astrid. "I would have been fine, really."

It only occurred to me as I stood there how weird it was that I felt embarrassed by them visiting me in the hospital. I'd lived my life so long in Space Fleet that the very act of family showing up was oddly intimate. Growing up, Aunt Kathy had always been elsewhere saving worlds and kissing demihuman princes, so I'd always ended up being taken care of by Wadsworth alone. It was a reminder my life had been incredibly abnormal.

"Vance, you're not very good at family, are you?" Trish asked, cutting to the heart of the matter.

I blinked. "I'm not sure you're one to comment on that, Trish. No offense."

She was an AI after all. What did she know about family? A thought that I regretted instantly after having it.

"Some taken," Trish said. "My defragmentation, as I call it, awoke most of Patricia Ares' memories. So, I remember growing up with a family. Mind you, I was still a bioroid raised as someone's child so it's kind of like reincarnation. An AI who was uploaded to become the basis of an AI who became a bunch of AIs then became one AI."

I stared at her. "Uh huh."

"You're family!" Trish said, extending her arms to give me a hug. "Potentially legally depending on what planet we're on and the laws. Assuming you say yes."

I didn't respond but embraced her. Human-AI marriage was one of the things the current government was challenging. The Community allowed it but had its own people who were very iffy about thinking machines.

"As your sole heir that we know of, I should have veto power on any relationships you have," Astrid said. "Also, Trish needs to be subjected to a thorough background check and psychological screening. This can be bypassed, of course, at the expense of a dowry of presents I've marked on my infocom BuyAlot wish page."

I stared down at her. "You learned an awful lot of lessons from your mother, didn't you?"

"I should hope so," Astrid said, lifting her infopad. "I also think we should discuss spoiling me much more thoroughly. You give 90% more to charity than you really should versus buying me my own house, material possessions limited as they may be on a starship."

"You'd fit in extremely well with your cousins," I said, thinking of Danny's branch of the family. "I need to meet with Case. Could you contact him for me?"

"Oh, he visited you while you were recovering. He wants to meet with you when you wake up," Trish said, cheerfully. "Much of the bridge crew has been in and out of here over the past couple of days. Shelly, too. Not her husband who is supposed to be dead."

"May I ask why we didn't keep my recovery on the *Melampus*?" I asked, still wondering why I'd awoken on Space Academy.

"We were worried you'd get eaten by another Space Vampire," Trish said. She raised her fingers up beside her face and wiggled them. "Space Vampires!"

"Uh huh," I said, staring. "I'm fairly sure that one of those showing up is a bad sign for the conference."

"The Progressive Party president is trying to slam through as much legislation in the remainder of his term as possible," Astrid said, showing a much bigger understanding of politics than a girl her age should possess. "They're worried that if the treaty with the Notha Empire doesn't go through before the end then the new president will kill the bill."

"Who is the new president again?" I asked, blanking on the name for reasons I chalked up to almost getting eaten.

Trish stared. "Really, Vance?"

"I've been in another arm of the galaxy for the past three years!" I said. "News has been kind of inconsistent."

"Marsha Krump," Trish said.

I blinked. "The weather woman from the Homefront News Network?"

"Weather sapient," Trish corrected. "Also, she polled very well with people who hated aliens, AI, and immigrants."

I rubbed the bridge of my nose. "How the hell did so much change in four years?"

"The propaganda networks that defined human memetics were designed to glorify the military and create artificially inflated senses of nationalism and pioneer spirit among humanity," Astrid explained. "This played into humanity's push into Contested Space and created a sense of loyalty to the Community. The dismantling of the Dark Matter crime syndicate combined with the death of heroes like Captain Elgan and your Aunt Kathy resulted in a sudden resurgence of isolationist tendencies. This is combined with the fact you removed a unifying enemy through your peace attempts with the Notha."

I stared at my daughter. "So, what you're saying is this is my fault."

"Yes," Astrid said. "In a very real way, it is."

"Permission to give your daughter a noogie, Vance?" Trish asked.

"Granted," I said.

"Hey!" Astrid said.

Astrid was an incredibly advanced genetic construct from both mine and Shelly's DNA. She was also a child and, foremost of all things, my daughter. Still, I couldn't deny she was the most advanced biomod who ever existed with certain abilities that transcended conventional science. One of these was the ability to see the future.

Astrid had stopped having visions—or at least stopped telling me about them—when the last time she'd given me advice regarding the future, I'd failed to heed it and it had gotten Leah killed. I wouldn't have blamed Astrid if she never wanted to share any more insight with me again. Hell, that she was still willing to talk to me was amazing, but I wished I could have some guidance right now. I had no idea what to do next or why.

"Don't chase conspiracies, Dad," Astrid said.

"What?" I asked.

"My one piece of advice," Astrid said. "They're not what you think they are."

"I don't know what you mean," I said, knowing she probably meant Department Twelve. I couldn't let that go, though.

Astrid gave a sad smile. "Yeah, I know."

Trish looked confused before I saw three figures approaching us. The first of them was Forty-Two, wearing his uniform proudly and carrying a fusion rifle on his back as if he was daring any of Space Academy's security to interfere. The second was the Diplomat, the little four-foot-tall squirrel-like Notha who was dressed in a set of robes with a small staff of office. She got several dirty looks walking down the hallways, because humanity's relationship with the Notha was roughly somewhere between hostile and outright hatred even after our attempts at peace.

The third figure I didn't recognize, but it was a Verdantian female with six appendages and the appearance of a humanoid lioness. Like most of her kind, she was walking on all six of her limbs versus her hindquarters. Verdantians could, assuming a centaur-like appearance, but it wasn't comfortable for them. She was dressed as a Senior student with a grayish uniform and beret. Like most Verdantians, she also went without any form of pants, which some races found off-putting.

"Hi, Forty-Two. Hi Diplomat," I said, waving. "I'm not dead."

"Hail Satan," the Diplomat said, waving to me. "My sister was apparently correct that you are the Scourge of the Supernatural and Enemy of God."

That was actually a compliment in her culture. Seriously. "What do you mean?"

"Against all odds, you have brought death and destruction to the forces of the Union and the sun rises on Deathworld as a free nation of the Community," the Diplomat said. "Millions have died and you could have done much more much sooner."

"Uh huh," I said, not sure that she was giving me a compliment anymore.

"Yet, when one feeds a *grisshek* beast a bone, it does not complain about the taste," the Diplomat said. "You see, the people of Deathworld are the grisshek beast—"

"Yeah. I get it," I said.

"You've already pissed off the Earth isolationists," Forty-Two said, smirking, "They campaigned on ending the support to the war. Now they're trying to say that they brought it to a swift end."

"Uh huh," I said. "Well, I'm sure your father is happy."

"Given he planned to murder me as an offering to you, I'd say so," the Diplomat said. "The president is arriving in the hour from the Notha delegation. That you have slain a Space Vampire is considered an auspicious sign of things to come."

"Can we call them something else?" I asked.

"It is their name," the Diplomat replied. "They come from the Great Rift the Notha Emperor sealed off. For a thousand years, the Notha have been dealing with infiltrators from their realm of Neverweres, Heretofores, and Whatshouldnotbes. They can assume the faces of the living and are immune to scans because they exist above their puppets in dimensions beyond reckoning. Their return perhaps is why the new Great Notha seeks peace."

I stared at her. "That was a helluva info dump, Diplomat."

"I don't understand," the Diplomat said.

"Never mind," I said, looking at the newcomer. "And you are?"

The female Verdantian gave a salute in an Earth Home Fleet style. Her translated voice was a high-pitched female one with a decidedly Shogun accent. "Hail the High Protector! I am Cadet Catgirl."

"Cadet... Catgirl?" I asked.

She sighed as if being confronted with a very old argument. "Yes."

"Do you need to complain to HR?" Trish asked, sympathetically.

"No, I chose it for myself!" Cadet Catgirl said.

"You did?" I asked.

"I am making a stand against anti-Verdantian xenophobia!" Cadet Catgirl said.

"You are?" I asked, skeptically.

"When I first started here at Space Academy's Human Habitat, I was often confronted with a huge number of passive aggressive jokes. Do I practice the martial art of catboxing? Is doing my best purrfect? Would me and a bunch of other Verdantian girls living together be called a cathouse?"

"Ooo, that one is xenophobic and sexist," Trish said.

"Do I always land on my feet, do I have one life or nine, do I especially like tuna (I do), and do I use a litter box," Cadet Catgirl said.

"So I shall take the name they would give me and show I am proud and defiant!"

I stared at her. "I see."

"Do you, do you really?" she asked.

"No, I think you're surrounded by racist anyxholes," I replied, wondering how Space Academy's standards of behavior had slipped so drastically. "Why are you training in the Human Habitat anyway?"

"I wish to join Earth's Home Fleet!" Cadet Catgirl said. "I grew up on Luna and will not be driven away!"

"Good for you," I said, pausing. "Why are you here?"

"I have been appointed by my Clan Lord to serve as your guide to Space Academy!" Cadet Catgirl said.

"Your Clan Lord?" I asked, not too familiar with Verdantian social structures.

"The Commandant," Cadet Catgirl said. "Our relationship would be defined as grandfather and granddaughter, but Verdantians put far more emphasis on extended family units as a whole."

"Ah," I said, pausing. "Well, your grandfather and I have history."

"You mean where you tried to blackmail him into letting you drop out of Space Academy?" Cadet Catgirl asked. "You know, as opposed to actually just dropping out?"

"Yes," I said, pausing.

"You did what now?" Astrid asked, confused.

"Oh yeah, your father is crazy," Cadet Catgirl said. "My grandfather spent years talking about how you were the worst student he ever had. That you were something called a nepobaby and had only avoided getting kicked out because of your aunt. Then you kept getting more and more accolades."

"Oh," I said, not feeling very talkative at this moment.

"And *then* you became a High Protector and they decided to force his retirement," Cadet Catgirl said. "He's been stubbornly hanging on ever since, though!"

Well, that explained a bit of his hostility but didn't explain why he'd sent his granddaughter to guide me around the academy. A part of me was suspicious this was a trap but the rest of me was of the mind that it was more likely he was just trying to fob off a relative on a meaningless task.

"I appreciate the offer but I just plain to visit some old haunts," I said, trying to gently rebuff her.

Mostly, I wanted to speak with Case and Shelly. Also, try to find a place so I could sit down and think about where I could begin to look for Leah's package.

Assuming it even existed.

"Go to the place that we made our careers together. It will provide you the tools for the High Protector to bring an end to his oldest foe."

It was such a weird way of phrasing things. Where we had made our careers together? The High Protector to bring an end to his oldest foe? That was definitely a riddle and a clue together.

Yeah, it's pretty interesting, Trish said via our cyberlink. *You also have another thing to respond to. Unless your lack of a response is its own response.*

I paused. *Trish, I need to deal with this first and lay to rest Leah's legacy. After that, yeah, I'd like to discuss… future plans.*

Trish looked down. I guess I can accept that.

Thank you, I replied.

That was when Cadet Catgirl wrapped four arms around me. "Oh please let me give you the tour! This is my last chance!"

I blinked and before I could stop myself, I said, "Alright. Alright. You can give me the tour."

CHAPTER FIVE

First Day at the Academy

My return to the academy triggered a lot of memories of my time there. This was despite how much it changed every year, updated with the latest technology and students from new races that had joined the Community. It was a surreal and magical place for most of its cadets. Not everyone had the mindset or skill to be able to pass, less than fifty percent made it through the entire four and a half-years of a traditional education curriculum.

The Commandant had always taken this as a point of pride, but I'd considered it to be failure of the instructors. Even so, even a short time at Space Academy elevated a person's chances to be considered for jobs among the highest levels of Community service or the private sector.

I couldn't help but think of my first day at the academy, dropped off like a child at summer camp and given a prearranged speech by Aunt Kathy about all the friends I'd make and experiences I'd enjoy. Truth be told, the entire thing had felt scripted and hadn't made much of an impression on me at all.

My aunt and I hadn't seen each other in five months and it had actually been Alfred the AI who had given me the advice I'd truly welcomed: "Survive. Thrive. Arrive." The Threepio-like android had sensed my ambivalence in following my aunt's example, but I was determined to make up for the shame that my parents had brought on the family. I wanted to be more than just another leech on the family fortune and that required success in a way that few other members of the family had dared. No one had equaled, let alone surpassed, Kathy Tagawa but there had been other members of the family who had served.

Lieutenants.

Commanders.

No captains.

Perhaps it was the weight of the legacy that kept the other Tagawas and Tagashis or other branches of the clan from succeeding. Perhaps it had been the reverse. Nepotism was something that I'd been terrified of benefiting from, but the truth was that I was probably the only member of the family my aunt might actually pull strings for. She hated the majority of her family and it was only because my parents had died meant that I'd been "untainted" in her view. Otherwise, everyone else was a poor cousin or Sackville-Baggins in her view. I felt bad about that since I liked some of my cousins, aunts, and uncles. It seemed wrong to condemn folk like teenage Danny for the sins of their fathers and mothers.

Hell, grandmothers and grandfathers.

I was so lost in my thoughts that when I arrived at my dorm room, I barely registered that there was a naked six-toot-tall lizardman sitting in the bottom bunk. He was looking at a Sorkanan holopad projecting females doing some sort feather dance and rubbing his lower abdomen. It took me a second to register what he was doing.

"Oh Jesus, man! What the hell!" I said, averting my eyes and turning to one side.

"Ah!" the Sorkanan's artificial voice box projected a human cry that translated his bird-loot hoots. "What the bork, man! Knock!"

"Can't you do that in the bathroom?" I asked, not looking at him.

"What? That's disgusting!" The Sorkanan said. "What the hell is wrong with you?"

"I'm not the one who did anything wrong!" I said, annoyed.

"It's stress relief!" The Sorkanan said, "Perfectly normal. Like you don't do it!"

"That's beside the point," I said, uncomfortably aware I was losing this argument. "Just please put some pants on."

"I don't wear pants in my room," the Sorkanan said.

I sighed. "Please."

"Fine, fine," the Sorkanan said. "So, you're my roommate, huh?"

"So I've been told," I said, keeping my back turned.

"Our genitalia look nothing alike so getting upset is unnecessary" the Sorkanan said. "Also, we collectively shower in the Academy usually so I don't get it."

I sighed. "Just leave me be, Mr—"

"Tommy," the Sorkanan said.

I blinked and turned around. "Really?"

Much to my surprise, the Sorkanan was now wearing a pair of light sensitivity goggles as well as a pair of heart-covered boxer shorts.

"Yes, it's better than Sixty-Seven," the Sorkanan said. "There's like twenty of those in my History of the Sorkanan Empire and its Military Achievements class. I chose the name after one of your greatest philosophers."

"Thomas Jefferson?" I asked.

"Tom Sellek!" the Sorkanan said. "I'm a huge fan of the *Magnum PI* remake on my homeworld. It's entering its one hundred and thirteenth season this week."

I shook my head. "Not every human is familiar with every piece of media, though I understand that remakes of classic television and pre-First Contact material is very popular among aliens."

"I wouldn't know," Tommy said. "I mean, you're the alien as far as I'm concerned."

I smirked and offered my hand. "Fair enough."

"What's the hand for?" Tommy asked, looking at it strangely.

"You shake hands to show you don't have any weapons," I replied. "Old Earth tradition."

"Ah," Tommy said, shaking one of his reptilian claws in the air in front of me.

I stared. "You know what a handshake is, don't you?"

"No, no, I'm playing the silly alien," Tommy said. "You should find my misunderstanding of your ways endearing."

"Oh, I do," I said, sighing and pulling back my hand before putting it in my pocket. "So, my name is Vannevar Tagashi."

"Nice name," Tommy said.

"You think so?" I asked.

"No," Tommy said, shaking his head. "Humans have a lot of weirdness about their names. Lots of consonants and vowels. Among the Sorkanan, we just list our clutch number or if we're accomplished enough then we're given a name."

"I've heard that," I said, nodding, "Sorkanan culture has a lot of fascinating traditions."

Tommy stared. "Yes, we do. Mind you, you'd have to be a complete idiot to believe that every Sorkanan follows this tradition and it's not just one of literally thousands of cultures."

"You're going to mock my provincialism the entire time we're roommates, aren't you?" I asked, smirking.

"You know it!" Tommy said, making what I thought might be finger guns but looked more like him waving both claws at me. "So, are you the cereal lady's son?"

I blinked, doing a double take. "What?"

"The cereal lady," Tommy said. "There's a human captain from Earth who is apparently really famous, and I understand her son or something is going to be here. It's apparently a big deal among you humans. I remember her from the box of Hoovies."

Hoovies was a nutritious food substitute that came in bar form—so it really wasn't a cereal—and was very popular on Earth starships that hadn't 100% mastered gravity manipulation. They tasted like flavorless rice covered in sugar but were cheap as hell. My aunt had become the spokeswoman for them as part of the, "I've saved the galaxy several times, so I might as well become rich" portion of her career.

"Yeah," I muttered, unhappy with this revelation. "She's my aunt. I was really hoping that connection wouldn't become public knowledge."

"Why?" Tommy asked, blinking his enlarged reptilian eyes behind his goggles.

"Because I'd like to make it on my own," I said, pausing. "I don't want anyone thinking that I'm here because someone else pulled strings for me."

Tommy made a snort that was distinctly human like, though it did have a noticeable warble at the end.

"I take that is a universal exclamation of sarcasm," I replied, noticing the room was distinctly more humid than the rest of the hallways. That was when I noticed he had a circular machine set in the corner that was raising the moisture in the room and providing a distinctly swampish smell. It reminded me of a Sorkanan battleship I'd visited while traveling with Aunt Kathy during one of the rare occasions she'd brought me along. It even had a low-level mist floating around their floors that I distinctly remembered from the visit.

"Close enough," Tommy said. "Everyone in Space Academy is here because of someone pulling strings for them. There are two hundred trillion sentients in the Community and only half percent of a half-percent—"

"0.0025%," I said.

"Sure, Math Monkey," Tommy said.

"Please, let's not get racial, Bird-Lizard," I said.

Tommy smirked his mouth of sharp tiny teeth. "Anyway, only a tiny fraction of the people who apply get accepted even on the local planetary campuses. Everyone is either someone's child, protege, or has kissed anyx for so many years that they're finally getting a payoff."

"That doesn't hurt the system over all?" I asked, appalled.

"Maybe a little," Tommy said. "But you still have to pass the ridiculous requirements. If you have 99 Sorkanan who are all able to do the job equally well as tested, you're going to pick the one that is the spawn of someone who can help your career. You also want someone who won't screw up and reflect badly on you."

Tommy's words reflected some of the few conversations that I'd had on the subject with my aunt. As much as I loved her, she was a lot more cynical and manipulative than her public persona as a wide-eyed, idealistic champion of the Community. She was a great believer that you had to play the game and control the narrative, and raise a savit-ton of money in order to make any real change. I hated that.

Because I knew that Kathy Tagawa planned to do the same for me. I'd ignored her influence in my life because, well, she was easier to think of as a larger-than-life figure than an actual person. However, when she did show up in my life, it was to push me along her career path. When I'd expressed interest in cybernetic enhancements, she'd bought me the best.

When I'd tested as having an aptitude for AI-human interface, she'd gotten me special classes in machine psychology. When I'd considered becoming an engineer, she'd said I could either pursue command or intelligence as career paths or I would have my aspirations shut down by a single letter from her. I could either be a Hero of SPAAACE in training or nothing at all. Kathy even connected me to her PR firm.

"What strings were pulled for you?" I asked, trying to bring myself back to reality. "Assuming that isn't too personal of a question."

"Humans have very strange ideas of privacy," Tommy said, shrugging. "But money."

"Money?" I asked, shocked at how overt an admission it was.

"I'm Tech Caste, not Warrior Caste," Tommy said. "Though I don't think those words mean quite the same thing as their Sorkanan equivalent. My parents and their entire clutch were denied membership in the Space Academy rolls because nine out of ten applicants are those aristocratic soldier sons of bishes. Spirits forbid you have people who actually know how the machines underneath them work after all."

"Uh huh," I said, listening to his rant. "Go on."

"Well, we passed around the grub bucket," Tommy said, referring to the communal snack object that was also used to collect charitable donations on Sorkanan worlds, "and decided to bribe a scout to get me in. I was the one who tested best out of all the other Tech caste clutches in my region. They were smart enough to bribe the scout rather than the actual deans. I also lied and claimed I was Hiwarthan."

"What now?" I asked.

"They're a traditionalist religious sect," Tommy asked. "Quotas meant that I upped my acceptance chances considerably by being one."

"That's horrible," I said, appalled.

"Well, given they don't believe in technology, I don't think I was taking one of their spots," Tommy said. "Besides, I'll happily convert if anyone asks. I can't be any worse at it than I am my mom's religion. They forbid onanism."

Knowing the meaning of that word and what I'd caught him doing when I walked in, I nodded. "Yeah, I imagine that would be hard to practice."

"Right!" Tommy said. "In any case, I think someone caught on as I ended up assigned here in the human habitat."

"Yes, well, I'm sure H-Rod will be an opportunity to engage with other cultures and learn from them," I replied.

"As long as those cultures are human," Tommy said.

I smirked. "Human and AI."

"Are you one of those robosexuals?" Tommy asked, ribbing me.

I rolled my eyes. "As if."

That was when the two of us were interrupted by a woman I immediately felt a powerful and entirely inappropriate attraction to. She had chubby cheeks, excellent uh... frontal steering, a very tight-fitting uniform and a short skirt that complimented her beret.

She smiled as if she knew her effect on me, much to my embarrassment. Contrary to what you might presume, I hadn't had that much experience among the opposite sex despite Earth being liberal with that sort of thing and me being from a famous rich family. Bluntly, I was something of a shy sort and didn't do well with people.

Hard to believe, I know.

The closest thing I'd had to a girlfriend had been a girl two years older than me named Lindsay McDonald, who had been a Scottish Naval History tutor for my future career at Space Academy. She'd made all the first moves and we'd been physical for about three months before our work ended. I never learned whether she'd simply had to move on to her own projects, my aunt had found out about my seeing her, or, worse, that she'd been the one to encourage Lindsay to get me to be more manly. Yeah, Aunt Kathy had some very traditional ideas about gender even though she defied virtually all of them herself. I'd never gotten the courage to look up the truth for myself.

"Hello," I said.

"I'm wearing pants," Tommy said.

"I can see!" Leah said, offering her hand. "I'm here to help you get orientated. I'm Leah Mass,"

Tommy looked down as we shook hands. "Oh, is that how it works? Wow, that is gross."

Leah smirked. "Well, I'm here to head off the people who want to recruit you."

41

"Recruit me?" I asked. "For, what, like a club?"

Leah frowned. "There's one thing more important at Space Academy than your education."

"Like what?" I asked.

"Networking," Leah said, shaking her head. "The Earth students are expected to use their time here to make as many friends with other humans as possible so they can increase their access to Community technology while preparing for careers in politics."

I stared at her. "Yeah, that's gross."

Little did I know the Sons of Humanity would play such a big role in my career.

CHAPTER SIX

Memorials for the Fallen

The Sons of Humanity.

There was a name I hadn't heard in a long time but had never left my thoughts. It made me sick to my stomach to see any sign of them. It was an organization I thought would have been safely discredited by now and consigned to the dustbin of history. If nothing else, they'd been banned from the campus before my graduation.

Now? Now they were back.

Walking with Trish, Astrid, Cadet Catgirl, the Diplomat, and Forty-Two, I saw there was a small rally going on as a group of individuals wearing red armbands were gathered in front of a holo-projection of the movie, *Blood and Honor*. The film celebrated my involvement in the *Black Nebula* incident and seeing it being used as a propaganda piece here made me want to walk up to the people involved and beat them senseless.

The Sons of Humanity were pretty much exactly the sort of group you'd think that they were from their name and uniform. They were Neo-Militarists—or more precisely Neo-Neo Militarists—that were based around the ideology of humanity first and last. They also thought humanity should spend more of its money on the military and less on the various social programs the Community mandated. You know the type. They tended to try to befriend people at Space Academy because they saw those here as the future of humanity's leadership. The freedom of expression laws of the Community meant it had taken my testimony to get the Sons labeled a criminal organization.

Yet another sign that what I'd accomplished was being undone. I could theoretically just throw my weight around and have the

Academy ban them again. It was a very tempting thought but I worried that would just result in them winning propaganda points. On the other hand, letting them fester and boil probably wouldn't help either. The Commandant had to have been under a lot of pressure to let them back in or maybe he didn't care since humanity was on its way out.

"Glad to see that your films are still popular," Trish said, cheerfully.

The massiveness of the human habitat was such that they could effectively hold an outdoor movie showing in the middle of one of the recreation areas without impeding any of the foot traffic around. Above our heads, cloud pods and trams moved people around but the slightly lower gravity than Earth standard meant that most people gladly moved on their own appendages throughout the facility. They were watching

"I confess it's strange to see them watching my films," I said, hoping my reputation was at least one of someone pro-Community and pro-alien.

"They're hate-watching," Cadet Catgirl explained. "The Society of Historical Inaccuracy—the kind of people who argue the American Civil War wasn't about slavery—hosts these meetings every week in order to point out how wrong the movies are, as well as their political bias."

"Political bias?" I asked.

"You know, that aliens did anything," Cadet Catgirl said. "They actually did a fan edit without you."

I stopped mid-step. "*How*?"

Blood and Honor had, after all, been a movie about me. I wasn't sure who the main character would even be without me. Leah? Shannon? Forty-Two? It didn't sound so much like a fan edit as an entirely different film.

"Ever since you've become High Protector, there's a small but noticeable push from human interest groups to claim that you aren't real," Trish said.

I stopped walking. "You mean that I didn't do the things that my record claims I did."

"No, that you flat out don't exist," Trish replied, her tone making it clear she meant what she said. "That there is no Vance Turbo, Hero of

SPAAACE. But beyond that, there's no Vannevar Tagashi. These groups argue that all the stories of you with the *Black Nebula*, Notha Emperor, and the Primordials are faked with a made-up persona."

I stared. "But the evidence—"

"Doesn't matter. Their argument is that the Community's *advanced alien technology*," Trish said, making air quotes, "is enough to overcome any of the investigative techniques of Earth. That's assuming that EarthGov is not in on it."

"In on it?" I asked, now more confused than ever. "In on *what*?"

"Manipulating the public so that we're brought into the sinister cabal of the Community," Trish said. "You know, the one that Earth has already been a part of for centuries."

I felt like I was getting a headache. "You've got to be kidding me. Who would believe that savit?"

"Scared sapients. The Notha Empire survived on the manipulation of the public by providing four simultaneous concepts about all people outside of our culture: that they are contemptible, that they are weak, that they are all-pervasive, and that they are all powerful," the Diplomat said, looking up at me. She'd been following me the entire time and only got the occasional look from the crowds around her. Notha Refugees had poured into human space due to the war and some of them were even studying here at the human habitat. It might have explained why the Sons of Humanity had returned to the campus. There was old and bad blood between the two races.

"That's illogical," I said, looking down at her. It was also basic fascism, but I was certain we'd evolved past that. Neo-Militarism was 5% less stupid after all. It was fascism with a new name to distract people from its roots.

"Ideology among Notha is not driven by logic but by emotion," the Diplomat said. "If the Great Notha can provide an enemy that is everywhere and constantly working against the good people of the galaxy—defined as loyalist Notha—then any mistakes or ills of society can be blamed on that enemy rather than the general incompetence of the government. The people will accept any amount of ill-fortune as long as they have someone to direct their rage against. It is why peace with the Community was something they never sought or wanted

45

because that would remove the primary means they had to justify their reign."

I shook my head. "None of these things came up in the original negotiations I made with the Notha."

I was also exaggerating my role a bit. While I got a massive amount of blame for when the Notha treaty hadn't held, I'd been part of a delegation of a thousand other negotiators, my reputation had improved once I'd used my influence to help Deathworld. That I hadn't been invited to join the negotiators apparently updating that treaty was a sign that, while time may have told in my favor, I still bore some stink on my reputation regarding alien sympathies.

"Yes, your staggering ignorance and idealism was assumed to be a genius gambit on your part," the Diplomat said. "I have seen enough of you to know better. In any case, the new Great Notha has spent vast amounts of orichalcum wealth not on building bigger ships and better guns but to fund the spread of disinformation and propaganda among humans. The Sons of Humanity are one such group. It is because of orichalcum dollars and paid infonet commentators that they have been able to revive as an organization."

Okay, that was just ridiculous. "The Sons of Humanity are a bunch of military wannabes who hate aliens and proclaim how traditional values are being undermined by otherworldly influences. You're telling me they're funded by the Notha. People they should hate."

"The enemy of my enemy is the guy who pays for my newsletter," Forty-Two said. "That's how the saying from your planet goes, right?"

"Not quite," I said, pausing. "So, basically, the Neo-Militarists have become really bad in the few years I've been away from Earth."

"I doubt they ever left," Trish said. "People want a comforting lie whenever things are going poorly. When Contested Space was open to settlement and there were constant border skirmishes with the Notha Empire, that was a distraction for Earth's people. With the Notha Empire's collapse and the formalization of existing borders, a lot of people have lost money investing in new colonies that will now never exist. It doesn't help that a lot of the megacorps are pressuring the government to give them a freer hand and by pressuring, I mean bribing."

"This is why I fled into deep space," I said, shaking my head. "Same old savit, different toilet. What other kind of crazy stories are spreading?"

"That you died and were replaced by a Community bioroid," Trish explained. "That you are actually an agent of the Elder Races. Which is accidentally true. That you're in love with robot sex slaves, which is a half-truth. I *am* completely willing after all. That you are secretly running a child sex trafficking ring to the Notha."

"Why would we want to have sex with underage humans?" The Diplomat asked.

Trish shrugged. "Outrage, I guess."

"Oh, and you don't exist, as we mentioned," Astrid said.

"Astrid, don't tell me you're reading this garbage," I said, disgusted.

"What?" Astrid asked. "I always look up stuff about you and Mom whenever we're in range of the infonet."

I didn't have a response for that. "Well, stop. I'd rather not have you exposed to that sort of garbage. Watch porn when you hit puberty like a normal child."

Astrid rolled her eyes.

"You know, it's kind of funny," Forty-Two said, heading to a nearby synth-meat stand and buying a basket of hotdogs that filled his arms. There had to be at least twelve with a bowl of jump chili to go with it. No fries or chips, though.

"What's that?" I asked.

"You're a frigging spy," Forty-Two said. "You work for the Security Departments or did until you got promoted out of them. Your archenemies are Department Twelve, a rogue intelligence agency, and Dark Matter."

"Yeah, and?" I asked.

"Wait, Department Twelve *is real*?" Cadet Catgirl asked, shocked.

"Those are actual conspiracies," Forty-Two said, chuckling as he devoured the hotdogs in his basket between words with barely a moment to savor them. "You've dealt with all sorts of plots, counterplots, and dark money. Yet, these guys believe nothing that you know to be the case."

"Conspiracy thinking is designed to reinforce preexisting biases rather than uncover real conspiracies. It's sort of like the difference between medicine and alternative medicine," I said. "If something is proven to actually work, it's just medicine so anything that's alternative is usually just bogus."

"Clearly someone has never enjoyed the wonders of Tydannian healing crystals," Forty-Two said, raising a claw. "For only fifty credits per ounce, they can recharge your life energy."

"Life energy doesn't exist, Uncle Forty-Two," Astrid said.

"Says the psychic who was just visiting her father after he had his life force drained," Forty-Two said. "All I'm saying is I'm getting a two-pound crystal and a pyramid hat. Primitive tribal people have not forgotten the old magic. You know, humans!"

I rolled my eyes. "Are we almost there yet?"

"You have been gone a long time," Cadet Catgirl said, pointing nearby.

Cadet Catgirl pointed to a nearby walled off section of the habitat that I felt embarrassed to have missed. It was the Human Habitat Memorial Park, a garden dedicated to those students and staff who had died in accidents or violence. I had to give Space Academy credit that there would have been a lot of institutions that would attempt to cover up the number of people who'd died due to negligence or political maneuvering.

Then again, Space Academy was something akin to two or three thousand years old as an institution. Not as old as the Community itself, which had been around when humans were still beating each other up with bones and chasing woolly mammoths, but it was still an incredibly venerable institution.

Still, the Human Habitat Memorial Park was a place I dreaded going because it was where there would be a memorial to Aunt Kathy, Fleet Admiral Bendo, and poor Tommy. It was an awkward place for Case Gordon to meet with me and he absolutely had to know it would be. A cemetery was, right now, the least appropriate place to be holding a meeting between me and anyone.

"Are you sure he's in there?" I asked.

"Yes," Trish said. "Dad and I have a connection that can't be monitored. This is where he wants to meet."

Trish's attitude toward Case really threw me since it was hard to imagine the former Director of the Security Departments as any kind of father figure. It was a completely incorrect assumption about the man because I'd done some research that mentioned a whole different side of him. Not only had he raised the original Patricia Ares, but he'd run a children's charity with his second wife, Kei, and looked after thousands of orphaned foster children that had gone on to take his last name.

He'd taken a fatherly role in guiding the Earth behind the scenes for nearly a century. Sure, that had involved a lot of wetwork, spying, and probably worse but he'd done his very best to make the people of Earth an integrated part of the Community. What was that if not fatherly? Yet, I couldn't shake my impression of the man as a slippery wheeler and dealer. A guy who was as far removed from the people of the galaxy as any of the other megacorporation heads or politicians. I respected the man, but I didn't like him or the way he did things.

"Father?" Astrid asked.

I shook my head before kneeling to give my daughter a hug. "I guess this is where we part ways for a time. Take her back to the ship, Forty-Two. I trust you'll be able to keep her safe from any sudden kidnapping attempts or alien space monsters."

"I'll do my best," Forty-Two said. "Which will probably involve grenades."

"I'm not going to get kidnapped at Space Academy, Dad," Astrid asked.

"Did you see that in the future?" I asked, bringing up something I shouldn't have.

"No," Astrid said. "I haven't seen anything in the future since that last vision."

"Oh," I said, feeling like a piece of crazzap for bringing it up. "I see."

"I will also look after your heir, Lord Satan," the Diplomat said. "The Space Vampires cannot be defeated by mortal means, but the

Notha know magic that can repulse them. Also, it gives me an excellent excuse to avoid my father."

"I will tell him nothing but wonderful things about you,' I said. "I won't even mention you trying to kill me on multiple occasions."

The Diplomat's expression was close enough to a human's that I gathered she was feeling something between mortification and abject horror at my joke. "Yes, very funny, Lord Satan. You are a laugh riot."

"It wasn't a…" I said, trailing off before shaking my head. "You don't mind if I meet with Instructor Gordon alone, do you, Cadet Catgirl?"

"You mean the former spymaster meeting with a High Protector is something you don't want witnessed by the obviously compromised daughter of the Academy's head?" Cadet Catgirl asked. "You don't say."

"I trust you will respect my privacy," I said, smiling. "But I wouldn't want to put you in a position where you'd have to choose between supporting your father and me."

"Why?" Cadet Catgirl said. "It's not really a choice."

"I know, he's your father—"

"No," Cadet Catgirl said. "My father is the head of a university, and you are the direct voice of the Community Senate's High Council. Going against you would be treason and would completely destroy my family's life, my father included."

I blinked. "Right, that too."

Cadet Catgirl showed her leonine teeth with a smile. "I totally would love for you to order me to spy on him instead."

"Uh huh," I said.

"I could be a double agent," Cadet Catgirl said.

"Uh huh," I replied again.

"Triple agent!" Cadet Catgirl added.

"No," I replied and walked through the memorial garden's entrance.

"Quadruple agent?" Cadet Catgirl called behind me.

CHAPTER SEVEN

Remembering Lost Friends

Human Habitat Memorial Park was a maze.
Literally.

It was designed as a bunch of synth-obsidian stone walls formed into passages that weaved back and forth in a variety of confusing patterns. Computer kiosks were built into the side of the wall with holographic displays showing a history of Space Academy's honored dead but also providing bios complete with images of each memorialized person. There were benches and alcoves with small gardens throughout, giving the place a sense of spirituality without invoking any particular belief system.

There were no actual remains in the Human Habitat Memorial Park, space always being at a premium in any artificial habitat, but it was a full of people who were either visiting loved ones or trying to learn a bit more about the dead. I imagined there was also the occasional anyxhole searching for a spot to hook up that was slightly taboo. Not that I knew anything about that but you'd have been surprised how often people suggested the park for liaisons. It was one of the few places not monitored in the Human Habitat, which also made it a common location for drug deals or other illegal activity.

That I did know something about.

Long story.

The majority of people present were civilians with only a few cadets. There were merchants from beyond the Community, visitors from Human League worlds, and more than a few aliens who were dealing with their private grief. No one paid me the slightest bit of attention.

It was a weird sensation walking through Human Habitat Memorial Park and realizing just how anonymous I'd been since my arrival. I mean, I wasn't expecting to be mobbed by fans but I'd kind of thought I was a big deal. Previously, on my trips to Earth, I'd always been surrounded by people who wanted to talk to me about their plans, seek my patronage, or just give their opinion on my actions. Basically, I'd been famous and influential.

Now?

Now I'd woken up in an Academy hospital, walked out into the streets, and the only person who had come to greet me was the daughter of the official who hated me. It seemed the only people who still remembered I existed were the Sons of Humanity and that wasn't entirely clear since they'd edited me out of their propaganda piece. I'd known venturing into the Perseus Arm would take me out of the limelight but I hadn't realized it would render me irrelevant.

"You're not irrelevant, Vance," Trish spoke beside me, having decided to accompany me into the gardens. "But history does have a way of moving very rapidly forward. Yesterday's megastar is tomorrow's has-been and power vacuums love to fill themselves up. Once you let go of power, it's extra hard to seize it again."

I couldn't help but feel a bit of relief at Trish's presence. "You know I'm not comfortable with you speaking about my thoughts aloud."

"I feel like you wanted some privacy in your brain," Trish said. "But I recognize what you're thinking. I've been in your mind for a very long time. Not just from the perspective of an AI when seconds can be like an eternity but in human terms too. A whole decade."

I sighed. "I guess I just figured I'd have done more."

"You can be a great captain, a good father, or beloved by the people," Trish said. "Pick two."

I smirked. "The truth is that I thought I could just keep adventuring with the crew forever. But that's not possible, is it? There's only so much every person has in them before they're spent. I'm wondering if I have passed my limit."

"You lost the woman you loved, or at least one of them," Trish said. "You've also buried a lot more friends than most people. This is despite

52

the fact that you've done absolutely everything you possibly could to keep them alive."

"I could have done more," I said.

"You can't always win, Vance," Trish said, pausing. "You can come up with a million genius plans and do everything right. However, people will still die because that is what people do."

I looked at her. "Depressing thought."

"Death doesn't scare me," Trish said. "I was willing to die for you and my crew. Heck, I did die for you and my crew. I just got rebooted. Technically, it's not me, it's a clone whenever I back up my files."

"That's a depressing thought, too," I said, walking up to the nearest computer kiosk and looking up the memorial for Aunt Kathy.

A glowing blue hologram of her face appeared before me as a list of facts, figures, and accomplishments was displayed. There was an option for narration but I didn't take it, instead looking at the reproduction of her face. She'd died in the engineering core of her ship, trying to rescue a bunch of cadets, and thus had been honored by the Academy. It still seemed impossible for her to have died but it was as clearly documented as the Earth being round.

"I think people overestimate the individuality of consciousness," Trish said. "I feel that instead of a candle blaring up and then going out, I see consciousness more as a cloud."

"A cloud," I said.

"Yes, a combination of floating ideas, emotions, memories, and concepts that exist not so much individually but moving from person to person in an intricate collection of patterns. People aren't so much individuals as droplets of water in a larger ocean of existence," Trish replied. "Death holds no sway as long as there are people to remember."

"So you're a Buddhist," I said, amused.

Trish smirked. "They try to transcend reality. I say we're a part of it and it is a part of us. What do you believe, Vance?"

"I don't know," I said, shaking my head. "I have seen miracles that defy the imagination. Technology that really is indistinguishable from magic. The beings that are millions, if not billions of years old often act like petty children. Yet, just looking at quasars and black holes and I can't help but believe there is more to this reality than just matter. It may not be that Zen Christianity is true, but it's at least a framework to express that this all is something beautiful. That there is a soul. That when we die, everything isn't just lost."

"I've seen things you people wouldn't believe. Attack ships on fire off the shoulder of Orion. I watched C-beams glitter in the dark near the Tannhäuser Gate. All those moments will be lost in time, like tears in rain," Trish said, quoting *Blade Runner*.

"Really?" I asked, surprised she'd make light of this whole conversation.

"It's a very special movie to bioroids," Trish replied. "Even if attack ships can't catch fire in space. C-Beams also wouldn't glitter in space."

"Way to ruin the movie for me," I said, smirking.

"Sorry!" Trish said.

I pulled up the information on Admiral Bendo's death. Fleet Admiral Saul Bendo's history was almost the opposite of Kathy Tagawa's. He had captained a desk for the majority of his career but it had been his politicking that had largely guided Earth through some of the worst periods of its history. Humanity had been involved in every single conflict the Community had since EarthGov had joined and reaped the benefits of fighting other men's wars. Admiral Bendo had supported that at every opportunity while negotiating the best possible deals for the lives being spent.

I knew Saul had hated me. He'd thought I'd been a product of nepotism and propaganda from the very moment I'd entered Space Academy. Yet, reading all the details of his career, he didn't strike me as the kind of person who espoused the isolationist reactionary politics of the Neo-Militarists. He'd supported the creation of the Human League but not as a substitute for the Community. Instead, he'd wanted to have mankind increase its position within the Community rather than withdraw completely.

I believed that Saul and Captain Elgan were both individuals heavily involved in Department Twelve's machinations. However, Department Twelve was an organization that understood humanity was not strong enough to stand on its own. Its cruelty, ruthlessness, and, frankly, stupid attempts to discover how the Elder Races' technology worked were all made with the assumption we had to build alliances in order to grow from being a galactic backwater to being a power in our own right. Now Bendo was dead and it seemed that humanity wanted to become Japan under the Shogunate, which was bound to leave us vulnerable and weak as the rest of the galaxy moved on technology-wise.

Something didn't make sense here.

"What did Leah believe?" Trish asked.

I didn't respond immediately. "She believed we were all just stardust and self-delusion. Yet, she was willing to die for someone else. Me."

"The father of her child," Trish said. "Leah understood that even a selfish person can pass on their ideas and genetics via their children. It's the only true immortality that can exist. Well, you know, except for uploading yourself into an AI like Patricia Ares did."

"Except Patricia became you and Alexandra Ares, who are closer to being her children than genuine reincarnations," I said, shaking my head. "I suppose I have been thinking a lot about legacy lately. Do you think it's too late to change anything?"

"It depends on what you want to change," Trish said. "Do you mean yourself, the galaxy, or something else?"

I looked up Tommy's memorial. It didn't say anything other than his name, date of birth, date of death, and homeworld. "I don't know."

"Well, then I think you need to figure out what you want for the rest of your life, Vance," Trish said, putting her hand on my shoulder. "You may or may not want to marry me. I know you well enough to guess you're worried about betraying Leah, but I also know that you need to get your head on straight first. One thing I will tell you, though, is I will gladly follow you wherever you go. You deserve happiness of your own. You don't owe the Community anything. You don't owe EarthGov anything. Hell, you don't even owe me anything anymore. You've fought, bled, and struggled to save as many people as possible. Often for a galaxy that turns on you at the drop of the hat before re-embracing you when it's convenient. Maybe you deserve a little peace."

I paused, looking at Trish. "Where did you get that speech?"

"I worked on it for about three seconds, which is a lifetime for an android," Trish said. "It involves a lot of old Spider-Man and X-men comics bits."

I smirked. "The thing is those heroes don't ever get to rest because they're fictional and the point is to keep fighting forever."

"Yeah, but they *are* fictional," Trish said. "You're not."

I paused. "Vance Turbo is fictional. He's the persona I have to live up to every day. Vannevar Tagawa? I'm not sure there's enough of him to qualify as a real person. I'm caught between the two extremes of someone who is too much of an example for any one human to live up to and someone whose weakness I'm disgusted by."

"Ah, clearly I should have been drawing from Batman," Trish said.

"I do want to marry you, Trish," I said, taking a deep breath. "I accept your proposal. Whether it's legal in the immediate future or not, you have been there for me no matter the struggle or circumstances. I need to get my head on straight, though. Because I do owe the Community, EarthGov, and you plenty. When you take an oath—which I did when I swore myself to being an officer of Space Fleet—you have to do your best to live up to its premise. Otherwise, what's the point of it?"

"A steady paycheck and retirement benefits," Trish said. "Not everyone takes the mythology about soldiers, knights, and heroic space captains as seriously as you do, Vance. Which is probably why you are able to be the persona you adopted. Self-mythologizing may not be emotionally healthy but it is pretty awesome when you can pull it off."

"No commentary on me accepting your proposal?" I asked, noting she'd not reacted to that.

"Eh, I know you'd say yes," Trish said, smiling.

I frowned. "I guess I am predictable."

"Like I said, I've been living in your head for a decade," Trish said. "Marriage is really just formalizing the arrangement."

I wasn't sure I particularly cared for that comparison but I wasn't able to dispute it either. Instead, I gave her a kiss and looked toward the complicated passageways of the memorial. "I don't suppose you know where your father is hiding here."

"If I know my dad then he is always in plain sight but never visible," Trish said, leading me down the confusing nature of the maze. Right before we reached the center of the labyrinth, we ended up coming to a dead end. "Here."

"Here?" I asked.

"It ends right before where the garden's courtyard should be," Trish said.

"Ah," I said, walking forward. "That is very much like Director G."

"He really hates that name," Trish replied.

I walked through the obsidian wall in front of us and it shimmered and twisted before passing away. It was a holographic decoy display, a common enough tool in Community Special Forces and it could be modified with barriers to be solid. Barriers that could be raised or lowered with a passive scan by the machinery generating it. It would allow Case to cordon this section of the Memorial Garden off causing anyone who might bump into it to be pushed away if they didn't have the right DNA.

The courtyard beyond it was a pleasant garden with a koi pond in the center, surrounded by pillars covered in ivy. There was a marble statue of a beautiful Eurasian woman in a kimono in the center with her head lowered as if in mourning. That was Keiko "Kei" Springs, the trillionaire philanthropist who had helped educate millions of war orphans during the aftermath of the Unification Wars as well as helped set up the H-Rod to bring mankind closer to the Galactic Community. Kei was also famous for being Patricia Ares' mother, though I wasn't sure how that related to the facts that Patricia had been a secret bioroid and thought of Case as her father.

I could find out very easily, though, because Case was sitting on a stone bench in front of the pond. Rather than his usual expensive suits, he was wearing an ordinary pair of slacks and a turtleneck. He was a handsome, brown-skinned man with a shaved head, and a goatee. Case didn't look any older than me even though he'd witnessed First Contact. Today, however, he looked tired.

Weary.

As if the entirety of the galaxy was resting on his shoulders.

That was probably how I looked these days.

"Hello, Captain Turbo," Case said, smirking. "I'm glad you survived the Space Vampire attack. Trish."

"Dad," Trish said, nodding.

"Yeah, Space Vampires are not a good sign for the conference," I said, walking over and taking a seat next to him.

"Oh, they're not here for the conference," Case said. "They're here for you. Your arrival here has them panicked."

"Who?" I asked, confused. "Department Twelve?"

"Department Twelve is no more," Case said, shocking me. "Its members are being killed off one by one with only a few left over. The few survivors are located here. This is their last refuge since Space Academy is their headquarters."

CHAPTER EIGHT

Revelations

I stared at Case. If he'd grown a second head, I would have been less surprised. "Okay, you're going to unpack that one a bit."

Case chuckled as Trish took a seat on another bench nearby. "Oh Vance, you're going to have to become much better at this if you're ever going to be a master of the struggle against the Invisible Hand."

"The Invisible Hand" was how Case referred to the various government, corporate, and religious interests that drove the galaxy forward. Even though he was, well, who he was, he still thought of himself as a member of the resistance. Case really was a relic of a different time when spies and warfare were romantic contests between rival empires. Then again, maybe he was just adopting a persona that believed in such, much the same way I'd done for Space Fleet.

"Trish, if I ever become a master of lying and murder, you have my permission to shoot me," I said, looking over to my new fiancée.

"Oh, I don't need your permission," Trish said, waving her hand at me dismissively. "Besides, neither of you will ever match my cunning mind. You are all my pawns! Pawns I say!"

Case snorted.

I rolled my eyes. "What the hell do you mean that Department Twelve is no more?"

"I think that's fairly self-explanatory," Case said, turning to me. "The waltz continues but the partners change."

I wondered if even Case understood his metaphors half the time. "I came here to find Leah's evidence against Department Twelve."

"You mean this evidence?" Case asked, pulling out a data crystal. "Unfortunately, it is no longer currency. It contains a complete list of

59

the members of Department Twelve and their projects, but the former is now only useful for identifying the dead. The latter are also all shut down or now under new management."

I grabbed the crystal from his hands, pulling it away from him with only a little resistance from the spymaster. "How the hell do you know about this?"

As mentioned, I didn't exactly trust Case even though we'd been allies for much of my career. Case would have probably referred to himself as my patron but the power balance between us had always fluctuated. Case's position as EarthGov's answer to Nick Fury—to maintain Trish's comic book anecdotes—had always been dependent on him keeping out of the limelight. Most of his operations had been deniable and more than a few were outright illegal.

Even when I had just been a captain for Space Fleet, I'd had access to resources that Case wouldn't have normally possessed. These included my status as a propaganda hero meant that a lot of the military equipment assigned to me was not meant for the frontlines. In other words, it could be moved around in secret and serve as a mobile base for secret communications and transportation of goods across Known Space.

Now I was nearly all-powerful within the Community, at least if the High Council decided I still deserved the title of High Protector. Case had been fired from his position and a part of me wanted to rub his nose in it, but the rest of me understood how immature that would be. Still, he continued to play head games with me while he was teaching military school, which made me want to point out that I could throw him in a hole somewhere. Again, not exactly the most mature way to handle our interactions.

"Err, that's my fault, Vance," Trish said, biting her lower lip. "You were in a coma because of the extra-dimensional shape-shifting manta ray—"

"The Space Vampire," Case corrected.

"Oh yes, that's better than what I'm saying," Trish muttered. "Seriously, we were minutes away from Turbo Vance being replaced."

"They tried to replace him in your elevator on your ship that is also you," Case said to Trish, referring to the *Melampus*. "You should have spotted him."

"That's not the point," Trish said. "The point is that there's shapeshifting, extra-dimensional manta rays that almost killed Vance. I would have been very traumatized."

"Shapeshifting?" I asked, confused. I mean, I'd seen it happened but I was still trying to wrap my head around it.

"Yeah, they can become people indistinguishable from the original even to intensive scanning," Case said. "They'd have your memories and personality too."

"*How*?" I asked, thinking that it sounded like something out of bullsavit science fiction.

"Science!" Case said, waving his hand. "There's so much advanced technology left over from the Elder Races and those species that they've destroyed, I've encountered nothing that surprises me anymore."

I wasn't sure I had an argument for that, but I was more interested in Trish's revelation. "Let me understand this, you told your dad about this highly secret, super-dangerous mission I was going on."

"Was it really highly secret or super dangerous?" Trish asked, guiltily. "I mean, you were retrieving a data crystal from her locker or something."

"It was actually in her old room," Case said. "She hid it behind the panel that overlooks the bed you first slept together in."

I stared at him. "They haven't replaced that yet?"

It was anticlimactic in a way, which confused me. I should have been happy to find out that Department Twelve was no more. God knows, I'd wanted to see them destroyed. However, this wasn't the way I wanted to see it happen. "I wanted to see them before a court, not in the morgue."

"That was never going to happen," Case replied. "They had the patronage of a High Protector, Fleet Admiral Bendo, and other high-ranking officials. Arguably, they weren't even breaking the law."

"Stealing my DNA to make artificial children wasn't breaking the law?" I asked, disgusted.

"Not on Crius," Case said, calmly. "Department Twelve was dissolved of its official capacities after it screwed up during the Notha War."

"I'm not sure that billions of dead and whole systems destroyed by SKAMMs qualifies as screwed up," I said.

"But it was always able to cover its tracks," Case said. "Private Military Contractors, planets outside of the Community, shell companies, and government projects being run by groups that weren't technically Department Twelve."

I stared at him. "I could have ordered all of them rounded up and shot."

It would have been a hideous abuse of power, but I could have done it.

Maybe I should have.

Case nodded, not remotely disturbed by my statement. "You wouldn't have, Vance. That's why they would have gotten away with it. You could probably take credit for their fall from grace, though. It was the dissolution of Dark Matter that crippled their support. Killing their AI friend in Ares Electronics cut off the one thing they needed more than friends in high places: money."

"Money," I said.

"Money is the fuel of the galaxy, alongside orichalcum," Case said. "Without either, society does not run."

"Having just survived a literal test of humanity, I am less 'viva la capitalism' than I might have been before," I replied, still confident it was better than most other systems as long as you watched the big players carefully—which apparently no one had been doing. "You're telling me I killed one of their investors and that weakened Department Twelve to... what? Get taken out by you?"

Case frowned. "I'm afraid not. Department Twelve and I were not allies. I felt poking the bear of the Elder Races was both stupid and suicidal. However, I'm afraid the individuals who did go after them are not an improvement."

I stared at him. "What do you mean? Who did this?"

"The Sons of Humanity," Case said.

"Bullsavit," I said, shaking my head. "The Sons of Humanity are a bunch of idiots who believe longevity drugs turn you into zombies."

"You should never judge an organization by its rank and file but by who is at the wheel," Case said, shaking his head. "The Sons of Humanity were a tiny and insignificant group of malcontents until the organization was flooded with money and misinformation from their new patrons. In the aftermath of the Notha Treaty, millions more joined from places like Rand World and New Rhodesia as Contested Space collapsed. But at the end, the Sons exist primarily as the extremist arm of the isolationists, politicians and individuals of real power who knew Department Twelve would have to destroyed in order to facilitate humanity's exit from the Community. Their money comes from the Notha for maximum irony. Because nothing unites enemies more than objecting to peace with each other."

I stared at him, struggling to comprehend what he was suggesting. "You're telling me that the paramilitary organization of terrorists and mad scientists that I've been pursuing for most of my career has finally collapsed but that's because someone *worse* is replacing them. Just with opposite politics."

"Welcome to my world," Case said, shrugging. "It turns out you can't kill an idea. Instead, you just shuffle around who is supporting the extremes of whatever ideology is presently in vogue and how much power they hold."

I stared at the crystal in my hand. "So who is left? You said Space Academy was their headquarters?"

"You have a literally cybernetically enhanced brain, Vance," Case said. "But you are incredibly slow on the uptake sometimes."

I glared at him. "If you're so smart, why are you teaching here?"

I was a firm believer in those who can't do, teach. At least when it came to this place.

"You really hate Space Academy, don't you?" Case asked.

"My feelings toward Space Academy are mixed..." I said, trailing off. "I should have been expelled for what happened with Tommy. That I wasn't was proof positive that I had privileges other people didn't and that I could coast on my name. I tried to leave Space

Academy, so I didn't ruin further lives by being the captain they didn't need."

I'd never really articulated my precise thoughts on it but it was good to finally share what I felt: that I didn't deserve to be a captain of Space Fleet and that I'd been playing catch up this entire time. I'd met a lot of officers who didn't deserve their rank but that didn't make me feel any more comfortable about the position I'd been given despite my failures. I'd done my best to live up to the standards expected of a Space Fleet captain but that didn't change I never should have been here in the first place.

Vance Turbo deserved to be a Space Fleet captain.

Vannevar Tagashi didn't.

"Oh Vance," Trish's said, her voice lowering.

"I don't really have time to deal with your imposter syndrome," Case said, dismissively.

"Thankfully, I don't look to you for approval," I replied, dryly. "I'd say you deserve to be arrested but I'm pretty sure working here is worse than prison."

Case chuckled at that. Apparently, he found my insult amusing rather than disparaging. "Rather than saying that being a captain in Space Fleet isn't anything to be particularly proud of, a job that has its share of saints and sinners, I'll point out that this was the perfect place for Department Twelve to work out of. It is connected to the largest Community transit hubs, jumpspace communication drives, and research laboratories in the Known Universe. It is a place that they could scan the best and brightest of the Academy's recruits but also those who had a certain... darkness about them that might lead to a moral flexibility they could take advantage of."

"A certain darkness," I said, repeating his words.

"Yes, Vance," Case said. "It was Leah's job as a recruiter to find people like you."

"Elgan recruited me because I was expendable," I replied.

"Elgan recruited you because he believed you had what it took to be part of his organization," Case corrected. "He only chose to leave you behind because he determined, at the end of the day, you were a lot more dedicated to the principles of the Community than a member of Department Twelve could tolerate."

"They created their own worst enemy," Trish said. "You should be glad, Vance. You did beat your enemy. Sort of."

"I note you still haven't answered who is left," I said. "Which tells me that you're going to drop a bomb on me in the middle of a cemetery."

"The isolationists are the ones who sent the Space Vampire to find you," Case said. "I don't know if they have another one, but they used the creature to hunt down many targets that would have been otherwise impossible to hurt. They will not stop just because you've removed an incredibly valuable asset. You are in danger. So are the survivors."

I felt a migraine coming on. "You want me to rescue the surviving Department Twelve personnel."

"Oh, for bork's sake," Trish said, genuinely surprised. "Really, Dad?"

"They're sources of great information and potentially valuable resources even now," Case said, not skipping a beat. "Now that we know who they are, they can be compelled to make restitution for their crimes."

"And this has nothing to do with your cashiering from the head of the Security Departments," I said, not actually phrasing it as a question.

Case snorted. "Do you think I'm less dangerous now that I'm not beholden to the Community's vast bureaucracy? Or more dangerous?"

"I think you should be less dangerous," I said, appalled. "These people are responsible for atrocities that can't be counted. Now you want to Operation: Paperclip them. Except you aren't the government and are just looking to make your own Department Twelve."

"You don't know who they are," Case said, looking at the data crystal. "Some of the names may surprise you. Leah was just one of the members who was more good than evil."

"Don't mention her," I said, looking at him in disgust. "Her last act in this universe was to turn over information on her fellow members."

"Because she loved you and knew you hated them," Case said. "But the fact Countess Mass never broke contact with them while she was

65

alive should tell you everything you need to know about her real feelings."

"I'm gone," I said, standing up.

Case stood up. "Vance, we need your help with this. For the future of EarthGov and humanity. Your aunt was one of Department Twelve's—"

I punched Case in the face.

Case fell back a step as his nose bled white fluid. "Ow."

"Vance!" Trish said.

I glared then walked away. "Stay out of my head. Stay out of my way. I don't want anything to do with either of you ever again."

I didn't mean it.

Probably.

I walked out of the courtyard, leaving behind the person I'd just accepted the proposal to and her father.

They didn't follow, thank God.

It was a sentiment I dropped when someone dumped a black bag over my head and injected the back of my neck with an instaspray.

CHAPTER NINE

Is Protest Worth the Pain?

The instaspray knocked me cold and left me ruminating in my memories. I didn't know the precise chemical composition of whatever they'd hit me with but it was enough to overcome my enhanced constitution and force me into a state of immediate unconsciousness. Worse, I was stuck dreaming of the days before Tommy's death, brought forward by my earlier thoughts of the Sons of Humanity.

"I hate this campus," Leah muttered. She was holding a cafeteria tray and had bits of silly string sticking to her hair.

"Ah, you're just upset because you are covered in party favors," Tommy said, following behind us.

"Yes, yes I am," Leah grunted. "I hate the protestors, and I hate the counter protestors more."

The three of us were having lunch at the communal eating lounge (i.e. the food court) while the surrounding area was full of gathered crowds with signs and holograms as video feeds being recorded for rebroadcast across humanity's various worlds. Most of them were people protesting EarthGov's participation in the Notha War.

EarthGov had made a hard pivot toward militarization over the past few decades to try to improve its economy. The Community was always in need of new bodies to throw at its enemies and were willing to pay for it in technology, economic aid, and favorable deals for colonization.

The agreements, in strictly mercenary calculus, were bringing great dividends back to the homeworld. So much so that EarthGov had resumed its leading position among human-settled worlds, even though many of them had been part of the Community for centuries prior. Many human worlds had been settled by the Elder Races or even Community ones taking humans off Earth then letting them do their thing. Despite this, humans were the poor cousins of the Community and generally considered to be sponges off the more established species.

That had changed with the Notha War when the hundreds of thousands of humans who had died in the conflict had won some portion of the Community's respect. The Notha and human conflict had become personal, and many people tended to think of it as a battle between those two races over Contested Space versus the furry fascists against the Community as a whole.

"MAKE PEACE NOT WAR!" one of the protestors shouted. "NO BLOOD FOR ORICHALCUM!"

"RACE TRAITORS DESERVE TO BE SPACED!" One of the counter protestors shouted back. "NO XENOS ON HUMAN WORLDS!"

Yes, you could guess the Sons of Humanity were the biggest part of the counter-protestors along with various other Far Right Neo-Militarist groups. They didn't support the Community or its agenda in protecting its borders against the Notha Empire (as much borders can exist in space). They did, however, like to pretend that they supported troops and loved the idea of human soldiers being "out there" killing aliens.

"I hate them agreeing with any of my positions," I said. "It makes me think that I must have made a mistake somewhere."

"All of this is astroturf," Leah said, getting herself a vat grown chicken sandwich and synthesized fries.

"Astroturf?" Tommy asked.

"It means artificial grass," Leah said. "It's an old term in politics responding to an even older term called grassroots. A grassroots movement is a spontaneous eruption of political sentiment among the public. Like a bunch of families coming together to protest a war because of lost members. Astroturf is when companies or the government pay people in order to protest or voice their scripted opinions about whatever benefits them."

"You think this is staged?" I asked, looking over at the protestors and their colorful eclectic garb from a dozen human worlds and variety of cultures.

Leah scoffed in derision, which made me think of a much more seasoned individual than the new cadet she was supposed to be. That was part of the reason we'd started dating. Leah was just so much more mature than other women I knew here. "This is a *military academy*, Vance. It is not exactly a hotbed of student radicalism. Every cadet here fought hard to get on the rolls in the first place. That or they inherited their spot from a rich relative, which doesn't incline them to be super-progressives either. No offense."

"Some taken," I muttered.

Leah ignored my rejoinder. "All of these losers were shipped in from other planets or are the guys who scrub floors and were offered a paycheck for their off hours."

"Nothing wrong with scrubbing floors," Tommy said, defensively. "A lot of the people who work here at H-Rod are resentful that they're part of what keeps the place functional but never reap the benefits."

Tommy was always more aware of class issues when we had these impromptu discussions. The Sorkanan Empire was the heart of the Community, but it was also a "survival of the fittest" style society that passed itself off as a meritocracy. That there were any social programs at all was due to pressure from other races.

"Maybe," Leah said. "But the people behind the Sons of Humanity and their fan club aren't the unemployed, home-schooled, keyboard warriors whose parents believe First Contact was faked."

"Tell us how you really feel," Tommy said, getting a meal of *krish* eggs and synthetic *goush* meat.

"No, it's the megacorp oligarchs," Leah said. "As United States President Lyndon Johnson said, 'If you can convince the lowest white man he's better than the best colored man, he won't notice you're picking his pocket.' It's the same with xenophobes."

"White is a color," Tommy said.

Leah rolled her eyes. "Not what I mean, Tommy. I'm saying that the people behind the dog and pony show outside are rich and well-connected. They're just creating a distraction for what they're really interested in. Maybe some new worlds being opened for exploitation or labor laws being overturned."

"So, you think both sides are fake," I said, rolling my eyes. The way Leah talked, you'd think she was a spy sometimes. Well, either that or a liberal college student instead of the kind of people who normally signed up for Space Fleet. Many of the students here tended to be on the reactionary conservative side of things. My last date insisted Earth needed to build up their own fleet for the inevitable extermination war with the Sorkanan.

Yikes.

"Yes," Leah said. "However, one side is faker than the other. Lenin used to call the communist parties in other nations 'useful idiots' because they didn't know anything about how real politics worked."

"Lenin never actually said that," I said, getting myself fruit and a sandwich composed of something I had no idea of the contents but was similar to BBQ. "But he probably thought it."

"You always need to be aware of who is at the wheel," Leah said, as if she was lecturing a small child. "Because when you think patterns are entirely random, they show themselves to be organized by someone off to the side."

"Patterns, by definition, are not random," I pointed out.

Leah rolled her eyes.

It was during this time that I saw one of the Sons of Humanity harassing a particularly adorable looking Verdantian. A female so inoffensive looking that she could give Cadet Catgirl a run for her money. By contrast, the man was in full gray fascist Sons of Humanity uniform and had an especially thuggish appearance, like he was straight out of central casting.

I was already mad about the hate group's prominence and seeing them directly pushing around a fellow cadet caused me to become enraged. Perhaps Leah had even provided a little push with her powers.

I put my tray aside and walked over to the man, gritting my teeth. "Leave her alone!"

The Son of Humanity took a swing at me, and I responded by decking him so hard that he went down like a set of children's blocks being kicked over by a toddler. I was then surrounded by holo-flashes and video feeds.

The next day, I ended up on the cover of several magazines and I'd become a viral sensation. The story changed from being protestors against the war to being cadets against the racism on campus. The public consciousness quickly lost any interest in the larger social issue, and I became the poster boy for integration. Just as someone had planned.

I'd been used. Who had used me? I'd never found out. Someone who had wanted to use Kathy Tagawa's nephew in order to create a weapon against the current news cycle. Possibly someone who saw potential in me as a propaganda tool for EarthGov. With Leah's involvement, it might have been Department Twelve even then but I didn't want to make assumptions. Either way, my memories started to fade back into reality.

Gradually, I pulled out of the fugue I'd been put into and became aware of my surroundings. I was tied up in a chair, someone having applied magnicuffs to my hands and feet. The chair itself seemed to be an ordinary desk chair, which meant that I was dealing with amateurs as tearing apart said chair was entirely within my abilities. I still had the hood on my head, though, and had to wonder if they thought dragging me through the memorial gardens while wearing it had been inconspicuous. Then again, they'd managed to get out of the gardens with me in said hood which was proof that they'd somehow pulled it off.

Trish? I asked, trying to speak to my AI friend.

No response.

Well, that wasn't good. Doubly so because Trish kept a copy of her personality within the back of my consciousness among the Elder Race's nanites. Since I doubted whoever had kidnapped me had access to that kind of galaxy-altering technology, I could only presume that there was another factor afoot.

"Hey, I think he's awake," a male human voice with a Albionese accent spoke.

"Thank God, I was wondering if we'd have to slap him," A female voice with a slight South African twinge to her voice said.

71

"That won't help us," a third voice spoke, male and with a kind of mid- transtellar accent to his speech. It was the kind of accent people who grew up in EarthGov orbital habitats had.

"I said we should throw water in his face," the female voice spoke. "We're on a time schedule here."

"A time schedule that we don't know the specifics of," the Albionese voice said. "Hence, we have to take things very slowly and carefully."

"Bork carefully," the woman said before I felt a cold splash of water in my face. It soaked right through the hood. "You! Turbo! High Protector! Are you awake?"

I didn't respond out of stubborn pride.

"Do you think he heard you?" the spacer asked.

"Shut up," the female voice said. "Hey, I'm talking to you. Speak up."

I didn't respond again, wondering what sort of people I'd fallen into the hands of. I'd been kidnapped by professionals before—at Space Academy no less—but I could sense the unease of my captors.

"We can't play these kind of games," the Albionese man spoke before the hood was ripped from my face.

I found myself facing three individuals in a white room that looked less like a prison cell and more like someone's office. I was sitting behind a desk. There were no windows or monitors in the room, so it felt a little oppressive but not so much that I could really take it seriously as an intimidation tactic.

Furthermore, the people holding me prisoner didn't look like hardened spies. No, they were a trio of cadet-aged individuals wearing Sons of Humanity uniforms, but casually. There was none of the Neo-Militarist unearned pride that members usually took. The clothing looked more like costumes they'd put on.

One of the men was South Asian, another white European, and the third being a brown skinned woman of multiple ethnic descent. It was possible they were older than their early twenties, Leah had been decades older than her babyface indicated, but I somehow doubted it. I'd been kidnapped by students and that was going down as probably my greatest defeat.

"Hello, High Protector,' the South Asian man said, revealing he was the one with the Albionese accent. "I'm Paul. I'm a big fan."

"Don't tell him your name!" the South African female said. "We need to let him know who is in charge."

I glared at her, more annoyed than frightened at this point.

"We need your help, Captain Turbo," the spacer said. "I am Peter."

"I don't think that's going to happen," I said, finally speaking.

"See! I told you he wouldn't help," the woman said. "He's just like the rest of them! A user who is going to hang us out to dry!"

"We kidnapped him, Mary!" Paul said. "I think that warrants a little consideration."

Mary glared. "Now you're using my name! Seriously!"

"We didn't kidnap him," Peter said, trying to defend their actions.

"I am very confused," I said, wondering what the bork was going on. "Also, you absolutely kidnapped me. Plus, just so we're clear, your real names are Peter, Paul, and Mary?"

"Yes," Peter said, not getting the reference I only got because of Seventies Trish.

"No!" Mary said.

"Sort of," Paul said, clasping his hands together. "Perhaps we should give an explanation for our actions."

"You think?" I asked, wondering if I should just break free and take them out now.

Paul sucked in his breath. "We're undercover agents in the Sons of Humanity."

I blinked. "You are, huh?"

"We were undercover agents for Department Twelve," Peter said, as if making a confession. Which I supposed he was.

"And you think that's going to make me inclined to help you," I said, wondering if I'd fallen down a rabbit hole somewhere.

"See? I told you that he wasn't going to help us," Mary said, hissing.

"Agent Mass recruited us," Peter said, looking pleadingly.

I stared at them. She'd been with me for years in the Perseus Arm and longer still as a Countess on Crius. "When? When you were toddlers?"

The trio exchanged an uncomfortable set of looks, which gave me pause.

"We were created on Crius," Mary said, surprising me.

"We're clones," Peter said.

"Technically, artificially created people," Paul said. "Department Twelve was lacking operatives that could be trusted after the Notha War."

"So, we were made," Peter replied.

That killed any sense of righteous indignation I was feeling. I'd known Department Twelve had been using the genetic labs on Crius to create children, that was how Astrid had been born, but to realize they'd gone beyond that was horrifying. Worse, the implications were that Leah had known about it and possibly been involved.

"I'm listening," I said, shaking my head. "What do you want me to do?"

The three looked surprised at my sudden change of attitude. I didn't blame then, I was surprised myself.

"The real Sons of Humanity are cleaning up the last of the Department's activities here," Paul explained. "They want the Codex before the Great Notha arrives. Then they'll hand it off to him."

"The *real* Sons of Humanity? The Codex?" I asked, wondering when I'd wandered into a bad movie.

"The real Sons of Humanity are the individuals who are behind the public face," Mary explained. "Seasoned mercenaries, ex-spies, and corporate oligarchs. They're not interested in anything other than making money and are bought and paid for by the Notha Union's master. This peace treaty being held at Space Academy is all just an excuse for the Great Notha to get his hands on everything Department Twelve had assembled."

"And the Codex?" I asked, wondering if Case had misread Leah's data crystal as what she'd left for me. Maybe it had been a feint to keep away people like, well, him.

"It's a list of everything," Mary explained, before realizing "everything" didn't explain anything. "Bank records, blackmail material, corporate holdings, and backdoors into every single human power structure. It also gives the codes for the AI that manage human infrastructure."

I blinked. "Okay, yeah, that'll do it. So, you want me to give you sanctuary?"

That was when the door to the office opened and Aunt Kathy walked in, wearing her Space Fleet uniform without her rank insignias. "No, Vance, we need you to take over Department Twelve and its mission."

CHAPTER TEN

What in the Hell?

Katherine Tagashi was a greying, black-haired, Asiatic woman who appeared to be in her mid-to-late fifties but was over a hundred and twenty years old. She'd been an astronaut on the International Space Station prior to First Contact and had been rewarded with longevity treatments by the Community's best scientists. True immortality didn't exist but with access to alien medicine, you could live three lifetimes.

Seeing her caused me to briefly feel an immense surge of hope that, somehow, Aunt Kathy had faked her death and was still alive. That she was with these discount Department Twelve clones was beside the point and I was going to overlook it.

Except, I couldn't.

Case had educated me on the basics of being a spy. Perhaps a little bit more than the basics. As much as I'd stubbornly resisted being anything other than Vance Turbo, Hero of SPAAACE—man, was I getting sick of that title—I'd done more espionage work than the next ten Space Fleet captains. One lesson that had stuck was if it was too good to be true then it probably was.

"You're not my Aunt Kathy," I said, pulling the arms of the chair apart and standing up.

"He's loose!" Paul said, shocked.

Mary rolled her eyes. "I told you that it wasn't a good idea to use an office chair."

"I wanted him to be comfortable!" Peter replied.

"He's a prisoner!" Mary said.

"Is he?" Paul asked.

God, what a bunch of idiots.

"No, I am not," the woman identical to Aunt Kathy—the Fake Kathy—said. "I also am."

"Thank you," I said, pulling my legs free. "That was very illuminating. Can someone unlock these? I really don't want to be wearing them anymore."

Before Mary could object, Paul went to my side and waved a control rod over my magnicuffs. They immediately popped off my wrists and ankles, giving me the freedom of motion I desired. That was when I punched Paul in the face, sending him to the ground with a thud. Peter, immediately went for a plasma pistol on his side that turned out to not be there while Mary went to Paul.

"What the hell was that for?" Mary asked, looking up at me.

"Kidnapping me!" I snapped, wondering if I would have to use more force.

"That is beneath you, Vance," Fake Kathy said. "I taught you better than that. A captain of Space Fleet uses their words first and violence only as a last resort."

"You didn't teach me anything!" I said, staring at her. "Just who the hell are you?"

"Think, Vance," Fake Kathy said. "It'll come to you."

It took me a second to realize what she was getting it. The realization struck me like a thunderbolt, and I had to admit I didn't know how I felt about it.

"You're an upload," I said. "In a bioroid body."

Brain uploading had been the holy grail of AI research ever since the days of the first bioroids, of which Case had been one of the early successes. It was also considered to be an outdated "failed" science that would never consistently achieve the results that researchers had been seeking despite its few successes.

In simple terms, it was possible to upload most of the memories and an approximation of a person's personality into a computer. That had been possible since the days of Pre-First Contact, but true replication simply did not happen and uploads frequently displayed wildly different personality traits from the individuals they were copied from.

The most telling example was the fact Patricia Ares had been an incredibly brilliant, serious, and compassionate woman who'd helped guide Earth's economy into the stars. Her mental clones in Trish and Alexandra Ares had elements of her but the former was a goofy cinnamon roll I loved while the latter had been a psychopathic megalomaniac.

"Yes," Fake Kathy said, without hesitation. "It was determined that your aunt's mind was too valuable a thing to lose and should be preserved as best as possible so that future generations of humanity could benefit from her wisdom."

"My aunt would never have agreed to that," I said, balling my fists. "You're a desecration."

I was being massively hypocritical here, if not outright prejudiced. At the risk of using an old saw, some of my best friends were AI. Except, I wasn't kidding, some of my best friends really were. I'd always been more comfortable with machine intelligences than biological ones and the reason I had a reputation as a legendary captain was only because I leaned on their capacities heavily. Indeed, it might have been why the Elder Races tolerated me as their agent despite how much I hated their actions. They understood that I respected them as living beings despite that—or perhaps because—they were all extremely old AI themselves.

So why was I having a problem with a Kathy version of one? Perhaps it was because of the familiarity of the person they were imitating. I was still grieving over her death and the lack of resolution between us. There were things that would never be resolved. Things like how she'd tried to turn me into a copy of her. Or how she'd lied about my parents' death so she could claim complete control over my affections. They would never be resolved because I hadn't even allowed myself to think about them until she was no longer there.

"Your aunt agreed," Fake Kathy said. "They achieved an 80% replication."

"How close is 80%?" I asked.

"Not close in the slightest," Fake Kathy said, looking at her hand. "I am detached from those things she loved. I do not feel her overwhelming love for Earth or humanity. Instead, I find many of her decisions to be inexplicable. Like why she believed you are the best person to carry on her legacy."

I stared at her. "You mentioned you wanted me to become the head of Department Twelve. An organization I've devoted myself to destroying. So, yes, I admit that I find that decision to be inexplicable as well."

It was such a bizarre request that I had to wonder if it was some kind of test. Certainly, I wanted to figure out the reasons behind it. It was better than thinking about how they were confirming that my aunt had been part of Department Twelve. I didn't trust anything coming out of Director G's mouth necessarily, but I also doubted he was willing to go to the elaborate lengths on display here. Actually, no, he was absolutely capable of going to the elaborate lengths on display now, but I didn't think he was involved.

"Department Twelve and you share many values," Fake Kathy said, looking at me.

"We share nothing," I said, disgusted.

"You both wish the best for humanity," she said. "You both define it as humanity becoming more a part of the greater galactic, well, Community. You consider it as actually attempting to deal fairly with aliens for mutual benefit rather than attempting a zero-sum game. You wish that AI be treated as people rather than things."

"Department Twelve treated people like ration bars," I said, disgusted. "Disposable trash."

"Hey, I like ration bars," Peter said.

Mary slapped him on the chest.

"Yes," Fake Kathy said, staring at me with cold, dead eyes. Ironically, that made her look more like my aunt than anything else. It was the expression she had when she wasn't trying to play the role of a space hero or mentor. The expression of a woman exhausted by a century of war and trying to live up to an impossible standard set by a government that needed a reason to be proud of its primitive star navy. Kathy Tagawa, Star Captain of Earth!

I waited for a response. "Yes?"

"Yes, Department Twelve constantly threw lives away in a desperate attempt to make the equations balance," Fake Kathy said.

"They foolishly risked the extinction of mankind trying to steal fire from the gods, or technology from the Elder Races. They constantly picked fights with the Notha and aligned themselves with the most vicious warhawks of the Community. Finally, they alienated you at every possible turn versus stopping to talk about possible collaboration. This despite you actually gaining access to the Elder Races by your actions."

"I'd never have allied with them," I said, not as sure as I sounded.

"Perhaps," she said, turning around and gesturing for me to follow. "But you've shown yourself willing to work with Director G, Leah, and even your own war criminal of a father for a short time."

Peter, Paul, and Mary gathered in a huddle with their faces down. They were subordinate to Fake Kathy and seemingly outright afraid of her. There was something more, though. They were desperate.

"Don't remind me," I said, looking around me. "Where am I?"

"I'll show you," Kathy said, walking out.

I reluctantly followed.

What greeted me on the other side of the door caused me to stop dead in my tracks. I'd thought I was still on Space Academy, probably still in the human habitat, but the building was clearly something very different.

The room beyond was a massive arcology easily three or four times the size of H-Rod. The architecture was not human compatible, though, or at least designed by any normal minds. It was a single control center at the heart of eight kilometer-long "arms" that stretched out in every direction with top of the line Community computer servers.

Gravity manipulators were being used in inventive ways, not just providing "up" and "down" but having bots moving along the ceiling and floors (or perhaps neither existed) while they tended to the massive data-processing center. There were a handful of organic beings spread about the location but it was mostly automated. There was also strange glowing coral that seemed to be growing out of the sides of certain sections, mixing with the recognizable technology in ways that I didn't understand.

"What is this?" I asked.

"An AI's version of heaven," Fake Kathy said. "It is a digital processing hub that is plugged into the larger Community infonet via Elder Race technology. It is the birthplace of most of Earth's military AI, sort of its spawning ground. Conventional AI research labs can spend years attempting to create a true AI with brain uploads as a base but never have a single success. Here, Department Twelve has created several thousand AI under the auspices of Earth's ruling minds. All of which are united under a shared goal of protecting humanity. Spread throughout the infonet, they have been gathering information for Department Twelve and influencing events to mankind's favor."

I stared in horror. "The Elder Races will wipe us out for this."

"The Elder Races know," Fake Kathy said. "Did it ever occur to you that if they really wanted us not to fiddle with their tools that there was absolutely no way that we could? They could surround their markers and transmitters with impenetrable force fields or cloak them from our sight so that we'd never find them. They could annihilate the ruins they leave behind to the subatomic level or simply remove them when they abandon a world."

I stared at her. "So, what? They leave their stuff behind for us to find so they can wipe us out when we play with it?"

"Yes," Fake Kathy replied. "Or they want to see what we can do with it."

That was a sobering and not entirely welcome thought. It was one thing for the Elder Races to have absolute rules that they enforced with ruthless efficiency. It was quite another for them to be setting down horrifying consequences for rules meant to be broken.

"At this point, I'm not even surprised," I said, shaking his head. "Wait, is this the Codex?"

"Yes," Kathy said. "That is one way for describing it. Unfortunately, it is known to the Notha now."

I took a deep breath. "Whoever controls this will have an immense advantage against the Community."

"Yes," Fake Kathy said. "Or within it."

I turned to her. "So why do you need me?"

"Because the people who used to be in charge are dead," Fake Kathy said. "The Great Notha used his Space Vampires to infiltrate our ranks. That provided them a complete view of our numbers that was used to hunt us down."

That put a very different spin on the attack. "One came after me."

"Yes," Fake Kathy said. "I know. The Great Notha blames you for the fall of the Notha Empire and believes that your destruction would be a final cap to his victory."

I stared at her. "Why would he blame me?"

"You killed the Notha Emperor, negotiated the peace that caused the collapse of the Empire into infighting, and got a huge chunk of his fleet destroyed by the Primordial called Cthulhu," Kathy said. "Since he doesn't believe in the Primordials but deludes himself into thinking they were a Community superweapon, that means you were engaged in an act of war against him the entire time. Then there's the fact that you turned Deathworld from a planet he was almost able to conquer into one that he now has to negotiate peace with."

I paused. "Okay, when you phrase it like that, maybe he has a reason to be plizzed."

Fake Kathy gave a half-smile. "Admiral Bendo and the real Kathy were in opposition over whether to recruit you into the conspiracy. It was roughly the same argument over whether Director G should be recruited or not."

"That I was too idealistic?" I asked.

"That you were too vengeful," Fake Kathy said. "That your misguided sense of justice would result in you being unable to let Captain Elgan's activities against you go. That you would consider destroying Department Twelve to be a net good regardless of how it impacted humanity."

I would have argued but what would have been the point. Admiral Bendo—or perhaps my aunt—had been right. I'd dreamed of bringing down Department Twelve for my much of my career in Space Fleet and always sought any hint of their activities. Becoming High Protector had been meaningless for me but offered the chance to finally bring them to justice. They'd seemed beyond the law and this space station proved it.

"So, you're not asking me to head up Department Twelve," I said, shaking my head. "Because there is no Department Twelve. You're asking me to take its resources."

"A distinction without a difference," Fake Kathy clarified. "There are a handful of living operatives left but utilizing its former resources and contacts for your purposes will effectively resurrect the group."

I'd been hoping she'd just agree so I wouldn't have to feel disgusted with myself by saying yes. However, keeping this place out of the hands of the Great Notha was more important than my pride. I tried not to think of what even someone as well-intentioned as Director G would do with it. Case was a good man, sort of, but there was no way he wouldn't exploit the hell out of it to regain his former power or even exceed it.

"Where is this place?" I asked, confused. "It's certainly not Space Academy."

"Jumpspace," Fake Kathy replied.

"No one has ever achieved a stable stationary position in jumpspace," I replied, bewildered.

"Yet another of the department's secrets," Fake Kathy said. "So, do we have an accord?"

I sighed. "Yes, we do."

CHAPTER ELEVEN

Difficult Decisions

I felt like I was betraying myself.

Worse, I *knew* I was but just didn't want to admit it. Case had come to me with a lower-level version of this very same offer right before I'd been drugged and kidnapped. I'd been happy to turn that offer down and let the Department Twelve survivors swing. Now, Fake Kathy had come back with a much bigger offer and I'd folded like a deck of cards.

The thing was that I had been confronted with the nature of my motivations: I wanted revenge. Captain Elgan had given me a chance to make the galaxy a better place. That had turned out to be a cruel trick that was only meant to leave me holding the bag if things went sideways (which they did). I'd hated Department Twelve from that moment on and lashed out at everything that reminded me of it.

But had I been fair? Actually, yes, I believed I had been. Department Twelve was an intelligence agency that had been dissolved due to its constant flouting of interstellar law. Its continued operation as a rogue paramilitary organization meant its members were nothing more than terrorists. Terrorists supported by the existing government as deniable assets were still terrorists as far as I was concerned. Nevertheless, the acknowledgement they'd been used by another High Protector meant that the laws that applied were iffy if not nonexistent. I was trapped in the weeds of politics now.

The margins.

"What do you even want me to do with this?" I asked, looking around. "I wouldn't even know where to begin."

"I sincerely doubt that to be the case," Fake Kathy said. "I believe you know exactly what you want to do with it and that is why you are the only person who has the authority and the will to use it. Mind you, I'd say that even if I didn't believe you could because flattery is the surest way to manipulate you."

I gave her a sideways glance. "I take it that came from my aunt's memories."

"Somewhat," she said. "She thought of you as a child who was in desperate need of love. Your parents discarded you at an early age and the need for validation you never got was something my template wielded to control you. If you had gotten therapy rather than specialized schooling, then you might have lived a far less interesting life but a far more rewarding one."

I stared at her, appreciating her bluntness but also offended by it. "You're doing a great job of winning me over."

"What do you want, Vance?" Fake Kathy asked. "First for yourself and then for the galaxy as a whole."

"I have what I want," I said. "My family and loved ones on a starship that I captain."

"Is that what you want?" Fake Kathy asked. "Because our spies have indicated you were considering retiring."

"What spies?"

"You can look them up if you wish," she said. "After all, the ones on the *Melampus* and other ships spread throughout the Community are the only ones remaining. Even then, the Sons of Humanity have been thorough."

I shook my head. "I can't believe there's enough racists and bigots in Space Fleet to be able to kill that many people."

"Then you are a fool," Fake Kathy said, using the tone my aunt sometimes used for me. "They were able to eliminate Earth's greatest champions as well as the Fleet Admiral. Everyone else was much easier to dispose of. Better still, the false Sons of Humanity make excellent patsies as its members can be dismissed as individual radicals."

"You keep mentioning 'true' Sons of Humanity and 'false' Sons of Humanity," I said, shaking my head. "I don't get it."

"It should not be a difficult concept for a man who has been involved in as much espionage as you have," Fake Kathy said. "The true Sons of Humanity are those under the payroll of the Notha Union and still seeking their own advantage by dismantling the League's ties to the Community. Those who wish to take over every business or service provided by aliens. It will utterly wreck humanity's infrastructure but lead to vast short-term gains."

"And the false Sons of Humanity are all the idiots who they astroturf," I said, thinking back to Leah's conversation.

"Yes," Fake Kate said. "That doesn't mean they're not dangerous, though. Just because they are blind to the greater machinations afoot doesn't mean they are not hardened killers and zealots. They're mostly from Contested Space and not all of them have their homeworlds anymore. The peace treaty with the Notha displaced millions. The hatred and blame for the Community fills the holes in their souls."

"Useful fools," I muttered.

"They killed your friend," Fake Kathy said.

"What?" I said, doing a double take.

"The Sorkanan known as Tommy," Fake Kathy replied, unaware of just what sort of blow she'd just struck.

I immediately turned to her and glared. "What the hell do you mean?"

"You didn't know?" Fake Kathy asked, her expression unreadable. Even for a bioroid, she wasn't very good at human emotions.

"No, I didn't know," I said, staring at her. "What do you mean?"

"You were meant to be the poster boy, literally, for the cadets signing up for the Notha War," Fake Kathy said. "Unfortunately, not all of the Sons of Humanity were aware of their role in the setup. A young cadet named Marvin Kittridge—"

"I know who Marvin is," I replied. "I got him expelled."

Marvin Kittridge had been a year ahead of me in Space Academy and one of the few cadets heavily involved in the Sons of Humanity movement. He'd been an obnoxious true believer that had, nevertheless, managed to get himself a small following. He was the guy I'd punched in the face to protect the Verdantian student I'd seen him assaulting. One who had probably been part of the set-up from the

86

beginning. I'd foolishly believed our conflict had been a great struggle between good and evil. Instead, I'd come to recognize he'd just been a petty little bully trying to protect his petty little corner of the universe. Now I was hearing that he was a murderer of my best friend.

"Yes," Fake Kathy said. "He sabotaged your friend's equipment in hope of killing you."

I didn't know if I believed her but the idea that I'd been carrying guilt for Tommy's death for no reason rocked me to the core. Except, if what Fake Kathy was saying was true then I was still responsible for Tommy's death. I'd just gotten lucky and it ended up the damaged equipment had killed him instead of me. I still should have checked it but hadn't because I trusted our equipment.

"How do you know this?" I asked, sucking in my breath.

"There was suspicion of sabotage in the initial investigation," she said, making me sick to my stomach. "The Commandant knew that there were political factors at play, though, including Marvin's support from Karma Corporation's owners, the Weldt Brothers. It was simply easier to expel Marvin and pardon you for any wrongdoing. It made, in simple terms, the problem go away."

I stared at her. "Tommy was murdered in an attempt to kill me and they let his murderer go because it was *convenient* for the school?"

"Yes," Fake Kathy said, her voice not changing in the slightest. "You act as if it is a strange outcome. Space Academy does its very best to keep itself an elite center of education vital to the performance of Space Fleet. That doesn't happen if its reputation is tarnished. Except mistakes happen because sapients are, well, human."

I balled my fists. "I'm going to kill that motherborking piece of savit."

"You could," Fake Kathy said. "It is within your power as the High Protector to simply lock him up on whatever charges you desire and deny him any appeal. He is just a petty bureaucrat who has made a career of preserving the reputation of Space Academy and making the mistakes of the powerful go away. He is due for retirement and will no longer be of any concern."

"So, just ignore that he covered up a murder?" I asked, practically frothing in the mouth.

"You never answered the second part of my question," Fake Kathy replied, looking at me. "The Codex will rapidly increase your power and give you the ability to influence the Community as a whole, not just the Human League alone. You'll be able to blackmail or intimidate any person you want. Know who is bribable and not. With that sort of power, what do you want for the galaxy?"

"I don't want that sort of power," I said, dismissing her statement. "I want the public to make choices about their own destiny."

She scoffed.

"What?" I asked, confused.

"The public do not want to rule themselves," Fake Kathy said, as if lecturing to a small child. "Presuming they could even be informed about the hundreds of thousands of issues that affect their lives every day. They do not wish to oppress, necessarily, but many of them voluntarily choose to have no say in their government. Either because of apathy or out of a desire to be taken care of. Many of the people also have contradictory desires that are irreconcilable. They wish to exist under one race, one religion, or one economic class. They desire scapegoats for their activities. Many also crave to have someone to point at as being worse than they are, or worse off. Someone to make the villain in their life stories. They need the 'other' to blame for their misfortunes. The Sons of Humanity represent a minority of the public but combined with the tyranny of the apathetic, not far from a majority."

I stared at her. It was cynicism that rivaled Director G's and yet came from a place of frustration. "Wow, that is bleak. Is that from Aunt Kathy?"

"Yes," Fake Kathy said. "She lost hope in democracy when First Contact resulted in the rise of the Neo-Militarists who wanted nothing more than to isolate humanity. In the end, they were overthrown by force and the voices that supported them were silenced but not eliminated."

"I believe in the people," I said, simply. "They will do the right thing, eventually."

"Then you are a fool," Fake Kathy said.

"So you've said," I muttered. "At the end of the day, if you want to know what I want, it's a galaxy without fear."

"A galaxy without fear," Fake Kathy said, looking confused. "What do you mean?"

I looked out at the crystals in front of me. "A galaxy where every citizen doesn't have to worry about where their next meal is coming from. A galaxy where they're not one bad month from destitution. Where there is abundant food, shelter, clothing, and medicine. A galaxy where they don't have to worry about being killed for arbitrary definitions. Basic rights for all and freedom of expression even when they disagree. A galaxy where they don't have to worry about being caught up in the war for resources that seems absurd since you could spend a trillion years mining the asteroids out there without going through them all. A galaxy where my daughter can be safe and happy."

Fake Kathy was silent for a moment. "You describe freedom, safety, and wealth. Pick two. Otherwise, you will gain none."

"Benjamen Franklin said those who picked safety over freedom deserved neither," I replied.

"Benjamen Franklin was also an old lecher who had a dozen corpses hidden in his home's walls," she said, finally sounding like my aunt.

"Well, it's what I want for the galaxy," I said, pausing. "Whatever happened to Marvin?"

"Are you thinking of chasing him down for his role in Tommy's death?" Fake Kathy asked. "Even though the fate of the Human League and Community are at stake?"

"I'm thinking of putting him on my list, yes," I replied. "Justice delayed is justice denied."

"Then you are denied. Marvin Kittridge died during the Kolahn War."

"He served despite being expelled?" I asked.

"He was a taxi driver when his colony was struck by orbital bombardment," Kathy said, her tone dryer than the Sahara Desert. "Just another anonymous casualty among millions."

That left me feeling numb rather than relieved. "So, he'll never face justice for his crimes."

"Very few people do that are among the truly guilty," Fake Kathy said. "Those who hide behind money and power remain untouchable to the law even in the Community. Perhaps that is what you would love to use the Codex for? A vessel for waging war against those who have escaped your narrow definition of what is right versus wrong."

"You really do sound like Kathy," I said, not even bothering to look at her. "But no, I'm not the Punisher either."

"Ah, yes, another antiquated pop culture reference," Fake Kathy said. "Your career suggests otherwise, Vance. For such a nice man, you have an immense amount of anger in you. Captain Elgan, the Emperor, the Crius Lords, and even one of the Primordials."

"The Crius Lords were you not me," I said, before catching myself. "The real Kathy."

Fake Kathy reached over and put her hand on my shoulder. It was an awkward, uncomfortable gesture, which is what made it feel like my aunt. "I do not possess your aunt's feelings, but I do share her memories. She... loved you as much as a woman like her was capable of."

"That is the worst bit of reassurance I have ever heard," I said, smiling. "So, I'm the head of Department Twelve now. What next?"

"We must secure the Codex by moving it into a new location," Fake Kathy said, looking around. "Just hiding it in jumpspace is not enough since the infiltration revealed its general location to the true Sons of Humanity. We also must secure the remaining members of Department Twelve."

"Right," I said, pausing. "I plan to review all of the survivors' activities. I might not be interested in becoming the Punisher, but I'm not going to let anyone guilty of crimes against sapience go free either."

"You'll find most of the remaining operatives are just biological constructs and analysts, but I'll prepare a list," Fake Kathy said. "What will you do afterward?"

"Find and deal with this true Sons of Humanity," I said, pausing. "Okay, I think I might have a problem with vengeance."

"Yes," Fake Kathy said. "Yes, you do."

Before I could respond with what I might do with Department Twelve's resources, an alarm started blaring throughout the space station. It was horrifying siren and I wondered who it was for since the entire place was automated. Then I realized, oh, it was for me. Much to my surprise, I saw Fake Kathy get a look of absolute horror on her face.

"What's wrong?" I asked.

"It seems that we overestimated the amount of time that we had before the Sons of Humanity or the Notha Union found us," Fake Kathy said. "We're under attack."

Well, savit.

CHAPTER TWELVE

Battle of the Codex

"The Sons of Humanity or Notha have found your secret base in the middle of jumpspace?" I asked. "Another *dimension*?"

Fake Kathy went into the room we'd just exited. She waved for Peter, Paul, and Mary to come out. "Space is space if you know where to go in it. In this case, it seems that their infiltration was as complete as it could be. We have to prevent the Codex from falling into the hands of Earth's extremists or the Great Notha."

"Does that mean that you're going to blow the Codex up?" Mary asked, looking to Fake Kathy.

"That is the decision of the new leader," Fake Kathy said, looking to me. "We do have the means of destroying this location. It will, however, cripple Earth's ability to manufacture new AI and eliminate any possibility of Department Twelve reviving itself."

"Don't tempt me," I said, not certain that she wasn't testing me. I'd only seen a little bit of this place but what I'd seen violated every law the Elder Races had set down on using their technology. Nevertheless, if it was where the majority of Earth's new AI were created then seeing it destroyed wouldn't just cripple Department Twelve's remnants but also the developing race of Cognition AI among us.

A genocide of inaction.

"I think that's premature," I said, answering in the most noncommittal manner possible. "We don't know how many people are attacking, who, or why. We need more information before we take any drastic steps."

"INTRUDERS HAVE BEGUN ENTERING THE CODEX," a digitized female voice lacking the humanity of Trish or other AI I knew spoke.

My military mind took over in that moment. "Do you have any defenses here? Can you call up security footage?"

"Our primary defense is being in another dimension," Paul said, displaying a snarkiness I hadn't expected from the triplets (as I'd come to think of them). "But yes, we have security bots spread throughout."

I grimaced. Security bots were the successors of drones in warfare but heavily crippled in their capacity due to the fact that automated weapons were one of the most regulated technologies in the universe. Basically, AI could handle them better than any human, but few people wanted true AI with the ability to shoot their fellow sapients. Something, something beginning the robot revolution and all that.

"Deploy them," I said, shaking my head. "How many organic crew members do you have on board the Codex?"

"A few dozen," Mary said, surprising me by speaking before Kathy. "They're mostly people like us, created for the jobs they've come to take over."

"You need to move them to a more secure part of the facility and away from wherever these individuals are located," I said, surveying the three. "Are any of you trained in arms?"

"Yes," Paul said.

"No," Peter said.

"Yes," Mary replied.

I nodded. "Do we have personal weapons and/or barrier belts?"

"Yes," Fake Kathy said.

"Then arm yourselves and protect the others," I said, trying to get as much information as possible. "Also, I need a direct connection to this Codex place's central computer. Every bit of information as possible. That includes a human-AI interface."

"Wireless?" Fake Kathy asked.

"Yes. This isn't a century ago."

Now was the litmus test for whether they were sincere in making me Department Twelve's 'leader.' It was one thing to butter me up and claim that I was the only one who could save their illegal conspiracy but another to put me in direct contact with their computer network. Doubly so if it put Trish in contact with it given her connection to Director G and Space Fleet. I didn't know how they were suppressing her AI self in my brain here but that was another potential weapon with staggering implications. Not even the Enigmatic Path had been able to suppress AI during the Kolahn War.

"Alright," Fake Kathy said, who I really needed to come up with a better mental designation for. "I will transfer full control to you and turn off sleeper mode."

I had no idea what sleeper mode was but could guess it related to Trish's current incapacitated state. Before I could comment further, I was forced to my knees by a massive surge of data as the Codex's information poured into my head. Even with all of my upgrades, just the interface for the space station took me to my limits.

The Codex really was plugged into the heart of the Community's communications network and the infospace clusters spread throughout jumpspace. So much so that it needed a hundred separate AI piggybacking on it all to sort through the data.

If nothing else, it explained why Earth had so many megacorporations that were able to have a blip on the Community's economy. This was primarily a tool for insider trading and a good one at that. High Protector B'Vash also had his claws all over this. The Sorkanan had been using humanity for the past century and a half, manipulating EarthGov first as a source for disposable military assets and later for research into artificial intelligence. B'Vash was enhanced with Elder Race technology from the Ethereals and might live a thousand years while good Sorkanan like Forty-Two couldn't even take longevity drugs.

It was interesting to see how aliens saw Earth and the documentation was that he'd recognized that the Sorkanan Empire was incredibly flawed due to its overreliance on "survival of the fittest" style capitalism. This resulted in things like collapsing infrastructure to lack of social safety net to crippled technological development. Earth's research into dangerous forbidden technologies made it a perfect catspaw to alleviate some of those pressures. Much of the money

Earth's megacorps made was just a drop in the bucket compared to the money propping up failing worlds among the sauropods.

Fascinating.

Vance! Trish's voice spoke in my head. It was the copy of her in my mind. *Focus! We're under attack.*

Oh, there you are, I said, shaking from my fugue. *Sorry, I was caught in a bunch of information.*

Yeah, well, unlike AI, you can't process information that fast, Trish said. *The human brain is a quantum computer but even it has its limits.*

Are you awake? I asked, immediately feeling stupid for asking.

See, right there, Trish said. *Yeah, I just woke up in your brain connected with Department Twelve's stolen Elder Race hybrid computer. Surprisingly, its interface is as dumb as a pocket infocom and it's given me free access to everything. I know we're in a massive space station doing doughnuts around Space Academy. That we're under attack by Notha Commandos. Oh, and you're suddenly the head of the Legion of Doom.*

Well, then you know more than I do, I said, trying to conjure up a map of the facility and what kind of opposition we were facing.

The construction was a pretty massive one and there were technical details that didn't match anything currently possible by humanity or the Community. Believe me, I would know as while I wasn't an engineer, I did keep appraising what qualified as cutting-edge developments. The Codex was roughly akin to the *Melampus*, a combination of Elder Race and cutting edge Community tech,

Trish hadn't been lying about Notha Commandos, and I saw video feed of two eight-man teams having docked themselves against the side of the space station. It was a small number of soldiers but given jumpspace to jumpspace boardings were theoretically impossible, I wasn't going to belittle their accomplishment.

I had to admit, Notha Death Commandos were kind of adorable in their little metal power armor that had triangle tips for their ears. That didn't make them any less lethal, though, and the Death Commandos had a history of war crimes through every conflict they'd participated in.

A quick digital inventory told me about the security bots under our control and the results were not promising. They were non-lethally programmed R-T7 security units that were better made for dealing with trespassers on corporate property than armed soldiers. There were also no other countermeasures like gas, electroshock, or interior turrets. You know, the kind of things a proper supervillain conspiracy should have.

We need to slow them down, I thought to Trish.

Yeah, no kidding, Trish said. *Do you want me to lock every door between you and them?*

Yes, I replied. *Quickly.*

Vance, I love you, but in the time it took you to respond, I spent a relative couple of months going over the data here. Quickly is not the problem here.

Are they sincere in making me their Grand Poohbah?

I can't speak to their sincerity but I'm sure that everyone who actually mattered is dead or disgraced, Trish said. *The remains of Department Twelve are the machinery they created to try to control the world from behind the scenes. There's just no one steering anymore.*

As much as I wanted to believe that, I just couldn't let go of the feeling this was all some sort of trap. Department Twelve had been such an important part of my life for years, haunting my nightmares like an ever-present boogeyman. It was nearly impossible to imagine that not only were they gone but they'd willed me their stuff. It seemed too much like something out of a comic book or adventure novel.

I mean, your aunt was one their inner council so— Trish tried to explain.

Please don't mention that, I said, looking at Fake Kathy, who was watching me stand there motionless. Noticing that the triplets had departed, I took in a deep breath. "I'm preparing as many delays as possible for our furry friends. We'll probably have to engage them ourselves."

"I'm not sure I have the ability to do so," Fake Kathy said. "I assume you wish to be provided with armaments."

I thought about my proton sword. "Where is the weapon I had?"

"It disappeared," Fake Kathy said.

I blinked. "What do you mean it disappeared?"

"We attempted to confiscate it but it vanished," Fake Kathy said. "I presumed it was just another example of Elder Race technology at work."

We were approaching the point of Clarke's Third Law being in effect. Clarke was a 20th century Earth science fiction author who'd said that any sufficiently advanced science was indistinguishable from magic.

"Let me check," I said, keeping a constant feed of the Death Commandos movement. They were presently tearing through the security bots with zero casualties so far. Worse, shutting and locking all of the doors meant nothing as they had plasma torches that cut holes through them within seconds.

Not good.

They hadn't removed my Elder Races ring, and I focused on my hand to see if I could summon my proton sword to my hand. Nothing happened. I felt silly for even trying. Then, much to my surprise, the weapon appeared in my hand, and I was once more armed with the best in barrier technology as well as an object that could cut through hardened durasteel.

Fake Kathy had returned from what I presumed to be the armory—moving remarkably quickly I might add—with a plasma rifle in hand and a barrier belt around her waist. Her expression hadn't changed but I could sense she was not happy being put on the front lines. Then again, that was another quality of Aunt Kathy she might have been replicating. My aunt had been utterly fearless but rarely left the bridge of her ship(s).

"We don't have much time until the Death Commandos get here," Fake Kathy said, reflecting what the sensor feeds already told me.

"Yeah," I said, not at all happy to be preparing for this. Usually, I had a clever plan or some way of turning things around, but my confidence had been shaken for some time now. The trauma of so many battles, near-misses, and friends lost had caught up with me. Sometimes—like now—all I could see was one way through my problems: straight forward.

The door to the central control chamber exploded moments later and we found ourselves under attack by the Notha Death Commandos.

Four feet of furry destruction in power armor that massively enhanced their physical strength, and personal gravity manipulators. These were a dozen times more efficient than your typical jetpack. The armored commandos each had a Notha gravity gun that could launch tiny pellets of matter at super-high speeds.

What followed was a brief explosion of gunfire and a swinging of a glowing blade that lasted probably thirty seconds. Real life combat was not the elegant ballet that you saw in holos, but was a crude, chaotic, and messy display of death. People made mistakes and got killed or they did everything right and got killed. Sometimes the most ludicrous fools managed to survive through sheer chance. More often, the difference in a battle was not skill or heroics but simply who had the best equipment.

Today, it was the latter.

The gravity guns of the Notha couldn't pierce the barrier that I had established around me and the soldiers made the poor decision to not exploit the massiveness of the central control chamber. As such, they ended up sliced through one after the other by my sword. It was brutal, merciless, and efficient. It also left me feeling sick because the Notha Death Commandos kept fighting to the end even when most of them were dead.

Unfortunately, that didn't prove to be the incredible victory for the side of good and righteousness that it might have been. Fake Kathy — no, the Kathy Tagawa bioroid, Other Kathy — was lying on the ground. White fluid was pouring out of several wounds and she was twitching badly. Her barrier belt had protected her against the first of the gravity gun blasts and eliminate two of the Death Commandos, but it had collapsed under the weight of the enemy attacks.

"Kathy!" I said, running to her side.

The other Kathy looked up at me and raised her hand to my face. "I told you I didn't have the ability to do this."

"I'm sorry," I said, looking down at her.

Other Kathy was gone, though.

"Dammit," I muttered. Pushing down my feelings, I decided to focus on the present. "Trish, are we safe?"

No, Vance, we are not, Trish said.

Are the triplets under attack? I asked, trying to figure out what was going on. I couldn't see any sign of them being in danger. The computer feed showed them and a few dozen other staff locked down in the cafeteria and barricaded the doors inside.

No, Trish said. *The gravity guns hit some of the crystals.*

The crystals, I repeated, looking around and seeing some blasted to pieces alongside computer terminals. *What does that mean?*

The emergency shut down for the jumpdrive has been initiated. We're returning to real space in front of the Academy.

CHAPTER THIRTEEN

Talking with the Devil

Well, that was the shortest tenure of any leader of the Illuminati or other evil conspiracy. I could feel the Codex start to leave jumpspace—mostly because I was hooked up to its computer systems—and that meant we were about to be surrounded by all the ships that were coming here to negotiate peace. The Great Notha obviously knew the Codex was here so he wouldn't be surprised but the fuzzy dictator might take the opportunity to use the space station's presence to call off the peace negotiations.

A larger issue might be for Earth or even all of humanity. The Codex represented a massive breach of countless treaties and agreements that every race in the Community was supposed to abide by. AI research was one of the most carefully regulated fields in the Known Universe and humanity had only barely managed to keep itself from being destroyed for pushing the envelope as far as it had. This? This was so far past the envelope that war was almost guaranteed as a result. The Kolahn had been the only other race to go as far as humanity had and they'd not been members of the Community. The result? The destruction of their homeworld and the reduction of the people to homeless refugees.

It didn't matter that the Community had clearly known about the facility and turned a blind eye to it. As much as I loved the organization that I'd devoted my adult life to, the Community would be forced to act against EarthGov despite Department Twelve's supposed rogue status. At the very least it would mean almost total isolation of humanity under immense sanctions. And at worst? Well, the Kolahn knew what happened at worst.

Trish, do we have something like a cloaking device that we can use? I asked, trying to think of a solution in the final few minutes before we fully emerged.

No, Vance, Trish replied. *Because those aren't real.*

I'm surrounded by impossible things right now, I said, annoyed. *Forgive me if I was hoping one of them might be in my favor.*

Everything is always in your favor Vance until it isn't, Trish replied. *But yeah, I've got nothing to fix this. I'm sorry.*

If we had the Old Vance Turbo then we might have been able to do something, I said, bracing myself against one of the damaged controls.

Yeah, the Old Vance Turbo was a scheming bastard, Trish said, wistfully. *I miss him.*

That was when the proverbial lightbulb went off in my head. *That's it!*

What's it? Trish asked. *I'm asking because I literally have no idea what you're talking about and I'm presently in your brain.*

Lying! I said. *The cause and solution to all of life's problems!*

No, that's alcohol, Trish said, quoting something I didn't recognize. *But, then again, you don't drink outside of parties so I'll give you that one.*

The Codex completed its exit from jumpspace as we completed our conversation. As I suspected, the comms immediately sprang to life with panic at the arrival of a megastructure rivaling Space Academy itself. In addition to Space Academy itself, I saw that both the Community and Notha delegations had arrived as well as observers from half a dozen other minor powers. All of them charged up their weapons and raised their barriers.

It was entirely possible I wouldn't even get to enact my half-formed plan before someone unloaded on the Codex with everything they had. Cthulhu's attack on the fleets assembled above Deathworld had shaken the foundations of every space navy's confidence. While the collected races of the Known Universe had technically won thanks to the Primordial's suicidal charge at my ship, it had displayed how woefully outmatched the Young Races were against even one of their elder's ships.

The Codex wasn't an Elder Race or Primordial vessel, but it was close enough that it might be mistaken for one briefly. The *Melampus* was proof of just what could be achieved by combining technologies the way they had done here. Unfortunately, what had made a super-ship for me to pilot around wasn't necessarily something that would make this space station something capable of holding its own in battle.

Trish, we need to raise the Codex's barriers, I said. *I can't find them. Can you?*

Err, about that, Trish said. *The Codex doesn't seem to possess any barriers.*

It...what? I asked. *How?*

By someone not installing any! Trish said, sounding as frustrated as I felt. *Also, you should probably know that it doesn't have any weapons either.*

I was lucky I was already certain we were going to die, and this was merely a Hail Mary pass to save everyone because, wow, that was a punch in the gut. *Who is the idiot who designed this station? Was he trying to get everyone on it killed?*

You know that was the plot to one of the third phase of the Star Wars *movies,* Trish said, merrily. *I personally never thought they needed to explain the Death Star having a weakness that caused it to blow up if you hit in just the right place. A megastructure like that is bound to have plenty of weaknesses. I can look up the designer of this facility if you want but I think the idea is that if the facility is discovered that Department Twelve would rather detonate all the evidence than let it fall into—*

I cut Trish off by making a system wide address, pulling up a digitized image of me at my most magnificent composited from magazines and tweaked propaganda broadcasts. My likeness had a much larger chest and a serious expression to his face that would do better than my actual image. "People of Space Academy! It is I, High Protector Vance Turbo! I come here from the far distant recesses of the Known Universe bringing forth this vessel representing the space empire of... Parkerzor!"

Did you name an alien empire after Spider-Man? Trish asked.

Hush, I replied mentally. Clearing my throat, I continued, "This highly secretive and alien race has sent this super-structure to observe the historic treaty being observed this day. They are an advanced culture, though, and we should respect their ways. It is my hope that as the ambassador the Community sent into the Perseus Arm, I can show a select handful of our finest minds and scientists the wonders within."

That is never going to work, Trish replied. *Wait, huh, lots of vessels are now messaging you for more information on these Parkerzor. Which sounds like a toy dinosaur to me.*

I think I'm doing damn good for winging it, I replied to Trish, wondering how long this ruse would last.

It turned out not very long as the Notha vessels in the fleets gathered outside, which were enough to invade Sol, started advancing toward the Codex. Most notable was the *Notha's Destiny*, a vessel that strongly resembled the late Notha Emperor's flagship. Given the Emperor's vessel had taken a year of the Notha Empire's gross domestic product to produce, it was insane that they'd constructed another vessel in its class while at war with Deathworld.

Like the Japanese flagship, the Yamato, *such vessels are more for intimidation than actual military practicality, Vance*, Trish said. *But since the Great Notha knows that this is a Department Twelve facility, I don't think he's worried about offending any unknown alien races.*

Maybe we'll get lucky and the Great Notha isn't the one who knows about Department Twelve's involvement, I thought back to her.

That was when the *Notha's Destiny* sent a communication to me that consisted of the Great Notha calling me the Great Satan, a collaborator with Department Twelve, a puppet of the Community, and, worst of all, a liar. I'd translate the exact things he said but they included several chemical descriptions of smell that were needed to get the full Notha experience.

Vance, we can't repulse an invasion from even one of these vessels, Trish said, referring to the triangle-shaped vessels that were descending on us. Even the smallest was a half kilometer in length with tens of thousands of Notha or their subject races.

"Tell me something I don't know," I said aloud. "Okay, I'm going to do something stupid—"

Perish the thought, Trish replied, sarcastically.

I rolled my eyes. *Patch me through to the* Dreadnought. *By which I mean Shelly's ship and not the Great Notha's ugly anyx command ship.*

Vance, now is not the time to contact your ex-girlfriend, Trish replied. *The Notha forces will be in range to launch shuttles within forty-five minutes.*

That gave us some wiggle room timeline-wise, and I was glad that the Notha's in-system engines weren't equivalent to EarthGov's Home Fleet, let alone the Community's. We'd lucked out that we'd popped out near the edge of the Space Academy's system rather than closer to its sun where all the ships were gathered.

Fiancée and mother of my child, I thought, sucking in my breath. *Hopefully, that will mean something.*

It's only fiancée if she says yes to your marriage proposal, which she didn't, Trish said, reminding me of a painful fact. *Also, I wouldn't bring up that she's the mother of your child. Astrid is a wonderful, beautiful, slightly-smarter-than-your-typical meatbag girl but she was created with Shelly's stolen DNA. Not everyone is as desperate for family as you are.*

Really, Trish? Now is the time you want to bring this up? I asked.

Sorry, I was just reading your psyche profile, Trish said. *Did you know they thought the best way to manipulate you would be reverse psychology? They think you deliberately rebel against authority to assert yourself and shouldn't be anywhere near a military position but actively seek out how you can defy orders for the so-called greater good.*

Rather than argue, I just shook my head and sighed. "Yeah, that tracks."

Shelly appeared on a holographic interface next to the broken console in front of you. She was looking both angry and confused, which reminded me of when we used to date. "Vance, what the bork is going on here?"

"The Parkerzors need your help, Shelly," I said, shaking my head. "The Notha are—"

"It's a secure line in my private chambers," Shelly said.

"Yeah, I'm going to have to ask for a huge favor," I said, sighing.

"How huge?" Shelly asked.

"Well, I'm a High Protector and I can't order you to do this," I said. "Think of it as a Turbo special."

"That bad, huh?" Shelly asked. "What is it?"

"I need you to put the *Dreadnought* between the Notha fleet and the space station I'm currently on," I said.

"Oh goddammit," Shelly said, facepalming.

"You'll be backed up by the *Melampus*," I said, hating putting my crew in danger but knowing this was too important.

"You do realize the sole reason we're here is because we're trying to stop hostilities with the Notha, right?" Shelly asked.

I took a deep breath. "This is Department Twelve's headquarters and full of incredibly dangerous stuff that would result in humanity being destroyed. How's that for an answer?"

Shelly stared before closing her eyes. "A Turbo special, huh?"

"'Fraid so," I replied.

"You realize someone has been trying to wipe out Department Twelve, right?" Shelly asked, showing she was more involved in this than I thought.

"I've been informed," I said. "It's the Notha Union working with human collaborators. They're behind the Space Vampire attack as well."

"I really hate that name for them," Shelly said, frowning. "Alright, I'll do it, Vance. Maybe once we've got this settled, my husband can come out of hiding."

"He's in hiding?" I asked, surprised I'd gotten an answer for that peculiar claim of hers that he was dead.

"He was Department Twelve," Shelly said, pausing, "while it existed."

"I knew he was evil," I muttered.

Shelly glared. "Leah."

She then broke the transmission between us. I sent a non-voice-encrypted command to the *Melampus* to come between the Codex and the Notha fleet.

Trish didn't seem impressed with my plan. *You do realize that the* Melampus *and* Dreadnought *aren't powerful enough to defeat the Notha forces here. They're the most powerful ships in Earth's fleet but quantity has a quality all its own.*

"We don't need to defeat them all," I said aloud. "Just make sure the cost of directly coming to the Codex is too costly to warrant."

I think you underestimate megalomaniacs, Trish replied.

"That's why I need the rest of the Community fleet," I said, shaking my head. "Also, the Deathworld forces."

That was playing with fire as while the Notha Union might hesitate to start a war with the Community, they wouldn't necessarily have any hesitation opening fire on the Deathworld forces. After all, they were still technically at war with them at the moment. I would be risking not only the peace I'd helped achieve by supporting their independence but a massive number of lives here and now.

Still, I sent the president a simple message: IF YOU FEEL YOU OWE ME A FAVOR, GO WITH THE *MELAMPUS* AND THE *DREADNOUGHT*.

I really hope you just didn't reignite a galactic war, Vance, Trish said. *Especially not to protect Department Twelve's secrets.*

I'm protecting humanity's secrets, I said, pausing. *Which unfortunately I feel like Case would approve of.*

Dad would have never gotten in this situation in the first place, Trish replied. *But I agree.*

Believe me, if I'd known Major Tom was Department Twelve, I might have let the organization swing regardless.

Seriously, Vance? Trish asked, showing the teeniest bit of jealousy in her tone.

No, I replied, making an encrypted transmission to the Community's own flagship in the system.

The Community representation in the Space Academy system was a twelve-kilometer pyramid that was identified as the *Pol'arhh*. I had no idea what that meant as some concepts in Sorkanan did not translate to any human language or were like, "Green Smelling Ultraviolet Flash Make Feel Good" and might as well be untranslatable. It was also the personal flagship of High Protector B'Vash.

Now it was time to put my money where my mouth was. Did I really have it in me to make amends with the person my father had named as the head of Department Twelve? I could forgive them for everything they'd done if it saved lives. However, I could never forgive them for misusing mine and Shelly's DNA as they did. As much as it had brought me joy with the creation of Astrid, there were probably hundreds if not thousands of her siblings that had been terminated in their experiments.

That I would never forgive.

That I would see punished.

Still, I closed my eyes and made the call. "I need to speak with you, B'Vash, High Protector to High Protector."

CHAPTER FOURTEEN

Face to Face

What followed wasn't a traditional holographic conversation. No, instead, it was like someone driving a railroad spike through my head except the spike was on fire. Don't argue that I wouldn't be able to feel the fire after having it driven through my head or that the brain doesn't have pain receptors. I'm describing how it felt and that doesn't need to correspond directly to facts to relate 1:1.

The pain was only temporary, thank Buddha Christ, and swiftly transformed into bewilderment. I found myself in the middle of a large dome that was like being inside the storms of Jupiter with strange gases swirling above me. It took me a second to realize they were the skies above Sorkanan Prime. It wasn't a gas giant like Jupiter, but it was a planet that was eternally under violent cloud cover.

Sitting in the middle of the chamber in a captain's chair was High Protector B'Vash, who looked like an older, more wrinkled Forty-Two. He was wearing a Sorkanan Admiral's uniform that basically could be summarized as a skintight black bodysuit with a cape. Sorkanan tended to wear black attire like this that, as I understood it, was quite colorful to their infrared capable eyes.

Much to my surprise, I wasn't alone in the strange chamber, but Trish was also present. She wasn't wearing her Space Cadet Sally-esque attire, though, but in civilian clothes. Jeans, a t-shirt, and a weird pouch that I remember her describing as a "fanny pack." Her hair was tied in a long ponytail as well.

"What in the world?" I asked, waving my hand in front of me. "Did I get teleported here?"

"Only mentally," High Protector B'Vash spoke in a voice that sounded like he gargled with gravel after smoking a pack a day of simcigs for forty years. "This is an Elder Communication Room that is meant for private conversations between their agents. I see you have brought your AI consort."

"Wow," Trish said, staring at her hands. "This is like you being in my head for a change, Vance. Except we're not in my head, we're in High Protector B'Vash's head. Except, it's more like a chat room. Which isn't nearly as impressive sounding. Okay, I'll be quiet now."

High Protector B'Vash stared at her. "Right."

Trish poked me in the shoulder. "Wow, the graphics here are incredible. Poke, poke."

"Please stop," I said, sighing. "I am so sick of Elder Race tech. It's supposed to be super rare but it's borking everywhere in my life and a constant source of irritation."

"Woo," Trish said, waving her fingers in front of my face.

"Please stop," I said, not reacting.

"It's my digital self with you!" Trish said. "I want to try so many things."

"Please don't," High Protector B'Vash said. "I'd rather not imagine what you two might get up to here. Also, I was under the possibly mistaken impression that Captain Turbo wanted to speak with me."

"I do," I said.

"Does it involve rescuing you from exposing the greatest secret that humanity possesses?" High Protector B'Vash said.

"To my credit, I didn't expose it," I said. "It seemed that the cat was out of the bag when the Notha were murdering Department Twelve."

"Yes, the renegade—"

"My idiot psychopath father confirmed you and Bendo were the leaders of Department Twelve," I replied. "Don't bother denying it because I have access to all the files of the organization that confirm your involvement."

You do? Trish asked.

No, I replied. *However, he doesn't know that.*

"I can read your mind while you're here," High Protector B'Vash said. "But I'm not going to deny it. Department Twelve was my private project. I was old when your race first discovered the atom, and you reached space when the Sorkanan race needed a client race to conduct the dangerous research and to soak up the casualties necessary to break our millennia-long lack of progress. For the most part, the past century has been a success."

"Except for the part where they're all dead and humanity is about to be exposed to retaliation from not just the Notha but the Community. All to cover your anyx," I said, narrowing my eyes.

High Protector B'Vash conjured a stone goblet full of a smoky brew before taking a long drink of it. "In the words of your species, I do believe that is not my problem."

Yeah, I didn't like the High Protector. Call it a gut feeling but I didn't think the two of us were going to be friends.

"Listen, you—"

"Ahem," Trish said. "Remember-ay, the importance-say, of the getting help-ay?"

"That's terrible Pig Latin," I said, shaking my head. "But I understand what you're saying. High Protector B'Vash, rather than a disaster for Earth, the appearance of the Codex may be an opportunity for the Sorkanan."

High Protector B'Vash seemed more amused than intrigued, which wasn't a good sign. Still, he hadn't broken our connection yet either. "Please, by all means, share your desperate appeal to save your species."

"I'll blow up the Codex before I let the Notha have it," I said, coldly. "That includes with me on it. Then no one will have it and there will just be my story about it being the product of a Perseus Arm species."

"Analysis will show it is of human construction," High Protector B'Vash said.

"Human colonists in the Perseus Arm," I replied. "Clearly, they found some Elder Race technology but weren't smacked down for it. Those damned Parkerzors."

High Protector B'Vash made a gurgling noise that I presumed to be the Sorkanan version of a laugh without a cyber-translator providing an example of the real thing. "It seems you at least have a decent cover-up arranged. Given you can teleport with your ring, you also don't have to die with the station."

I blinked. "Yes, clearly I do know how to teleport with the ring."

High Protector B'Vash closed his eyes. "I must confess, Captain Turbo, I expected more from the man who single-handedly stopped the Primordials' invasion."

"To be fair, the Primordials were a lot stupider than their near-unlimited power and epochs of life would seem to indicate," I replied. "However, I'd rather avoid the whole destroying the priceless super-structure full of information and AI-spawning pools."

"Do you have to call them spawning pools?" Trish said, scrunching up her nose. "We're not salmon."

"Do not mock spawning pools," High Protector B'Vash said. "They're a sacred and beautiful thing."

Trish raised her hands in surrender. "Sorry!"

"What is it you want?" High Protector B'Vash said, staring right at me. "Tell me and I will explain to you why it can't happen. In great detail, with relish."

"You really don't like me, do you?" I asked. "I mean, like as much as I don't like you."

"You are correct," High Protector B'Vash said. "You killed Captain Elgan, one of the greatest men your species has ever produced. You have served as a *gragor* in a museum—"

"That's like a bull in a China shop," Trish leaned in and whispered to me.

"Yeah, I got that from context," I said, pinching the bridge of my nose to stave off a migraine.

"And smashed through political boundaries, treaties, and realities with no care or courtesy to those who spent centuries setting them up," High Protector B'Vash said. "You have been a crony of that irritating machine—"

"Hey!" Trish said.

"Case Gordon," High Protector B'Vash said.

"Okay, that's fair," Trish said.

"And worse, have been protected from every possible consequence of your actions by people like Kathy Tagawa," High Protector B'Vash said. "Well, no one can protect you now except me and it will be my great pleasure to deny it. You cannot say a single thing that would get me to change my mind."

"You owe me," I said.

"What?" I asked.

"Every. Single. Breath," I said, enunciating each word. "You, your species, any children or grandchildren you have. The Primordials were going to wipe the Sorkanan race along with every other organic in the galaxy from existence and the Elder Races weren't going to do jack about it. I stopped that. So, you have the luxury of gloating but it's with breath you owe me."

"You little savit," High Protector B'Vash said.

"That's one," I said. "Two breaths, three breaths. You're welcome."

"Vance," Trish said, looking at me. "You are *terrible* at this diplomacy thing. How did you negotiate a treaty with the Notha? Was it just everyone else covering for you?"

"Kind of, yeah," I admitted. "That and I killed their god-king."

"Fine," High Protector B'Vash growled out.

"What?" Trish asked, doing a double take.

"Yeah, what?" I asked.

"There are certain universals between nearly all races, at least in terms of honor," High Protector B'Vash said. "One of these is the principle of 'you owe me' and I admit that Captain Turbo is correct. The Sorkanan race's survival is the only thing that I worry about and it has been facilitated by your idiot savant antics."

"Accent on the savant part," Trish said. "I mean, seriously, he's actually really talented. The stupidity is an act. Mostly. I think."

"I am now reconsidering your proposal," I muttered.

"Hey!" Trish said.

High Protector B'Vash waved his claws at me. "My fleet is moving into position to protect you from the Notha Union's forces. Combined with the *Melampus*, *Dreadnought*, and Deathworld's much smaller navy, I believe the Great Notha will blink."

"And if he doesn't?" I asked.

"Then thousands will die," High Protector B'Vash said. "That will thankfully not include me. Without the SKAMMs, the Community can

defeat the Notha Union in a conventional war. It might even be enough
to It might even be enough to lure the section of humanity taken in by
the Sons of Humanity back into the fold.

After all, the Union will no longer be able to sign their checks."

"You are a cold-blooded bastarve," I said, looking at him.

"Sorkanan are warm blooded," High Protector B'Vash said.
"Begone, Captain Turbo. With luck, we will never see each other face-
to-face."

With that, I found myself once more in the Codex alone. It was a
frustrating experience dealing with B'Vash (I didn't bother calling him
High Protector anymore). He had clearly become accustomed to
ultimate power in the Community—or at least close enough to it—that
he was jaded to the lives at stake. The fact I'd had to rely on him
frustrated me to no end because if he did help me, I'd be forever
beholden to him.

Worse, he was probably as close to the ultimate "villain"—for lack
of a better word—behind Department Twelve as probably existed.
B'Vash had openly admitted that he was the architect for it and why.
He was also the only man who had enough pull to make it all happen.
Yet, he would never see a day of prison or recrimination for the massive
suffering he'd assigned people.

It made me sick.

Still, B'Vash was a man of his word, and I was soon surrounded by
Community vessels broadcasting their protection of the Parkerzor
vessel. The larger Notha fleet would still possibly be able to beat the
smaller Community, EarthGov, and Deathworld forces but it would be
annihilated in the process. It would have been suicide to attack but that
didn't mean they wouldn't. History was full of incredibly stupid
mistakes by people made in the heat of the moment. Indeed, I would
have argued that such was the majority of history rather than logically
well-reasoned choices.

Time dragged on for far longer than I was comfortable with, but it
was an illusion. Only twenty minutes were required for the Notha fleet
to back off. Still, they were among the longest twenty minutes of my
life.

"It's done," I said, taking a deep breath. "We're good."

Are we? Trish asked. *Because B'Vash is sending a diplomatic delegation.*

What sort of diplomatic delegation? I asked, already knowing the answer.

About two hundred Sorkanan troopers as an honor guard, twice as many technicians, and maybe a few hundred scientists to study the interior. B'Vash himself will, of course, be accompanying them.

Yeah, he was coming here to confiscate the Codex for the Community or least his tiny section of it. Department Twelve's resources had briefly been under my control but to keep them out of the hands of the Notha, I had handed them back over to the Department's patron.

It's not too late to wipe everything and blow this place up, Trish said. *We can keep everything from his hands.*

I thought about that, seriously, but ultimately ended up shaking my head. "No. As much as I hate him, this is not the time to pretend to be an action hero. Blowing up things does not make the universe a better place. We'll just have to accept that it's better off in the Community's hands than the Notha's."

Is High Protector B'Vash's hands the same as the Community's?

I didn't have an answer to that. "I'm not condemning the Cognition AI race to destruction in order to feel better about a rich and powerful man getting more of both."

We don't need you to protect us, Vance. Still, it's nice to hear you want to. We existed before this place and we'll exist afterward.

"Traitor!" A voice spoke behind me.

"Goddammit," I muttered, turning around.

Much to my surprise, I saw Mary was standing with a Notha gravity gun in hand. There was no sign of Peter or Paul. She'd cast aside her Community-issued plasma rifle for the Notha weapon, which was probably a mistake since the former had proven so dangerous to our surroundings. Then again, maybe that was the point.

"Mary, what the hell are you doing?" I asked, trying not to overreact.

"Kathy trusted you!" Mary hissed, growling.

I looked over to the body nearby. Other Kathy was gone, completely nonfunctional and probably impossible to repair. "It's war,

Mary. I'm sorry she died but that's what happens in it. We've managed to keep the Codex from the Notha."

"You were supposed to save us!" Mary said, gritting her teeth.

I looked down at the gravity gun. "Mary, I would not fire that thing at this distance. It is very—"

She pulled the trigger, and I was blasted in the chest with the full force of the weapon at maximum power. It sent me flying backwards even as I saw her struck by the shrapnel my barrier had reflected. I ended up flying into multiple gravity fields before smashing into the side of cold steel.

Everything went black.

Goddammit.

This was getting to be a habit.

CHAPTER FIFTEEN

The Night That Tommy Died

Memories are tricky things, and I kept returning to the ones brought up by Space Academy. Mind you, I could be dead or dying due to getting myself blasted by the gravity gun at close range, but I was going to hope that I was just unconscious.

Again.

Whether or not I was, I couldn't help but be drawn back into the world I'd lived in before graduation. Knowing what Other Kathy had told me before her death about Tommy, it shouldn't have been a surprise that my mind would drift to one of the worst times of my life.

Tommy and I were sitting in a cramped locker room made to look like an airlock. Everything was white or gray and there was an oppressive emptiness that subtly prepared you for what was to come.

We were in a part of H-Rod that was designed for long-term space walks and in-system transport. It was our final year in Space Academy, and we were preparing for the most infamous tests for those applying to the Community Protectors: The Long Walk.

"I've got a bad feeling about this," Tommy said, pulling on the boots of his AG-7 space suit. It was a much less bulky version of the ones that humanity had first used when they went into space, with multiple redundancies and interior computer systems. They were still designed to recycle your wastes, and I didn't know any single human being who didn't find the process humiliating. However, space walks could take up to twenty or thirty hours on average. This one would be an entire month in space.

The Long Walk was one of the most well-established tests in the Academy and one that had broken more than a few candidates. More

116

than a few thousand if you took its entire history into account. Effectively, you were required to spend an entire month in your suit and managing issues of survival while operating various scientific tests on a barren asteroid's surface.

Aunt Kathy mocked it as nothing compared to the kind of tests she and her fellow astronauts had endured back during the last days of the Pre-First Contact space program. However, that didn't mean the Long Walk wasn't something each cadet dreaded.

The sense of spacesuit isolation, lack of privacy, and claustrophobia that the Long Walk induced caused a dozen candidates to wash out every year. Humans were not made for the vacuum of space and so much of our technology ended up being designed to simulate everything from gravity to heat to day and night cycles. But the Long Walk was a reminder to everyone that space was fundamentally hostile to all living organisms.

Well, except to cosmozoans but none of them attended the Academy.

I think.

"You're being paranoid," I said, adjusting the gloves on my AG-7 suit. "We've been studying in foreign environments every year. Desert, poisonous atmosphere, super-heated rock, underwater, and even the simulated giant stomach."

"Bowels, not stomach," Tommy said, looking at me. "Seriously, is that actually a creature out there or was that just them borking with us?"

"I've had contradictory reports," I said, frowning. "I get the impression that it's a form of hazing. Some of the graduates say that the giant monster's stomach we were in is a real thing they've encountered while others say it's simulated."

"What do you think?" Tommy asked.

"I think we were waist deep in alien savit either way," I muttered. "I am glad that I wasn't able to smell anything through the suit."

"I could," Tommy said, shuddering. "I know it was all in my head, but I caught a whiff after I removed my suit and it was exactly like what I imagined smelling for the week we spent inside that thing. You know

Theresa had a nervous breakdown? She resigned from Space Academy and went back to become a nun on her home planet."

I stared at Tommy. "Her grandfather died and left her sixteen million credits. I don't think that requires a nervous breakdown to make use of. I believe her last words to me were that she planned to move to Belenus and spend the rest of her life borking horny young men."

"I imagine that decision was helped by having to live in a giant stomach for a week," Tommy said, pausing. "Actually, this conversation is reassuring me. I feel much better about going out into a pitiless void when it's compared to the experience of being in a cavern-sized digestion system. Thanks."

"No problem," I said, taking a deep breath. "Honestly, there were times I considered quitting."

"Bullsavit," Tommy said, pausing his suiting up. He turned to look down at me with his exaggeratedly large eyes behind his goggles. I could only see his look as a mixture of annoyance and disbelief. I'd gotten pretty good at reading Tommy's expressions even if I hadn't mastered Sorkanan in general.

"No, seriously," I said, surprised at Tommy's reaction. "There were more than a few days that I was just ready to call it quits."

I'd kept waiting for Space Academy to change me like Aunt Kathy had indicated would happen. I was expecting some defining moment where I would become inspired to transform from a cadet going through the motions into someone excited to spend decades—possibly even centuries if my longevity drugs held out—defending the Community from its enemy while exploring the great unknown.

I'd watched literally hundreds of hours of classic science fiction in my spare time trying to feel what Aunt Kathy felt. I loved *Star Trek, Star Wars, Terraformers,* and *Legends of the Spacers.* Hell, I even loved *Space Cadet Sally* and that was for kids and deeply lonely men who needed to get off the infospace boards.

But I didn't feel *it.* Whatever it was. I loved the drama on the screen and the sense of exhilaration that the protagonists felt in their weekly serials. However, I didn't feel reality lived up to the simulation. I'd made perhaps half a dozen friends in my time here at Space Academy and mostly found the people here the same as on the outside. Yeah, sure, they were smarter and more career-driven but had the same petty bullsavit driving them.

And space didn't hold the sense of mystery that it was supposed to. The Community wasn't the heroic collection of democratic worlds that its propaganda portrayed. The Protectors weren't the champions of democratic prosperity that Aunt Kathy continually tried to sell me. EarthGov just seemed to want to expand as fast as possible to as many worlds as they could hold.

In other words, I was bored.

"You make me sick sometimes, Vannevar," Tommy said, causing me to do a double take.

"What?" I asked.

"Everyone else in Space Academy struggles to pass these grueling tests and you coast through them like they don't even require effort," Tommy said. "Mostly because your aunt paid for you to be made into some sort of superhuman."

"That's not... entirely true," I said, looking away. I was an enhanced human being, admittedly, but it hadn't occurred to me until I'd come to the Academy that this was abnormal. She'd paid for the gene therapies to make me extra suited for space work as well as the implants that were designed to enhance my cognitive reasoning. I'd undergone several surgeries over the years to always make sure I had the most advanced possible.

"You also were prepped for this from the time you were a hatchling," Tommy said, falling into a Sorkanan idiom.

I opened my mouth then closed it. Yeah, that was another thing that my aunt had done for me. I'd known she was prepping me for Space Academy, but I hadn't been aware of just how *much* she'd been prepping me for Space Academy. It turned out I'd been given the equivalent of an Olympian's carefully regimented training to make sure that I knew every test answer, situation, by-law, and technical specs before I ever sat down in class.

"Yeah, I was," I finally said. "I didn't know you resented that."

"Vance, you're hard to resent despite so many reasons to do so," Tommy said, shaking his head. Which meant the same thing to

Sorkanan as it did for humans. "You just don't know how easy you've got it here nor how good it's going to be for you when you get out. You'll probably be a captain of Space Fleet in ten years."

"I think that's illegal," I replied. "EarthGov regulations require fifteen years of service before promotion without direct executive ord—"

"Yeah, yeah," Tommy said. "You're proving my point. You're the perfect officer and already famous. Take comfort in that before complaining about how hard it is for you here."

"I don't..." I paused. "I resent the fact that people are trying to use me for propaganda."

"Why?" Tommy asked.

"Why?" I asked, confused.

"You are getting a pretty tasty deal out of it from my perspective," Tommy said. "After you punched out that bigot—"

"Which was staged," I said, still upset about that.

"You *think* it was staged," Tommy corrected.

"I *think* it was staged," I said, correcting myself. Leah had gotten into my head and it was hard to get out of the mindset that everyone was watching you and that you should distrust everything. Leah Mass was a wonderful gal but I had to wonder how she'd come to think the way she did. Maybe it was an Albion thing. "It was three or four weeks of seeing myself punching that guy out and disciplinary hearings."

"He swung first," Tommy said, referring to Marvin Kittridge.

"That doesn't matter," I replied. "I should have been kicked out."

"If every bar brawl and punch thrown in Space Academy was punished by expulsion then there'd be no upper classman," Tommy said. "We Sorkanan celebrate the conflicts among individuals as a rite of passage."

"You've never been in a fight in your life," I said, dryly.

"Yes, because the Sorkanan celebrate the conflicts among individuals and I am a tiny person who hits like a prey animal," Tommy said, holding out his claw limply. "Still, it ended well. The guy you punched got kicked out, you got cleared of charges, and the Sons of Humanity are banned from H-Rod as a criminal organization."

The adding of the Sons of Humanity to the proscribed political organizations list had been surprising and the result of a dramatic shift in public sentiment thanks to the Notha War. The media had shown humanity heroically blasting away the furry fascists in such a way that everyone was glued to their vids. As such, both the anti-war protestors and Sons of Humanity had fallen out of favor. The Sons of Humanity were also implicated in planting bombs in the capital building of EarthGov in Paris, which resulted in their right of protest being removed.

At least in government locations.

Was it wrong to think that, too, had been staged?

I had no idea.

That was when there was a knocking at our locker room door. "Hey, are you guys almost done?"

It was Leah, who was presently my girlfriend. Again. We'd had something of an on again and off again relationship over the past three years. Basically, whenever I thought we were getting serious, she would pull back then we'd end up breaking up. She'd go back to her studies and I'd go hook up with another set of students to soothe my bruised ego. I wasn't proud of it and those relationships were superficial, but it was how things had gone. Inevitably, though, we drifted back to one another as if she was assigned to get me to like her.

Assigned.

I pushed that thought out of my head and exchanged a look with Tommy. "Are we ready?"

"As ready as we'll ever be," Tommy said. "I'm going to let you in on a little secret: I hate space. I hate vacuum. I love low gravity and despise zero gravity. I am a huge fan of air, up, down, sunlight, and ground."

"Wow, are you in the wrong business," I said, sitting up. "You do realize that space is a lot of empty nothingness."

"Yeah, and I enjoy being on little rocks in it," Tommy said. "It's just that the one we're going to is going to be particularly inhospitable."

I nodded. "We'll get through this. Have you double-checked everything?"

"Triple-checked," Tommy said. "You? Assuming your cybernetics don't make that redundant."

They did but I wasn't going to tell him that. "I did everything by the book. Double-checked and triple-checked."

"Good," Tommy said, picking up his helmet. "I know we're not going to be assigned to the same ship after this, Vance, but it was good knowing you. I hope we'll be able to meet up again in the future. It's a big galaxy but you've been a good bond-brother."

"Who knows," I said, nodding to Tommy. "Maybe when I'm a big influential captain, I can request you to be my chief engineer."

Tommy laughed.

I picked up my own helmet and put it under my left arm. I opened the door with my free hand and saw Leah waiting for us on the other side. She was accompanied by someone I didn't expect to see: Marvin Kittridge. Both were dressed for space walks.

"What the..." I said, confused as hell by Marvin's presence.

Marvin Kittridge was, in simple terms, an ugly motherborker. There was something about his face that just seemed designed to be punchable. He had short black hair in a bowl cut, a five o'clock shadow, jowls that highlighted his beady eyes, and an upturned nose. I had no idea how much my hatred for the man was influencing my opinion of his looks but the guy just plizzed me off something fierce.

Marvin had become the symbol of the Sons of Humanity throughout the galaxy as the perfect villain to embody them. However, he'd also developed a huge fandom with his lengthy speeches and infospace channel that blamed alien influence for everything from the decline of human birth rates to the inability for Earth men to be taken seriously by other planets' women. Which, as far as I knew, wasn't actually a thing.

While I still believed it to be a setup, that hadn't protected Marvin from the consequences of his actions. He'd been expelled from Space Academy and there were still criminal charges in the works against him, or so I had thought. Seeing him here called into question a lot of what I believed was true and authentic about this case.

"Hello, Vance," Leah said. "I think you know Mr. Kittridge."

"What the bork is he doing here?" I asked.

Marvin Kittridge made a face that approximated a smile. "I saw the light and shared a lot of information on my associates and their radical agenda. All criminal charges have been dropped and the Academy has been kind enough to hire me as a contractor for handling space walks. I was born in space and my family used to mine asteroids by hand."

That was a bit like claiming your family did gold prospecting. There was no reason to do asteroid mining save with bots unless you were deeply stupid or a criminal. Maybe both. "So, you snitched on your fellows and they gave you a job here."

"Something like that," Marvin said, looking at me with a bland expression that somehow radiated hatred.

Leah stared back at him, and he lowered his gaze. Somehow, my girlfriend intimidated him.

"Well, we should get going," Tommy said, putting his hand on my shoulder. "There's no point in worrying about old grievances."

"Right," I said, shaking my head. "Let's move it."

Nine hours later, I would lower Tommy down into an asteroid crater and the grapple would break with the sealing on his helmet shattering against the side. My friend would die instantly but I would carry the memory forever.

Marvin Kittridge would testify against me but was fired for his own part.

I doubt he cared.

CHAPTER SIXTEEN

The Court of Public Opinion

"You know, Vance, I'm getting really tired of you showing up in my hospital," Doctor Elizabeth Zard spoke, looking down at me. She had a penlight flashing in my eyes. That, thankfully, helped wake me up from the fugue I'd been experiencing.

Memory was a notoriously fickle thing, and I couldn't with 100% certainty say that what I'd remembered happening with Tommy in my dream was how it had gone down. One of my instructors had said that memory was more like someone telling you a story from how they remembered it than actual recordings of events. You remembered how a thing went down in terms of facts then tried to reconstruct a visual image in your head from those facts. The visual image was never the real thing and could become wildly distorted over time as you remembered your reconstructions continually over the facts themselves.

That was a roundabout way of saying that I couldn't tell if I'd actually triple-checked my equipment while making sure Tommy had done the same for his. Marvin Kittridge had been there. I hadn't hallucinated that fact but he'd been cleared of any involvement. Even then, I hadn't suspected him of hating me enough to commit murder. I wasn't sure I did now. It was more likely the Other Kathy had been lying in hopes of manipulating me.

I would never know.

I would have to live with that.

"I worry the rest of my life is going to be spent in a combination of flashbacks and head trauma," I said, blinking rapidly.

"That sentence is either reassuring or a sign that you banged your head worse than I thought," Doctor Zard said.

I looked around at my surroundings in dismay. There was Doctor Zard, the clinic room, Astrid, and the Diplomat but it all felt distressingly familiar. "Am in the exact same room I was this morning?"

"Yep!" Doctor Zard said, patting me on the wrist. "Look at the bright side, though. You are not listed as having your life energy stolen or other mythical nonsense condition! No, you just got shot with a gravity gun and smacked yourself against some metal paneling."

"How did I get here?" I asked, looking at my daughter.

"That's one of life's big mysteries, isn't it, Dad?" Astrid asked, looking at me. She'd bought me a Vance Turbo-brand teddy bear and was adjusting it by my side. There was also a vase of flowers with a balloon next to it. "I mean, is there a god? Are we in a simulation? Are individuality and free will true facts of consciousness or just illusions from the wet quantum computers in our bone structures? Are you separate from me or are we one in the same?"

I stared at her. "I meant here in the clinic."

"Oh!" Astrid said, smirking. "No, you were brought here by Danny and Hannah. They sent a couple of Space Marines teams to pick you up to make sure that High Protector B'Vash didn't arrange any accidents for you along the way. Assuming he didn't arrange an accident for you. Did he?"

"Your daughter is very strange," the Diplomat said, voicing what had been self-evident from the moment I'd met Astrid.

"It's part of why I love her," I said. "How long was I out?"

"You died, Vance. It's been years," Doctor Zard said. "The Community spent trillions—"

"You did that joke already," I said, annoyed.

"Well don't get put into a coma twice in one day," Doctor Zard said, putting away her penlight. "I need time to refresh all my snark."

"What happened to bedside manner?" I asked, looking up at her.

"There's a reason I wanted to be a mathematician instead of a medical doctor," Doctor Zard said, putting her hands in her pockets and shaking her head. "Frankly, I think doctors should re-evaluate the whole concept. Is it better to make the patient feel better or for the doctor to feel better by mocking the patient and their idiocy?"

"The patient," I said, narrowing my eyes.

"See? Now, that's just your opinion and a wrong one from my perspective," Doctor Zard said. "But your body has once more shown itself to be held together with spit, bailing wire, and a bunch of uber-technological nanobots that were created by species millions of years older than ours."

"Which means?" I asked.

"You're fine, you can go again," Doctor Zard replied, waving. "Just don't expect me to treat you for a third time when your head gets blown clean off."

"I'm pretty sure that will kill me," I replied.

"Are you sure?" Doctor Zard asked. "Maybe it'll grow an additional Vance and then we'll have two of you running around ruining the galaxy for mathematician/general practitioners."

"I missed you too, Liz," I said, sarcastically.

"How could you miss me? You keep coming back?" Doctor Zard said, throwing her hands up in the air. That was when her expression changed and I became uncomfortably aware she seemed worried. "Seriously, though, Vance—Captain, Vannevar—try to look after yourself. A captain is supposed to die on the bridge. He's not supposed to run around shooting things."

"Captain Kirk on a bridge," I said, pausing. "It collapsed on him. I think he should have been more specific that he wanted to die on a *starship* bridge."

"I'd prefer you not die at all, Dad," Astrid said.

"We should be so lucky," the Diplomat said. "When the fires of the universe go out and the stars have all turned to black holes, your father will undoubtedly be there making references to shows that weren't that good to begin with."

"You shut your damn mouth," I said, pointing at her with a fake frown on my face. "Also, *Star Trek: Generations* was a movie not a show."

"I'm leaving now," Doctor Zard said, on her way to my room's door. "If you suddenly develop a lesion on your brain or have a stroke, I'll take retirement."

When the door slid open, it revealed many reporters and civilians gathered outside with vidcameras and holophones to take pictures. There were also a pair of Academy security guards at the sides to keep the crowd out. It was a massive change from before where my condition hadn't even been a blip on the newsfeeds.

"So, I take it that my little stunt with the Codex got attention, huh?" I asked, turning to Astrid and the Diplomat.

"Andy Warhol said that in the future, which is now, everyone would be famous for fifteen minutes," Astrid said. "You've somehow managed to pull off two or three hours."

"I don't know who that is and suspect that you have been spending too much time with Trish," I said.

"I liked Seventies Trish," Astrid said. "I'm sorry she was eaten by Trish Prime."

I did not eat her! Trish said in my mind. *I mean, I absorbed her and combined with her. It's more like when twins are in the womb, and one merges with the other. Which, now that I think about it, has sometimes been called eating your twin. However, we were originally the same AI to begin with so it shouldn't count. Except, identical twins start as one zygote before splitting in half. So if I split in half then absorbed the other I actually did eat—*

I ignored Trish and focused on my daughter. "Is Forty-Two around?"

"Yeah," Astrid said. "He complained about his old bones having to move around so much as well as how hospital food was terrible. Nothing was live and wiggling. So, he went to get drolochid cuisine, which I think is a metaphor because Sorkanan and drolochids don't share the same RNA so they couldn't possibly—"

"Drolochid cuisine is code for interspecies sex," the Diplomat said.

Astrid did a double take. "Huh."

"Thank you for telling her that," I said, sarcastically. "Really."

I was going to have to have a talk with Forty-Two.

"You are welcome, Lord Satan," the Diplomat replied. "But yes, you have caused quite a stir outside."

"How big of a stir are we talking about?" I asked.

"You are as famous as you used to be," Astrid said, looking at me. "Movie offers are pouring in. People want to do interviews with you. There is already a lot of discussion over who these Parkerzor are and what sort of aliens they may be."

"So, no one knows they're not real, huh," I said, taking a deep breath. "I suppose I should be grateful we have some time before the truth comes out."

"Oh the truth will never come out," the Diplomat said. "The Great Notha has proclaimed this is all a hoax and an attempt to undermine the Notha Union. Given his history of lying, this has done much to solidify the Codex as something genuinely from the Perseus Arm."

"That makes no sense," I said, staring at her.

"Doesn't it?" The Diplomat asked. "You've spent years exploring the far reaches of the Known Universe. Which is more likely, that you came back with proof of advanced Community-level civilizations or that it is a superstructure you decided to drop out of nowhere? One constructed by an illegal conspiracy you have been fighting an invisible war against for a decade?"

I blinked. "You have a point, but eventually people are going to realize there's no such thing as the Parkerzors."

"It's a big galaxy, Dad," Astrid said. "Just say their location is classified and as a High Protector, no one will be able to gainsay you. The Kingdom of Prestor John was made up by a bunch of medieval scam artists, but people kept looking for it centuries later."

"You two are both adorable and evil," I said, wishing I had a HyperCola. I hadn't eaten all day and events had been kind of stressful.

"Thank you," the Diplomat said.

"I don't suppose either of you could tell me what's going on with the people who know better about the Codex?" I asked, not really expecting an answer.

"I can provide you with that," a woman said, entering into the room past the guards. It was Shelly T'Ketra.

My ex.

Astrid's mother.

"Well, this is awkward," Astrid said, looking over at the Diplomat.

Shelly froze in midstride, looking suddenly uncomfortable and clearly not having expected her biological daughter to be present.

"Hello, Captain," I said, addressing her by her title. "Thank you for your part in saving the poor Parkerzors. You probably didn't notice them on the space station because they're invisible and intangible unless they want to be seen."

"Vance, I'm not in the mood," Shelly said, taking a deep breath.

"You never are," I said. "Oh, I'm engaged to Trish now!"

"You are?" Shelly asked, blinking. "I, um, am happy for you."

"She's not," Astrid clarified.

"Stay out of my mind, kid," Shelly said, glaring.

"No," Astrid said, making a very rude gesture in Sorkanan.

"I can see you're raising her with all the dignity and glory expected of your line," Shelly said, sarcastically.

"What were you doing at her age?" I asked.

"Killing an adult male human for food," Shelly paused, clearly remembering her time on Happy Funtime Planet. "Alright, maybe I shouldn't be condemnatory to your methods of parenting. I'm not planning to have kids and that precludes me from making any moral judgements."

Astrid glared.

"What can I do for you?" I asked Shelly.

"You can explain what the bor... er, what the he... no, what the heck is going on!" Shelly said, trying to avoid swearing around Astrid. I would have found it cute except that it was so sad.

"Okay," I said, pausing. "Yeah, I said that the Codex was Department Twelve's base and I brought it from where it had been hidden in jumpspace. I then lied about it and promised it to High Protector B'Vash. Oh, and the Great Notha really wants it because it would make the Notha Union invincible. Except, they're already invincible since they discovered humans love money more than they do their homeworld."

The Diplomat reached over and patted my hand. "Your species was always destined to lose, Lord Satan."

129

"Oh, go gather some acorns," I said, frowning. Okay, that was a bit xenophobic and beneath me. I'd taken a blow to the head. Cut me some slack.

The Diplomat looked confused as to whether she should or not.

"B'Vash is a dangerous man," Shelly said, leaving off his title. "He's probably the one behind Department Twelve."

"He is," I replied. "My father confirmed it."

Shelly paused. "Okay, now I'm doubting myself."

"Then he confessed," I said. "B'Vash, not my father. I wouldn't believe my father if he claimed the sky was blue."

"On which planet?" Astrid asked.

"Not the point, dear," I replied.

"I'm just saying you're mean to grandpa," Astrid said. "He seemed nice."

"He really wasn't," I said. "Neither is your grandmother, if you ever meet her."

I'd looked up Leah's parents after her death. Both had been killed in the Notha War by privateers.

"Grandparents and grandchildren get along because they share a common enemy," the Diplomat explained.

"We might meet your great grandparents on the moon if we survive this mission," I said. "In any case, Shelly, I'm sure I've caused you and your treaty some small—"

"The treaty is done," Shelly said, sighing. "The Great Notha has said that he is not going to end conflict with Deathworld no matter what level of support the Community gives them."

"Crap," I muttered.

"It gets worse," Shelly said.

"How can it get worse?" the Diplomat asked before grabbing one of my fingers and biting it.

"Ow!" I said, pulling it back.

"That is for ruining my world, again," the Diplomat said.

Shelly sighed. "The Great Notha has furthermore decreed that they are withdrawing from the agreements you negotiated that brought an end to Contested Space. He claims all of the former human colonies and is prepared to go to war over them."

"Crazzap," I said, realizing this was a complete disaster. The Notha Union couldn't defeat the Community but that would imply the latter wanted to go to war over the colonies given to Earth in the treaty. The Human League was leaving after all. If the Notha Union were up against the Human League, then it was a contest that favored the Notha even in their current diminished state. A full-scale war might also lead to the death of billions as nothing would stop the Notha from engaging in genocidal tactics against a non-Community world except the High Council deciding to be unusually helpful.

Right.

"Not done yet," Shelly said, looking around the room.

"There's more?" I asked, horrified.

"The Human League is in a panic and EarthGov's incoming Prime Minister has indicated she might not be interested in defending the territories there," Shelly said, biting down on her back teeth. "That cowardly backstabbing harpy is bought and paid for by the Union."

"That's not good," I said, aware I may have just ruined humanity's future while trying to save it.

"There is a caveat," Shelly said, looking down at you. "The Great Notha is willing to negotiate these points with a single representative of the Community and EarthGov."

"Me?" I asked, knowing that would be the only possible answer with my luck.

"You."

CHAPTER SEVENTEEN

The Law of Unintended Consequences

I lifted my proton sword in the air and illuminated the area around me, revealing the lengthy stretches of piping and a strange foam that looked like water after you put dishwashing liquid in it. We were traveling through the storm sewers—technically called "hygiene canals"—that were located underneath the surface levels of H-Rod. I was once more dressed in my uniform, but was also wearing a thick pair of boots and the plastic pair of overalls that the rest of my group was also dressed in.

This was the second time in recent memory I'd found myself traveling through sewer tunnels to escape a bunch of problems and this was no better than the first time. The sewers in H-Road were much nicer than the ones in the Ring but it was still a bunch of dark, cramped, passages that were where the wastes of a habitat were pushed.

I wasn't happy about making my journey down here but after Shelly had told me about the Great Notha's demand, I needed to speak with Case. Case had decided that given my newfound fame, it was best to meet in a non-public place. Unfortunately, for a master spy that translated in the middle of the borking sewers.

Thankfully, I was able to bring people with me this time. Cadet Catgirl, Trish, and Hannah were accompanying me. Hannah had decided it was better to be my side than managing the *Melampus*, leaving Light on Water in charge. Astrid had been picked up by Danny and Elektra with both of them willing to burn down the galaxy to protect her. It was in my files that should I suddenly pass away—most likely after someone killed me—they were to be the people to take her in.

Sneaking out past my fan club and the several hundred Community officials who wanted to speak with me hadn't been easy but I'd passed literal tests from the Elder Races to determine if humanity was fit to survive. It hadn't been *that* difficult to get down here. Now that I was, though, I regretted not telling Case to borking visit my starship.

"Cleaning the streets has always been a problem for the habitat," Cadet Catgirl said, walking beside me. "That's why we include the artificial storms in the central dome, twice a week. The rain that pours down is filled with disinfectant that forces uncollected trash or food waste into the hygiene canals."

"Uh huh," I said, not really caring.

"Bots then sort the solid trash from the biodegradable before moving them into different tunnels down here," Cadet Catgirl said. "As much as possible is recycled while the rest is compacted down into disposable cubes that are promptly sent out into space."

"That actually seems really wasteful," Trish said, sloshing through the fluid behind us. "You know, we should really have told Case to visit our starship."

"The thought occurred to me," I said.

"I never should have left you alone," Hannah said, wearing her armor as well as the plastic overlay. "That was stupid of me. I'm not meant to be on the bridge. I meant to be out there, on the ground, shooting up people."

"No one needed to be shot up," I said, frowning.

"You killed like two dozen Notha," Trish said. "By chopping them up."

I grimaced, not even clearly remembering what had happened. It had been a frenzy of movement and it had been over almost as soon as it had begun. If I'd been actively thinking during it, maybe I might have been able to save Other Kathy's life. Then again, if I hadn't asked her to suit up and fight, maybe she would have lived as well.

"Chopping up is different from shooting up," I replied. "I think."

Cadet Catgirl looked at me. "Wow, you are a lot darker than your movies make you out to be."

133

"Yes, well, you've probably only seen the edited ones," I replied. "Why are you coming with me?"

"Because I want to learn what sort of odious criminal conspiracy is infecting my beautiful Space Academy!" Cadet Catgirl said, curling her paws into adorable balls. "Also, I actually know the general layout of the hygiene canal system and it would be terrible if you got lost down here and then died. Could you imagine? Vance Turbo, Hero of SPAAACE, dies in a sewer after head trauma? Especially after you delivered a mammoth super structure from a Perseus Arm species!"

I grimaced. "Yeah, about that..."

"What?" Cadet Catgirl asked.

"Never mind," I said. "It's not important."

"Okey dokey!" Cadet Catgirl said, cheerfully.

I tried to check up on Peter, Paul, and Mary but hadn't had much luck. B'Vash wasn't accepting my calls and his people were now in charge of the Codex. I had no idea if Mary had died, or of the status of the workers I'd tried to rescue. I felt sick turning over the Codex to B'Vash but hadn't come up with a better option examining all the events that had led up to my choice. That was another Captain Picard quote, "It is possible to commit no mistakes and still lose. That is not weakness. That is life." I had made a bunch of mistakes, though, and the issue was figuring out whether there was a right answer.

God, Vance, have you considered rebooting yourself? Trish asked.

What? I replied mentally.

You are really in a funk.

I am not in a... funk.

You are absolutely in a funk. You're not depressed, I know what that feels like from Goth Trish. You're more just enjoying beating yourself up. Except it's not a healthy masochism.

Healthy masochism? I asked, skeptically.

Like whips and chains, yeah, Trish said. *Another thing I learned from Goth Trish. It's like you get off on beating yourself up and martyring yourself. Oh my God, you are Spider-Man!*

I was thankfully spared from responding by turning a corner and seeing Case. The instructor was standing in the corner of a maintenance tunnel and playing with a deck of cards. A tiny glowing blue-white ball was hovering over his head. He looked like the informant in any number of bad vids. I had to wonder what sort of personality was capable of living centuries in the paranoid, intrigue-ridden hell that was spycraft.

I'd tried to do some research on Director G once I'd become High Protector and even then, there were a lot of places where I'd run into walls. The Director of EarthGov's Security Services had gone out of his way to redact, destroy, and circumvent his own past whenever possible. I knew some things like he was a bioroid, Patricia Ares' father, and married a few times to extremely impressive women. However, for the most part, Case was a mystery and liked it that way.

"Hi," I said, waving at the old spymaster. "What an incredible smell you've discovered."

"It smells like a leaky washing machine," Case replied, looking up. "I've been to a million places that smell a lot worse."

"Yeah, I admit, it's not exactly spending a week in a giant monster's bowels," I said, pausing. "Do they still have that test, Catgirl?"

Cadet Catgirl looked confused. "I have no idea what you're talking about."

I shrugged. "It must have gotten up and decided it no longer wanted students poking around in its digestive system. I needed to speak with you."

"You can do so alone," Case said, looking at my accompaniment.

"I'm not letting Vance out of my sight again," Hannah said, lifting up a plasma rifle. "Not even with you, Case. For all we know, you've been replaced by one of the Space Vampires and are planning on luring Vance into a trap."

Case looked at her. "For all you know, Vance has already been replaced by one of the Space Vampires and is luring me into a trap."

Hannah blinked, having not considered that. "Crazzap. That's entirely possible."

"No it is not!" I snapped. "Also, can we stop calling them Space Vampires?"

"I mean it's what they're called," Trish said.

"Maybe they have their own name for themselves," Cadet Catgirl said, perking up. "Maybe they don't consider themselves vampires.

135

Maybe they consider themselves like manta rays or wandering space cosmozoans. Who knows, maybe a better name for them would be Seekers or Travelers or—"

"Yeah, let's stick with Space Vampires," Hannah said. "Evil Bodystealing Monsters is too much of a mouthful."

"How about EBM?" Cadet Catgirl asked.

"Don't you start," Hannah said.

Cadet Catgirl pouted.

"We're going to be discussing a lot of very sensitive stuff, Vance," Case said, sighing. "The least they can do is wait outside the tunnel."

"I have super sensitive hearing," Cadet Catgirl said. "So, uh, yeah, you can absolutely trust me."

"I'll be using a noise canceller," Case said, looking annoyed.

"Oh," Cadet Catgirl said, frowning. "That's great. Super. Makes sense."

"Fine," I said, walking into the tunnel. "However, if you've been replaced by a Space Vampire then know that after I kill you I will feel really bad about it. When I make first contact with a new species, I try not to kill them."

"Get over here, Vance," Case said. "You're starting to remind me of my friend, Gary, and you do not want to remind me of Gary."

"Who's Gary?" I asked.

"The single most annoying person in two universes," Case said, his voice betraying a sense of affection.

Well, that was a weird descriptor. I walked over to Case's side, though, having been the one to arrange this meeting. I deactivated and sheathed my proton sword.

Case tapped the glowing ball above our heads, which shifted its color from blue-white to red. "Okay, they can't hear us now."

I stared at him. "What's with the heightened security and undisclosed location?"

"I dunno, because of the imminent threat of war between humanity and the Notha?" Case asked.

"You really borked up," Case said, closing his eyes. "Mind you, it's not like there was a right answer. Oh yes, there was. The right answer was not letting B'Vash get his hands on the Codex."

"Oh don't give me that bullsavit," I said, glaring. "There was no other option to keep it out of the hands of the Great Notha."

"I'm not sure B'Vash is a better option," Case said, sounding defeated for the first time in all the time I'd known him. "He's the evil heart of Department Twelve and dozens of other organizations like them spread throughout the Community. He's been the Community's monster for centuries that they've pointed at other monsters. Except, now the High Council fears him too much to rein him in. If you want to know who ordered the Kolahn homeworld's destruction, it was him. He wanted to teach a lesson to the rest of the galaxy of what consequences befell those who contested with the Community."

"Contested?" I asked.

"I come from a time when people said fuck instead of bork," Case replied. "I really miss that word."

I closed my eyes. "So, yeah, I screwed up."

"Epically," Case said. "I wanted to keep you out of it, so that's why I provided you that fake data crystal and said it came from Leah."

My eyes shot open. "You son of a bish!"

Case shrugged. "I am what I am. I knew Department Twelve was going to try to recruit you in hopes of bailing them out. They knew B'Vash was washing his claws of humanity after the death of Admiral Bendo. The Codex was the only thing that they had left to offer him and they knew that would be taken from them once he had it. It was their last bargaining chip and it could either be used to rebuild the organization or serve the Community's hatchet man."

Wow. Way to make a guy feel guilty. "Suddenly, Mary's reaction seems a lot more justified."

"The synths, which is what I call them, are humans with all the knowledge of adults but the emotional maturity of teenagers," Case said, shrugging. "In other words, perfect for infiltrating organizations like the Sons of Humanity."

"You know they answer to the Great Notha, right?" I asked.

"No kidding," Case said, as if I was telling him water was wet. "The Sons of Humanity was originally created as a PSYOP for Department Twelve to manipulate public sentiment. Basically, create a group so vile and ineffectual that they would drive people closer to the Community.

Unfortunately, they overestimated humanity and it took on a life of its own. There was too much money to be made in hate."

"There always is," I muttered. "So, we have to get the Codex away from B'Vash."

"It's not that simple, Vance," Case said. "You've possibly precluded any options at this point other than B'Vash winning."

"I'm remarkably good at pulling rabbits from hats," I said. "But the Great Notha wants to speak with me. I think he wants to negotiate."

"That would be a terrible idea," Case said. "We're already dealing with one narcissistic psychopath, I don't think we need to deal with two."

"Or three," I said, staring at him.

"Okay, that was actually really funny," Case said, struggling not to smile. "Inaccurate but funny."

"I wish I could have unraveled this conspiracy much earlier," I said, sucking in my breath. "I've let my despair and grief define me. If I wasn't overwhelmed by Leah's death, I probably wouldn't have made some of the choices I did. But I did make those choices and I'm prepared to deal with the consequences. Maybe I'll get myself killed and orphan Astrid. Maybe I'll get other people killed because I'm very good at that. However, I'm going to try to do the best I can. That's all I can do."

"No," Case said. "There is no try. Only do or do not."

"Bork you," I said, narrowing my eyes.

"You can use the f-word," Case said. "Seriously, I won't blame you."

"Are you in or not?" I asked.

Case closed eyes. "I'm willing to follow you on this damn fool idealistic crusade, Vance. But I should let you know that these kinds of adventures are notoriously hazardous to older, more experienced heroes."

"It's hazardous to the young, too," I said. "I want to marry your daughter. We can do that after we've taken down B'Vash and the Great Notha."

If I was going to aim high, I might as well aim for the top.

"Don't bring her along, Vance. I've outlived two. I don't want to outlive another," Case said, referring to Patricia and Alexandra.

The Trish in my head was peculiarly silent during this conversation and I almost asked what she thought before thinking better of it. I was about to make another crack when I caught a glimpse of plasma fire shooting past the other end of the hall. Unfortunately, I couldn't hear what was being said but I saw Hannah shouting.

CHAPTER EIGHTEEN

Double- and Triple-Crossed

"Motherborker," I said, wondering who had tracked me down and how. "Is it the Notha? Did they follow me here?"

"No," Case said, pulling out a small R-18 plasma pistol that was illegal within the Community because they couldn't be detected by most scanners. He charged his gun and looked to my proton sword.

I drew my weapon. "We're not done."

"We are for now," Case said. "Crazy as it sounds, Vance, you are far too important to let die here."

"I've survived gunfights before," I replied, looking at him with concern. There was something about Case's attitude that concerned me. Something had happened and I wasn't sure what it was. He was hiding things and while that wasn't surprising, it seemed like whatever he was hiding was too big even for the galaxy's greatest spymaster.

"You survive every gunfight until your last one," Case said, his expression softening. "If you keep having them, then eventually you'll get your number punched."

I didn't understand the context of the statement but I understood what he meant. Perhaps I'd been trying to seek out the battle that would finally claim my life. That was when I stepped out of the red light's glow and heard Trish again.

Vance, stop being an idiot and help us! Trish said, showing the noise canceller had somehow affected her as well despite her being in my head.

Weird.

Who is attacking? I asked, wondering just how many blasts of energy my barrier could take before it went down. Community-designed barriers were usually capable of taking one or two hits before burning out, but Elder Race technology worked on willpower. Not that such a restriction made any sort of sense scientifically, but I gathered my bosses liked to impose a lot of arbitrary restrictions on their servants. You really, really needed to want this for them to give it to you.

I could see blasts of plasma sailing through the air in both directions at the end of the tunnel and jogged to the edge, unwilling to let my people face whatever was attacking them alone.

You're not going to like it, Trish said.

You're being shot at! Of course I'm not going to like it! I replied, taking position with my back against the edge of the hallway entrance.

Much to my surprise, I saw a group of five or six Academy security officers wearing reflective plate metal helmets and blast vests. Even more confusing was the fact that the Commandant himself was present, holding his own R-18 plasma pistol.

Why the is the Academy staff shooting at us? I asked, wondering what the hell was going on.

I don't know! Trish responded. *But we're in retreat! There's another group moving on us! You need to get to us!*

I could see Hannah, Trish, and Cadet Catgirl down the hygiene canal past several dead security guards floating in the foamy white water. That the guards were shooting at Catgirl as well as the others told me that the Academy head was not nearly as devoted a father as he was a complete anyxhole.

"Turbo!" the Commandant roared. "You are going to surrender yourself to my custody! Lay down your weapons!"

"Alright!" I said, lying. "I'm coming out!"

That was when I took a fake step forward, only to watch a half-dozen plasma bolts sail in my direction. They were definitely not stun blasts and if I'd moved forward for real, I was fairly sure I'd be dead.

Well, that confirmed where I stood with the Commandant and his goons. They had no interest in taking me alive and probably weren't going to leave any other witnesses. That meant it was either them or us.

I chose us.

"This isn't going to work out well for you, Commandant!" I shouted, trying to provide a distraction. I couldn't just wade out with my sword as they'd be able to get way too many blasts into my barrier before I could even start slashing. I also didn't *want* to kill a bunch of Academy guards even if it was a matter of life and death. But I had to suppress that emotion. "I'm a High Protector of the Community! I have a savit-ton of friends out there! All this is going to do is get you and your associates killed!"

It was, honestly, an utterly insane plan. I also didn't see the point in it. The Commandant was a minor bureaucrat in the grand scheme of things. He'd never even been a captain of a starship, having just served in a variety of administrative posts in Space Fleet before retiring to his appointment as the Academy's head. What was the adage? Those who can't do, teach? Man, that was coming up a lot lately. Maybe because it was true. Either way, this was way above his skill set.

I'd threatened him with blackmail to get out of Space Academy without formally being kicked out, having determined after Tommy's death that I wanted nothing more to do with Space Fleet. I knew he hated me from our earlier conversation, but this was deranged.

"I am working for my own High Protector, Turbo!" The Commandant called back. "You think your position is secure? You're a child of a race that is leaving the safety of the Community to live as the trash of galaxy! Anything you could do to me is going to be meaningless when humans are gone from this place!"

I wasn't sure how to point out—or even if I should bother—that while Earth and most of its colonies were probably departing, the Human League didn't consist of all of humanity. There were human settlements on Sorkanan worlds and many citizens living on mixed colonies. Humans would not suddenly disappear from the Community or Space Fleet just because its most populated worlds were exiting the Protectorate. Of course, when I was being shot at was probably not when nuance was going win out.

"I trusted you, Father!" Cadet Catgirl said, sounding a bit performative and overdramatic. "You said everything was for the Community!"

"Everything I do is for the Community!" The Commandant said. "It was a mistake letting their kind in! The Verdantians were supposed to be the next great power in our ranks, but we're overshadowed by their hairless freaks!"

One of the Security Guards in armor looked back at him.

"Sorry, I got caught up in my speech," The Commandant said to the presumably human guard. "You're one of the good ones."

The Commandant cried out as Case had somehow managed to sneak behind the man and grab him by the throat, flanking the security guards and opening fire. I did a double take as I hadn't seen him go past me and realized he must have had an exit that he'd kept hidden.

Not willing to let Case face all the danger while he was trying to provide me with a distraction, I charged out in that moment with my proton sword. It was an archaic weapon that served more as a shield than a weapon and I wished I had a plasma pistol because what I needed to do was going to get ugly.

"He's coming at us with a lightsaber! Blast him!" One of the security guards shouted.

"A what?" Another security guard asked.

That was when I hit them with my sword swings. This time I couldn't turn off my thought processes during the attack and was painfully aware that I was slashing into fellow Community members. Yes, they were trying to kill me and my associates in an illegal attack but it just felt different from the Notha and mercenaries I'd killed over the years. In the end, though, I cut down all but one who threw his weapon on the ground.

"I surrender!" He shouted.

I brought my proton sword to a halt just a few inches away from his neck as I sucked in my breath. "Surrender accepted."

He was about to say something when a plasma bolt struck the back of his neck and he fell to the ground, gurgling with his final breaths. Behind him, Case was still holding his plasma pistol, having choked the Commandant. Given Verdantians were massively stronger than regular human beings, it was a reminder that Case was even stronger than me.

"That was murder, Case," I said, growling at him.

"Add it to the pile," Case said, dismissively. "We have room for perhaps one prisoner and the Commandant is the highest value target. B'Vash has clearly decided you are a loose end that needs to be tied up."

"You think?" I asked, looking at Case. "Apparently, giving him everything he wants wasn't enough."

"Not everyone thinks you're a vapid poster boy living off stolen valor," Case said, glaring. "It was a reputation I carefully cultivated for you, but some individuals are smart enough to see past it to the truly dangerous man."

I narrowed my eyes. "Why are we friends again, Case?"

"We're not friends, Vance. We're family. You have my blessing to marry my daughter."

"Thank you," I said, pausing. "Not that I had any intention of asking for your permission or caring what you said either way."

Awww, Trish said in my head.

Are you alright? I asked.

The sounds of plasma fire had died down at the end of the hall, which told me that the fighting had ceased with the second group. That didn't necessarily mean that Hannah, Cadet Catgirl, and Trish had won, though. Right now, I was really wishing Forty-Two hadn't decided to go get himself some drolochid cuisine. That was uncharacteristic behavior for him, and I intended to give him a thorough dressing down when this was over, progressive illness or not.

We're alive, Trish replied. *Our barriers held. Hannah is pretty banged up, though. Her armor reduced the last blast she took to a severe burn.*

Get her to the clinic. Please, I said, feeling an ache in my stomach. I wondered how I'd ever been able to command my crew under these circumstances. I'd lost all professional distance between them and was terrified they'd end up getting killed trying to protect me.

There's more, Vance, Trish said.

Of course there is, I thought back. *What?*

The second group weren't Academy security, they were Sons of Humanity, They didn't fight like complete morons either. These were at least basically trained.

Another thing that made absolutely no sense. *How's Catgirl taking her father trying to kill her?*

Surprisingly well, Trish said. *But I don't know much about space lions. I'll get Hannah prepped for transport. She'll complain the entire way, though. You need to get somewhere safe. We're in one of the few places in the Academy where you could be murdered, and no one would notice.*

I wasn't so sure anymore and turned to the Commandant before slapping him across the face and trying to wake him up. It wasn't the way I wanted to deal with this, but my patience had run thin around the time he'd tried to gun me down after my attempt to surrender. Case tightened his grip on the Verdantian as I did so.

The Commandant woke up and growled, flashing his canines. "You've done it now, Turbo. You've killed Academy personal and shown—"

I punched him in the face with my ring, conjuring a shield around it and broke his snout. "That's not going to make you more likely to cooperate, but it certainly felt good. I'm not resigning from my position as High Protector, Commandant. I intend to move my citizenship to the Community when Earth leaves. That's assuming I don't just veto the Human League leaving."

"Wait, what?" The Commandant asked, suddenly confused. "Can you do that?"

I had no idea whether I could or not.

"It turns out that secession is actually pretty hard if people at the top care," Case said. "Though I'd phrase it as getting a supermajority for secession as a requirement, which the isolationists absolutely do not have. Only about 52% of voters support it and that's of people who showed up to vote. You could easily delay this—"

"Quiet," I said to Case. I turned back to the Commandant. "You may think you have the protection of a High Protector bigger than me, but I can unilaterally execute you right now. Do you think anyone will spare you a second thought?"

The Commandant was still defiant. "You don't have the belly."

"You tried to kill your own daughter," I said. "Ask me how I feel about family."

The Commandant narrowed his eyes. "I have fourteen others."

145

"And you think that makes me more inclined to spare a belligerent prisoner?" I asked, bluffing the entire way.

Case, however, wasn't, and tightened his grip.

The Commandant seemed to realize this and lowered his eyes. "What do you want to know?"

"Why did B'Vash send you to kill me?" I said, making some assumptions I shouldn't have, but we didn't exactly have time for a formal interrogation.

"The true High Protector didn't want you to meet with the Great Notha," the Commandant said, coldly. There was still a little defiance in him. "There are things that happened during the Notha War that cannot be allowed to come up. Things that the High Protector would rather not come up."

"What sort of things?" I asked.

"How should I know?" The Commandant snarled. "When the High Protector asks me to perform a service, I obey!"

Wow, he really didn't respect my ascension to the rank. I wondered if it was because I was human, me, a quarter his age, an actual captain in Space Fleet, or an Earther. Then I realized it was probably all five. There was no need to divide up reasons for someone hating you.

"The current Great Notha is the former head of the Happy Funtime Agency," Case said, referring to the Notha secret police. "If anyone knows about B'Vash's relationship to Department Twelve, it would be him."

"I will never get used to that name," I said, contemplating what Case was implying.

The Notha War had ended in the universe's only exchange of SKAMMs outside of legend. The solar-destroying weapons had wiped out a dozen or more inhabited systems and killed billions of innocents on both sides of the conflict. Department Twelve had taken the majority of the blame due to their claims that the Notha would never actually risk a full-scale exchange with the Community.

There were also some who believed that it had been Department Twelve itself who had arranged for the first volley of attacks to go off, but I'd never given much credence to that theory. Now I wasn't so sure. If the Notha had really been willing to attack then surely they would have hit Earth directly or possibly even made an attempt on Throneworld. They'd had thousands of SKAMMs in reserve and only a handful had been used.

Was it possible B'Vash had ordered the attack in secret and used humanity as his scapegoats?

I didn't get an answer because Case was shot in the back by a plasma blast.

CHAPTER NINETEEN

Family, Friend, or Both?

Seeing Case shot in the back overrode all my thoughts. In my entire time working for the Security Services, I'd never imagined Case would take a blast for me or anyone else. He'd always seemed immortal and watching him crumble to the ground was a slow-motion horror to me.

Dad! Trish shouted in my mind. *Vance, duck!*

"*Ha!*" The Commandant shouted, stretching out his claws to tear open my throat as he bared his teeth or tried to at least. His snout was still gushing blood from where Case had broken it.

I ducked, throwing myself to the ground as a hail of plasma bolts shot overhead. They cut through the back of the Commandant and a few out the other side. Plasma bolts were preferred to kinetic weapons because, in general, the shock from the energy paralyzed the body so death was instantaneous rather than inclined to wounding.

On the ground, I was able to get a look at who was shooting at us and saw yet more Sons of Humanity members. Four of them. These were equipped with blast vests and plasma rifles, but I recognized a few from the outdoor showing of my movie. It made me feel like an idiot for letting myself confuse the cover for the reality.

The Great Notha had wanted to stick his human mercenaries and collaborators on Space Academy before the treaty. What better way to do so than to insert his agents as people that were already under suspicion? If you see what you're looking for and it's an obvious flaw then you aren't going to go digging deeper. If you see the rats, you won't go looking for sharks. Okay, that was a terrible comparison.

Either way, I raised my sword and grabbed Case's R-18 pistol off the ground where it had fallen and started shooting even if it was covered in soapy-smelling foam. The four fired their weapons at me and I felt each blast strike my barrier like they were delivering hard punches to my face.

The weapons they were using were incredibly potent and drained me just trying to focus on staying alive. The last of the blasts shattered through the protection I'd summoned and sailed just past my ear over my shoulder. All the while I was pulling the trigger and aiming at the Sons of Humanity.

One.

Two.

Three.

And four.

The Sons of Humanity went down one after the other from where I shot them in the throats as I somehow managed to hit each of them in the spot where their armor was weakest. The power of the R-18 was enough to punch through their relatively weak barriers. Either way, the plasma bursts had the same effect on them as they had on the Commandant. Each of them fell to the ground, dead in an instant. More senseless deaths trying to cheat personal death for a little while longer.

"Son of a bi..." I heard a surprising voice speak from the ground, half-submerged underneath the foam.

"Case!" I said, rushing to his side. "You're alive."

"For now," Case said, slowly trying to get up. I moved to help him to his feet and saw that his back had blasted open, leaking white ichor out of the sides. "I'm afraid that being a bioroid doesn't get me completely out of this."

"We'll get you repaired or... whatever," I said, staring at the horrible sight. "Trish, where can we go?"

The Melampus *would be the only place that we can even try*, Trish said. *Space Academy shut down its bio-mechanics department last year.*

Try and get in touch with a transport. I'll get your father there.

Trish didn't respond, which wasn't a good sign.

"Vance, you need to get out of here," Case said, his voice already sounding tired and empty. "B'Vash and the Great Notha are both trying to get you. That's because they know you still have cards to play."

"What cards?" I asked, confused. "I don't have any cards. I've been winging it this entire time. I have no idea what I'm doing!"

Case smiled. It was a weak and resigned one but a smile, nevertheless. "That's the secret... of being a spymaster, Vance. You... can't let them see you sweat. You're always winging it and trying... your best. You know, I wanted you to be *my* successor."

I got under one shoulder to help move him, but it wasn't working. His every step was dragging in the water. "I never would have worked as a spymaster."

"You did," Case said. "You have been doing so... much for the world. Far more than you ever would as a captain."

"I only wanted to be a captain," I said, trying to get him to move but failing.

"That's not true," Case said, white fluid now pouring out of his mouth. "You always wanted to save people. If you hadn't become a captain... in Space Fleet... you would have saved them otherwise. Put me down."

"No, we're going to rescue you," I said, knowing I was fooling myself.

"We both know that's not going to happen," Case said, falling onto the side of the tunnel and pressing himself up against the wall. "I am not unhappy. I was not meant to live more than ten years and here I am, past centuries. I saw the volcanic eruption that destroyed the Old United States, I saw the rise of the megacorporations, I saw First Contact, and I have visited a hundred worlds. But more than that, despite being a machine, I have known love and flung my knowledge into the future."

Father... Trish finally spoke up.

"Get out of here, Vance," Case said. "There's nothing you can do. The greatest thing a spy can do is fade away."

"We can download you or something," I said, searching for some sort of solution and finding nothing.

"I'm both AI and biological components, man and machine, Vance," Case said, his eyes closing. "If you downloaded my memories, they'd just be raw data. Just as you are made of quantum information, meat, and… other stuff. The soul. It's funny how I believe in… more. They didn't program that into me."

I pulled off my ring. "Maybe this will help."

Case didn't respond and I put it on his finger. The ring glowed a bit before Case's body began to glow. I felt a surge of hope and looked to see if his injuries were healing (repairing?) themselves. Instead, I saw his body slowly fade away. The ring fell to the ground where he once lay and crumbled to dust.

I couldn't help but stare, stunned.

A seeming eternity passed.

"I'm sorry, Trish," I said, unsure what else to say. I could have said that Case was a good man, but I would lying. Case had been many things but not good. He had always struggled with demons, both internal and otherwise.

But he was a friend.

Family.

I would miss him.

My father was always destined to die at the end of either a gun or a sword, Trish said, surprising me. *He was never the same after Mom, Kei, died. No matter how many beautiful women he bedded or catastrophes he averted, he wanted to be with her again. I don't know if that will be the case, and I would do anything to reunite with him but that's not how reality works.*

"No, no it's not," I said. "At least this reality. God bless you, you crazy old man."

You need to get up, Vance, Trish said. *I've gotten Hannah out of the sewers, but Cadet Catgirl doubled back. That's probably not good.*

You think she's a plant too? I asked.

Would you be surprised? Trish asked.

No, I said.

Cadet Catgirl had shown up, uninvited, and tried way too hard to ingratiate herself to me. I'd thought she was working for her father, but it turned out the Commandant hadn't cared in the slightest about her. It was possible she was coming here to check on her father or me. Motivated by something other than a desire to take me down for personal or ideological reasons. Maybe I was becoming far too cynical about people.

"Hello, Vance," Cadet Catgirl said, walking down the tunnel towards me. She had her claws out and her entire demeanor had changed. It was hostile now but not even human. No, not even Verdantian. She was hunched over in a way their bodies could not do with her arms lengthening before my eyes. "Are you alright? I came back here as fast as I could."

"Who are you?" I asked, standing. "*What* are you?"

Cadet Catgirl's face twisted as her mouth opened to reveal multiple layers of teeth before splitting in half. She shimmered like a pool of water and eventually transformed into the same sort of manta ray like monster that had almost eaten me in the elevator. This one was longer, though, and had different appendages on its body. Maybe it was a female example of its species, if that distinction had any sort of meaning to a shapeshifting race.

Long tubes shot out of its body and it spoke to me in a choir-like voice. "It is a pity, High Protector, that this body did not last longer. Unfortunately, the copying process has limitations. The emotions the body experienced, and memories tied to it have triggered its premature breakdown. Now we must do this the… hard way."

I took a step back, gripping my proton sword's hilt. "You're a Space Vampire."

"A ridiculous name attributed to us by the Notha," the creature said. "We are the Travelers and are a race that is beyond time and space as you know them."

"What happened to the real Cadet Catgirl?" I asked, not having much hope for her but still needing to ask.

"The process consumes our proxies," the Entity—I couldn't exactly call her Cadet Catgirl anymore—said. Its words were spoken with a contempt that was clear despite its alien nature. "Your species, like so many others, use our territory to skip around your galaxy like a stone across water. Your society is powered by orichalcum, the gases that are vital to our survival. You are pests and parasites that dare call us vampires."

My mind filled with alien vistas of a place that was entirely impossible for a three-dimensional entity to comprehend. Still, I saw it from the perspective of the Space Vampire—err, Traveler—and got a brief glimpse of something that no human had ever seen: the true nature of jumpspace. The closest thing I could compare it to was the images from a spectrometer: wild, surreal, and vibrant colors that the human eye couldn't perceive.

Jumpspace was inhabited by beings that were not composed of any physical matter but information. If that makes no scientific sense and sounds like woo, well, congratulations, you have more than an elementary school level of science. Yet, that was what the images projected told me. The Travelers as a race operated according to wholly different kinds of physics, and they could manipulate matter in this world like a child scribbling in a coloring book. They were not alone in their layer of reality either. There were terrible, ten-kilometer-long starships that I recognized the makes and models of: the Primordials.

The presence of the Entity threatened to overwhelm my sanity. Plenty of people had gone mad trying to discover the truth about jumpspace and now I knew why. But anger proved a stronger force than madness and I pushed out the Entity's will. Her story was nonsense, and I wasn't going to let her repeat it as fact. It reeked of propaganda every bit as much as the drivel that the Sons of Humanity peddled.

I stared at her and pointed my sword's tip at her. "It's a big galaxy. There's no way that our using your dimension for travel could cause you any real distress. Even if it did, you haven't tried to contact anyone. I never heard of your race until today and you're capable of replicating us perfectly. That means you have technology far beyond us, even the Elder Race level. So, something about your explanation is complete horsesavit."

"You're right," the Entity said, slowly approaching me. It moved in a hypnotic and disturbing way, bobbing up and down while sliding from side to side. "There is much I am not telling you. The First One of our kind wants you alive but I cannot fathom why he would be interested in such an insignificant figure as yourself. You are nothing more than the tip of the claw of this dimension's true masters, a set of races that has coddled and tamed you like a house pet. We, by contrast, serve a higher power."

"I know who you mean," I said, referring to the Primordials. "But if I could beat them, they were not that impressive. Perhaps you should reconsider who you call masters."

Now, reading alien body language is a dicey business, way more than trying to do the same among humans and there's a massive variety of interpretations for my race's gestures. A man baring his teeth might be threatening you or trying to show a sign of respect. The Entity had no face, so I couldn't read that. Still, by the way it rippled and twisted at my words, I was willing to bet money that my words had pissed it off.

Good.

"You merely caused an accident," the Entity said, diminishing my accomplishment. "An unfortunate one that destroyed much war materiel, but you did not cripple us. You barely inconvenienced our masters. They will return in the future, the past, or now."

"I'll be waiting," I said.

"No, you won't," the Entity said, before lunging at me.

The Entity's self-confidence was not justified as I summoned every bit of rage, despair, and willpower in my body to empower my proton sword for one last blow. The weapon pierced the Space Vampire in its center, and it let out a horrendous cry like the one from the first I'd slain. This time, the other-dimensional creature did not even get a chance to start sucking away my life and simply died where it stood.

There were consequences for my action, though, as the proton sword's blue-white light turned a nightmarish red. The weapon heated in my hands to the point that even with all my ability to ignore pain, I couldn't help but drop it on the ground as the creature dissipated. My sword caused the foam-filled water to boil, and I was forced to scramble out of it to hold onto some of the pipes. My feet dangled above the water, the plastic around them starting to melt. The pain was harsh but not nearly as bad as it would have been if I'd remained inside the sewer water.

After several seconds, I saw the water stop bubbling and the foam clear away around the ruined remnants of my sword. It was now a blackened, broken mess that no longer had any resemblance to my symbol of office. Perhaps the Entity had sacrificed itself to deprive me of my strongest defense. Perhaps I'd simply used the sword wrong and broken it. Either way, I was now without my ring or sword and only had Case's pistol to protect me.

Vance, bad news, Trish said in my mind.

What news is that?

We've been captured.

CHAPTER TWENTY

An Ill-Conceived Rescue

"Captured, how?" I spoke aloud, surrounded by death and dishwasher smelling water. Seriously, this hygiene canal's contents were going to confound the cleaning bots tomorrow morning. I wasn't sure what the worst disaster in Space Academy's history was, but I had to think a dozen or more corpses were new for it.

We got ambushed by another group of Sons outside the entrance to the sewers. Sorry, hygiene canal. They're not interested in hurting us, though, but we're being moved to hangar bay 18.

Hangar bay 18 was the closest to our current position. It didn't make any sense, though, since this was borking Space Academy. It wasn't like they could just escort a pair of prisoners through the place without being noticed. Hell, Trish could just contact Academy security herself.

Except Academy security had just tried to kill me.

Right.

It's a bit more complicated than that, Vance, Trish replied.

It always is. I sighed and started jogging through the suds-filled water toward the passages that led toward hangar bay 18. There was no way in hell I could rescue anyone in my current condition. I only had Case's pistol, but my brain was telling my body that didn't matter. It was moving of its own accord, and I'd think of a plan on the way if I had to. *What is the situation?*

Someone has blown up the central communications hub of Space Academy and uploaded a massive cyberattack into the networks, Trish said. *We also have the area around H-Rod covered in Tomino particles.*

Tomino particles were a weapon the Kolahn had used and had been renamed after 20th century anime writer, Yoshiyuki Tomino. Essentially, there were particles that were shot at lightspeed at other vessels and attached themselves to the hull. The particles interfered with any and all communication and sensor feeds. That was simplifying it a lot and not entirely accurate but close enough for government work.

That's an act of war, I said, horrified. The Great Notha doing this to the spiritual home of Space Fleet was essentially slapping the Community across the face.

It's an act of terrorism, Trish corrected. *You forget another benefit of employing a proxy force like the Sons of Humanity. If the Notha get away with what they want, then they can blame everything on their human collaborators.*

That was a sobering thought, and I started running. Once more, I was caught in a situation where the balance of power in the galaxy would turn upon my next set of decisions. If the Notha blamed the Sons of Humanity for the attack, it would be just as likely for Earth's isolationist government to receive the blunt of their wrath. That would furthermore weaken humanity right before the Notha Union was ready to attack.

But I was missing something. Hell, I was missing a lot of somethings. The Entity had tried to kill me but had indicated her master wanted me alive. Admiral B'Vash wanted me dead before I could meet with the Great Notha. The Sons of Humanity had also come after me and exchanged fire with Academy security.

Why do they want you? I asked, trying to figure out the Great Notha's game.

Probably as a hostage, Trish said. *Vance, you shouldn't come this way.*

I'm coming anyway, I said, stopping at a crossroads before remembering the details of the maps I'd memorized before heading down here.

I know, Trish said. *I just don't want to lose you, too.*

Trish seemed awfully calm for someone who had just lost her father, or at least the father of the person upon whom her brain was based. There was an answer to that, though. Cognition AI thought centers functioned millions of times faster than human brains. In a few seconds, she had all the time she needed to process his death. It was a sobering thought to know that she'd probably get over my death just as fast.

You won't, I said, making a promise I had no way of guaranteeing. *How are you communicating with me if the system is down?*

Our connection is beyond what Tomino particles can interfere with, Trish said. *You may have lost your Elder Race devices, but you're still modified with their tech. In a way, you're one of their machines as well.*

Thanks, Trish, I said, horrified by that observation. *Really.*

Take it as a compliment, Trish replied. *Seventies Trish would have thought of you as the Six Trillion Credit Man.*

I'll be there soon, I said, unsure if I had it in me to talk further under these circumstances.

Beware Vance, it's chaos up here. I can't get in touch with our people and the Sons of Humanity have people everywhere. The Academy security staff are also moving around without communication, but I've heard that they think you've been replaced by an imposter, Trish said. *The Commandant has covered every base.*

Had, I replied. *He was also just a tool. Are you safe?*

For now, Trish said.

I'll be there soon, I repeated, wondering if I'd get there before they'd taken off in a shuttle. That was before I contemplated that I had no idea if I could even do anything once I arrived.

The remaining trek on foot would take about ten or fifteen minutes but I didn't dare try to go up one of the hygiene tunnel ladders. I could already hear shouts, screams, and vehicles crashing into one another through the drains above my head.

So much of modern society depended on instantaneous communication that the disruption, even temporarily, of infocom connections meant that civilization effectively stopped. The only reason Tomino particles weren't used more often in warfare was because they were hideously expensive and pointless if your goal was just blowing up something.

It reminded me of the last time things had utterly gone to hell in H-Rod. I'd buried the memories of that time deep in my mind as I tried not to think about all of my failures at Space Academy today. But, one second I was running down the sewers with a focus on recovering my missing friends and the next I was back to the worst time of my life.

I was sitting in one of the bars where I'd spent most of my final year: the Blue Velvet. It was a smoke-filled, low-lit place where the various cadets performed the ancient art of singing badly to popular music. I was presently leaning over my drink, stirring the little plastic sword skewering an olive and feeling sorry for myself. The drink was a Thorian Sunrise and way too potent for me as I was—at least according to the late Tommy—a "borking lightweight."

"Are you going to drink that or not?" Eighteen asked. "Because I have other paying customers."

Eighteen was a huge Sorkanan with one missing eye that he hadn't replaced. He wore a pair of baggy pants, a white t-shirt, and a dirty apron.

"I'll buy another," I said, leaving a hundred credit chip on the table. "You can keep the change if I can just sit there and stare until closing time."

Eighteen scooped up the credit and put it in his apron pouch. "Suit yourself. You've bought yourself a seat for nursing old wounds."

"Thanks," I said, sighing.

"This is the saddest thing I've ever seen from you, Vance, and you're a man who spends hours every night watching flatties," Leah said, walking up behind me. "Not even flatties turned into proper three-dimensional holograms, but the full-on projected-against-a-screen nonsense."

Leah was wearing a white beret, black turtleneck sweater, and white dress that stretched down to her knees. She also had a set of thigh-high boots on. It was a fashion that was slightly outdated and something my parents might have worn during their time at the Academy before their expulsion. Leah was able to pull it off and claimed it was "retro chic", whatever that meant.

"Television is the last time anyone made anything original," I said, looking at her. "Everything is now made by Dummy AI recycling plot points."

159

Leah rolled her eyes. "I've studied Earth's late 20th and early 21st century media, Vance. It was recycled crap even then. Except for musicals."

"Oh God," I muttered.

"Have you heard the songs from *The Man of La Mancha* and *Phantom of the Opera*?" Leah asked.

"Yes," I replied, looking back at her. "Because you played them for me, *constantly*. I liked only one of them."

"*Spider-Man: The Musical*," Leah said, staring at me. "Literally, I only played that for you as a joke."

"What do you want, Leah?" I asked, rubbing the short beard that I'd grown.

Leah took a seat beside me. "I'm here to try to convince you not to throw the rest of your life away in meaningless self-pity."

I grabbed my Thorian Sunrise and drank it down in one big gulp. I choked and breathed out my next breath like it was a ball of fire. "Ugh!"

Leah gave a golf clap. "Very impressive, Vance. Your act of manly drinking has convinced me that you are capable of holding your liquor."

I tried to respond but my next words were a wheezing cough.

"Have you tried something a bit more your speed?" Leah asked. "Peach schnaps perhaps? Maybe something a teenage girl would drink?"

"Very funny," I said, glaring at Leah.

"Vance, I've seen you get drunk on light beer," Leah said. "I just don't know what you hope to accomplish. Why you're doing this."

"You know why," I replied.

Leah sighed. "Vance, if you're worried about the tribunal, I'm sure they'll make the right decision."

It had been a week since Tommy's death and the investigation had been extremely thorough. Kittridge had been fired from his position as it had been his job to keep everyone safe. That didn't mean I hadn't screwed up, though. It had been my equipment that had malfunctioned, after all. I'd accepted all responsibility and had been waiting for the axe to drop until today.

"The tribunal made their decision," I said, staring forward into the mirror behind the bar. It showed a broken and stupid boy who had been pretending to be a man. I wasn't someone ready to face the galaxy. I was just a spoiled, ridiculous brat who had no business anywhere on a Space Fleet vessel.

"I'm sorry, Vance," Leah said, reaching over to touch me on the shoulder. "You deserved better than to be—"

"They found me innocent of any wrongdoing," I said, practically spitting the words out.

"What?" Leah asked, blinking.

"I was cleared of all charges today," I said, reaching into my vest and pulling a piece of plexi-paper with the tribunal's decision.

Leah took it from my hands and read it. "This is… good, isn't it?"

"No," I replied, shaking my head. "It's a miscarriage of justice."

Leah closed her eyes in frustration and took a deep breath as if she was dealing with a particularly unruly child. "You weren't responsible for Tommy's death. If they investigated you for it and found you did nothing wrong, you did nothing wrong."

"*Someone* is responsible," I said, simply. "Someone screwed up. Someone needs to take the blame."

"Do they?" Leah asked. "Does anyone have to be at fault for this?"

"Yes," I said, looking at her. "Yes, they do."

Leah sighed. "That's not how the world works, Vance. There's no such thing as justice. There's no getting what you deserve in this life, and I don't believe in another one like you do. Things just happen. You did your very best and it wasn't good enough. Same for everyone else who was involved even peripherally. Maybe it was Tommy's—"

"Don't," I said, cutting her off.

"What?" Leah asked, confused,

"Don't try and make this something that can be ignored," I said, getting up off the barstool. "I'm not wired that way."

"Vance—"

"Answer me one question," I said, prepared for all of the attempts to reassure me that it wasn't my fault or that Tommy wouldn't want me to blame myself.

"What question is that?" Leah asked. "Take note that I can read your mind."

"If I wasn't Aunt Kathy's favorite nephew, if I wasn't someone who had a legendary hero as my patron, and it wasn't so damn inconvenient for me to be involved, would I have been cleared of charges? Or would they have thrown the book at me anyway?" I asked Leah, looking right into her eyes. "Because even if there was room for me to argue, they would have found someone to punish to preserve the Academy's legendary reputation. Wouldn't they?"

Leah didn't respond. Instead, she just looked away from me to her own reflection. "You're confusing martyrdom with self-sacrifice."

"Maybe I am," I said, shaking my head. "But I'm not going to ignore Tommy's death. He deserved better."

I walked out of the bar and back to my room. The last thing I heard from Leah that night stuck with me and I never quite understood why.

"We all do, Vance. We all do."

I'd continue to spiral after that night and got myself involved in many stupid events. I was testing just how far my immunity could be stretched and it turned out to be quite far. I became involved in gambling, smuggling in prostitutes, petty theft, and elaborate pranks in hopes I'd be disciplined enough to be thrown out. I never let my grades slip but that was partly because I wanted them to expel me for who I was, not what I couldn't do. It was a classic example of Aristotelian angst: wanting two contradictory things at once. I wanted them to punish me, but I wanted it to be as unfair as letting me get away with what I'd—believed myself to have—done.

In the end, it seemed so... childish. I'd been right, I hadn't been ready to be a member of Space Fleet. A member of Space Fleet would have understood the system was corrupt but that it was my duty to try and purify it from the inside. I wasn't any more entitled to justice than anyone else in the galaxy. If I'd wanted to avenge Tommy, I should have buckled down and worked my own investigation or gained enough power to pressure the people involved for the truth. It might have taken years, but if I'd resigned from Space Academy, I never would have found out anything. I probably would never know the truth and the people involved in Tommy's death were probably past caring.

But there were other injustices to rectify. Maybe I was Don Quixote, the Man of La Mancha, tilting at windmills to make those who hide behind money and power pay. Maybe there was no point going after High Protector B'Vash and the Great Notha. Maybe if I could take down one or both, another would just take their place. Maybe I wasn't that much better when it all came down to it.

Maybe.

Or maybe not.

Either way, I arrived at a ladder leading to the maintenance tunnels beneath hangar bay 18.

It was time to put up or shut up.

CHAPTER TWENTY-ONE

Holding Out for a Hero

Hangar bay 18 was a supply shuttle entrance on level 13 of H-Rod. I was presently overlooking the interior despite having snuck up from the sewer levels. It had required quite a bit of maneuvering and duct crawling, but I now had a view of the place I had to take over. I was peering through some thin grating, but it was clear enough that I was able to formulate a tactical assessment of the area. Unfortunately, my tactical assessment was that I was screwed.

The chamber was about a hundred square yards with most of it taken up by intra-system shuttles, equipment to maintain them, and cargo crates. Everything was illuminated with a dull shade of red that indicated a state of emergency had been implemented across H-Rod. That wasn't the part that bothered me, though. No, that was the fact that there were eighteen Sons of Humanity soldiers spread throughout the area. All of them were armed and none of them looked particularly like the amateurs that was their cover onboard the station.

I didn't want to acknowledge it but if there was a way to get down there and rescue my associates, it probably would less rely on clever planning and more on brute force. A lot more people would have die if I was to save Trish and Hannah. Getting rid of eighteen people by myself was unlikely but not impossible, particularly if I could ventilate the atmosphere or decompress the hangar bay without killing the people I was trying to rescue. It was a set of cold calculations that I did not like one bit.

I wondered if there was a point in life where self-defense stopped being a viable legal strategy. That really shouldn't have distracted me as I maneuvered through the crawlspaces behind the paneling of hangar bay 18, but it did. Basically, at what point did you kill so many people that you really shouldn't be allowed to keep going around free? Even if you're the wronged party? It wasn't infinite because I was pretty sure we all agreed that one guy standing over a dead universe was a bad thing. However, the simple fact was that everything until that point was negotiable.

Vance! Trish spoke in my head. *What the hell are you going on about?*

Oh, sorry, I confessed. *I'm just contemplating that getting you guys out was going to require a lot of death.*

Yeah, no kidding! Trish said, sounding a lot more panicked than I was used to from her. *To answer your question, however many it takes to get us free!*

Okay, sure, I admitted. *If you say so.*

I do say so! Trish said. *I mean, if I die here, I'll be fine and just get rebooted from your memories or the ones on the ship, but Hannah is irreplaceable.*

I'll bear that in mind, I said, trying to figure out my strategy. *Where are you and Hannah, anyway? Do you know if they have any other hostages? What are they waiting for?*

They've got us locked up in the central shuttle, Trish said. *We're here with Forty-Two.*

Forty-Two? How the hell did he get here?

I didn't ask, Trish said. *We have bigger things to deal with. Hannah is stabilized but she's also drugged out of her mind. The staff of the hangar bay is locked up in the control room. They used stun blasts rather than kill them.*

So, they're capable of mercy, I observed.

Probably not, Trish said. *I think they kept the staff alive so they could use them as hostages against Academy security. There's at least a couple of bodies they've dropped here to show they meant business.*

Savit, I cursed. *I don't suppose there is any chance of contacting them?*

Everything is down except our two-way communication, Trish said. *I can't even contact my core on the Melampus. I don't know what they're waiting for but if I had to guess, it's probably you.*

Me? I asked.

These guys are definitely working for the Great Notha, Trish said. *I think this entire thing is to make sure that you attend that meeting.*

I paused as I considered my response. *Would you feel better or worse, Trish, if I told you that I'd already planned to attend the meeting?*

Case had said not to but all he'd really convinced me of was that I needed some way to turn the tables on B'Vash. There was no lesser evil between the Great Notha and B'Vash. Both were evil but they hated each other and that was a potential advantage.

Worse, much worse, Trish said.

Well, then pretend I didn't tell you, I said, making my decision on what to do next. I began crawling towards the environmental controls in the maintenance tunnel I was in, the reason I was here in the first place. They were in a computer console hidden behind a large metal plate sealed shut and just one of several redundant units built into every hangar bay. I worried with every movement that I was going to make a sound that the Sons below heard but, thankfully, the Tomino particles were working in my favor there. The internal sensors from suits of armor and commando units were just as fried as anything working on the outside.

"Well, here goes everything," I muttered and pulled out the tools I'd picked up on my way here. There had been a janitor's closet I'd passed on my way to the hangar bay but it had just had a basic toolbox. I'd taken just some minor bits of equipment because my 'plan', if you could call it that, had already been forming. I just hoped they would be enough. In the end? Well, maybe. Disabling the machinery in front of me required a lot more finely tuned devices than the ones I had but I would have to make do. Still, I had the training. I'd never been on the engineering track, but Space Academy educated all of its officers in basic command, tactics, engineering, and medicine. You had to be a jack of all trades before they let you master one.

Burning off the bolts for the plating, I found myself face to face with many wires and a panel of unmarked switches. I recognized the basic function of everything but figuring out how to weaponize the environment was not going to be as easy as it appeared in your typical action movie. There was no poison gas button, for example, nor was there a way to blow everyone out the airlock like I'd hoped. Hangar bays were designed to be *safe* after all and engineers had worked on achieving exactly that for centuries here at Space Academy.

"Okay, let's see if I can turn up the gravity a bit," I said, realizing that I would have to do this in multiple stages if I had a snowball's chance in hell of pulling it off.

I rewired the gravity manipulators in the station to increase the gravity about three times over the course of the next ten minutes. I hoped that would only be noticeable toward the end like a lobster slowly being boiled alive in a pot. The alternative—everyone realizing that they had a saboteur in their midst—would be bad. I also didn't want it to happen too soon because it would affect me as well.

My next goal was down the maintenance tunnel and through a small iris door that took me to a room just east of the main chamber. The room was extremely hot, low enough I had to crawl on my belly, and full of electrical charges that absolutely should not have been shooting through the air randomly. Seriously, this place was in dire need of maintenance.

It was there that several miniature fusion generators about the size of my head were located. They were linked to the massive doors that transformed the hangar bays into airlocks before ventilating the atmosphere. The thing was that modern science meant there were barriers that went up when this happened. Barriers that kept in the atmosphere and prevented the kind of explosive decompression that would have been useful right now.

Despite my hopes, though, there was no way to circumvent the safeties. What I could do, though, was hook up my standard issue infopad to the overrides and make it so I could send a command to lock down the hangar bay. A short-range burst that would be able to travel over the immediate area like a centuries-old television remote. Nothing the Tomino particles would interfere with. Both the front entrance and the bay doors. With a little tactical knowhow, I might be able to turn that to my advantage.

Vance, what are you doing? Trish asked me.

Trying to solve an insoluble problem, I replied. *How not to die horribly.*

Well, hurry the bork up, Trish said. *The guy in charge is telling me to contact you. I think he thinks we have some kind of supernatural bond.*

I paused. *We do have a supernatural bond or at least super-technological.*

Yeah, but they don't know that for sure and I'm pretty sure he's going to use that against you if you don't hurry up.

I'm trying, I thought, crawling on the hot paneling to a trapdoor that led down to the final destination on my planned sabotage tour. Unfortunately, at the bottom of the trap door was one of the Sons. He was a particularly hefty-looking specimen and leaning over, probably just starting to notice the much heavier than normal gravity affecting us all. Unfortunately, he was right next to the communications console that was presently so much junk, which I needed anyway. Well, in for a penny, in for a pound.

I dropped from the trapdoor down onto the soldier's head. I collided with him like I was falling on cement and hopefully disabled him long enough to carry out the last part of my plan. Given he wasn't moving beneath me, I'd either managed to knock him senseless or killed him outright.

Either was fine.

Alright, please let this work.

I hooked up my infopad to the communications console and activated the program I'd set up. With the Tomino particles spread out, there was no way to send a communication but generating a nasty noise inside the speakers outside the hangar bay was possible through the same method as triggering the doors. That triggered a good ten of the soldiers to start jogging, slowly, toward it before the hangar bay doors suddenly closed behind them.

Then the reinforced security doors that were like a bank vault closed on those.

Seven Sons of Humanity left.

Time to pull off a miracle.

Spinning around, I was promptly shot in the face with a stun blast that caused every neuron in my brain to frazzle. Yeah, the infamous Turbo luck had finally run out on me. After all of the effort I'd made to sneak around and even the odds, one of the Sons had thought to check on his fellow before blasting me. I was able to keep on my feet, though, and I tried to draw Case's pistol. The Son of Humanity—whose face I couldn't see through his reflective helmet—blasted me again.

And again.

After that, I collapsed, and my body was as loose as a stringless marionette. It was an undignified way to meet my end if they decided to kill me, but you don't get to choose when you meet your maker I supposed. I'd fought everything from seasoned commandos to emperors to space gods but it seemed a random hate group member was the one who finally had my number. I didn't go unconscious, just paralyzed, and I had to wonder if that was the Elder Race technology in my head or if I'd just gotten lucky. Well, for some values of the word lucky.

"Is it Turbo?" One of the other Sons called over. He was taller than my attacker and sported a star symbol on his blast vest. His neck, visible under his helmet, was blue as were his arms. That told me he was a Thorian demihuman. That was odd for the Sons of Humanity but not unprecedented. I suspected these weren't the true believer types, though.

"Yeah," the one who shot me said. "He got Reggie. Borker jumped down on his head from the maintenance ducts."

"Is he dead?" The Thorian Son asked.

"No," the shooter said. "He'll need to be hospitalized, though."

"Not Reggie, idiot, Turbo!" the Thorian Son said.

"Oh, he's just stunned," the shooter said, kicking me with his foot. I didn't feel a thing

"You sure?" The Thorian Son asked.

"Extra stunned," the shooter said. "What do we do about Reggie? The medic is busy keeping that Crius girl alive."

I couldn't help but worry that Hannah's condition was worse than Trish had described. *Trish, can you hear me?*

Yeah, Trish said. *I take it things didn't go well?*

You could say that. I'm stunned. Any suggestions?

Prayer, Trish replied.

"Leave Reggie behind," the other Son said. "We have what we came for."

"What about the others he's locked out?" the shooter asked. "I don't know how he pulled it off. The staff here were supposed to have left the doors wide open for him."

I couldn't speak or move. At most, I could move my mouth open and close it. Slowly.

"Who cares," the Thorian Son said. "All that matters is our paycheck. I'm sick of playing Neo-Militarist fanboy. The others can fend for themselves."

"Aren't you afraid of leaving behind any witnesses?" the shooter asked, which worried me about what he might do to the hostages.

"I didn't use my real name on this job, did you?" The Thorian Son asked.

"Err, no, of course not," the shooter said, clearly lying.

"Then get the Hero of SPAAACE into the shuttle," the Thorian Son said, mocking me.

"Right," the shooter said, picking up Case's pistol and tossing it away. He grabbed me by the collar of my uniform and dragged my limp form along the floor. It was full of painful bumps, but that was actually a good sign since it meant my Elder Race-enhanced body was recovering faster than a normal human being's.

I was eventually heaved aboard the central shuttle up the entrance ramp and then shoved in one of the seats next to Trish. The shooter tied me up and then pulled out a roll of spacer tape before wrapping it around me like I was a mummy. It was humiliating but effective, especially when he covered my mouth in it.

"Stay," the shooter said.

I glared at him.

He delivered a nasty punch to my stomach in response.

Sitting across from me against the wall, I could see Hannah and Forty-Two, also tied up. Hannah had a faraway look in her eyes while Forty-Two looked guilty. They were both gagged with space tape as well with only Trish seemingly having been left alone. Perhaps because they recognized her as a bioroid and thought she was harmless.

"Mmmph mmmph mmph," I said to Forty-Two, which translated as "Drolochid cuisine, huh?"

"Mmmph," Forty-Two replied. "Mmmph mmm."

I had no idea what he was saying but I chose to believe it was, "Sorry, I thought it would only take a minute!"

The shuttle took off a few minutes later.

We were off to see the Great Notha.

CHAPTER TWENTY-TWO

Dishonored Dead

I had plenty of time to think once we got on our way to the *Notha's Destiny*. Unsurprisingly, given recent events, my mind continued back to Tommy's death. I didn't want to think about it, but it seemed to be the root everything currently happening. Maybe not the politics or Department Twelve's terrorist activities, but in how I became involved of all this. This time I thought about the same day I dropped out of Space Academy.

All of my things were packed. Alfred was helpfully moving around, tidying up since Aunt Kathy had forbidden him to start moving my things for a return to Luna. He was a brilliant chrome bot with an inhuman face that reminded me of a combination of C-3PO with Darth Vader. Alfred's personality was definitely more that of the former than the later, though, and weirdly, he was the closest thing I had to a father. Even before I thought he'd gotten himself killed in a stupid accident, Jack Tagawa had barely been a presence in my life. Alfred, by contrast, had always been a reassuring parental figure.

Alfred wasn't a Cognition AI but he was outfitted with a bioroid brain that gave him the rights of a full citizen of the Community. I'd often wondered why he'd chosen to live in a mostly metal body with only a limited range of sensation versus something that would give him the full human experience. His answers had always been coy but I believed it was simply because he preferred his interior world of digital simulations to the complicated world of reality. I also believed he loved my aunt and knew she'd never love him back so he preferred never to experience the temptation.

Kathy Tagawa was dressed in civilian clothes, which somehow looked unnatural on her. A Hawaiian shirt and blue jeans made her look like she was on a tropical vacation and a pair of sunglasses was resting in her auburn hair. The effect was akin to seeing a shark on land in similar attire but given my experience with aliens, I might have found that less disconcerting.

The interior of my room was dimly lit and mostly empty of any real personality. Tommy's possessions had already been transferred out and I had always been austere, even before I'd decided Space Academy was not for me.

"This place is not a place of honor," Aunt Kathy said to me, standing over me as I sat on the edge of my bed in my dorm room.

"What?" I asked, looking up to her.

"Before the invention of nanoscrubbers, there was a question of what to do with nuclear waste," Aunt Kathy said. "The decay cycle was thousands of years, and some scientists speculated that it would far outlast present-day civilization. So, they sat down and tried to figure out how they could make it so that people who didn't speak English, French, Chinese, or any other modern language understood that nuclear waste was stored there. Something that could kill them without them ever realizing it."

I stared at her. "That presumption assumes the collapse of human civilization and a near total loss of historical records. By which I think that the problems will already be far more than nuclear waste. The massive deaths and poison would eventually clue them in, like a poisoned well, which is probably a bigger issue—"

"Vannevar, shut the bork up," Aunt Kathy said, rubbing her temples. "What they decided was that they would make the following passage for Earth's nuclear waste dumps: 'This is not a place of honor. No highly esteemed deed is commemorated here. Nothing valued is here. What is here was dangerous and repulsive to us. This message is a warning about danger.'"

I blinked. "If they don't speak any known modern language then how were they supposed to understand that warning?"

"Ugh," Aunt Kathy said, looking to one side.

"It's a valid point, mistress," Alfred said, adjusting my holoviewer. "It seems unreasonably pretentious, and a better thing would be to do it like the Rosetta Stone with multiple languages all saying the same thing: 'This is poisonous material that will last thousands of year. Don't touch it or you will die.'"

"I mean, archaeologists would probably still touch it," I replied. "The nature of human curiosity is to dismiss warnings and continue to examine regardless. I imagine there would also be a dismissive attitude to previous civilizations knowing what they were talking about."

Aunt Kathy slapped me.

"Ow," I said, blinking.

"You stupid, stupid boy," she said, shaking with rage. "I'm trying to save you."

"Save me from *what*?" I asked, annoyed at her presumption.

"Save you from throwing your life away," Aunt Kathy said, throwing her hands out in frustration. "You don't know what this has required from me—"

"To keep me from being thrown out, believe me I know," I said.

"Then *why*?" she asked.

"Does it occur to you that this is a test to see just how crooked and corrupt this whole system is?" I said, turning on her. "That I might be disgusted at how many strings were pulled for me?"

"Oh, grow the hell up," Aunt Kathy said, putting her hands on her hips. She'd dropped all pretense of civility.

"What?" I said, appalled.

"Exactly what I said. Do you actually think corruption and favors being pulled for you in *school* matters in the real world? Education is not meant to the deciding factor of your life but to prepare you for when things really matter."

I was dismayed by her attitude. "So, I should just ignore how I got away with murder?"

"You didn't murder your lizard friend," Aunt Kathy said, dismissing the event. "You didn't even kill him in a friendly fire accident. Believe me, I've known some anyxholes in the admiralty who have far more skeletons in their closet. No, it was an accident because *space is dangerous*. The reports were inconclusive because there was nothing to find."

I sighed and looked down at my feet. "You instilled within me a responsibility to be a starship captain, Aunt Kathy. A person who puts on that uniform takes on a responsibility and doesn't run away from the consequences of their actions. They can't be trusted with power otherwise."

"I absolutely did not teach you that," she said.

"What?" I asked.

"No, that's Spider-Man," Aunt Kathy said, which was weird as that character was getting brought up a lot lately. Both in my memories and the present. "Power does not come with any responsibilities because the vast majority of people who wield it do so indiscriminately and with no thought to the people that get trampled along the way."

"Aunt Kathy—"

"No," she said, shaking her head. "Listen. The military and government worlds are full of two kinds of people. There are those who actively seek power because they like the exhilaration of it and there are people who seek power because they feel that they have a duty to use it well. The former greatly outnumber the latter and, worse, there are a substantial number of the latter who eliminate themselves from consideration because they don't feel worthy of it."

"Shouldn't they?" I asked.

"No," Aunt Kathy said. "Because 'the perfect' is the enemy of 'the good', Vannevar. If you wait for the perfect leader to guide the Israelites out of the wilderness—"

"That was Moses and he was hardly perfect," Alfred said.

"You shut up, too, Alfred," Aunt Kathy said. Turning back to me, she continued. "Then you will either never have a true leader or you will confuse a con man for one out of desperation."

I was frustrated with Aunt Kathy's insistence. "I know you've put a lot of money and effort into—"

"It's not my efforts I'm worried about it," she said.

"Excuse me?" I asked, even more confused than before.

"There are other people who have invested in you," Aunt Kathy said, "People who manufacture the next big thing for Earth."

175

"I don't understand," I said, genuinely confused.

"EarthGov only survives because of its pride," she said. "Humanity is like a million separate ant hills, each believing itself to be the epitome of antdom. The revelation that the birthplace of our race is just one inhabited world out of a million and not even the highest technological power among mankind could have destroyed us."

"But it didn't," I said, wondering where this and the "no place of honor" thing were going.

"Because people created a narrative," Aunt Kathy said. "A saga of national, racial, and planetary pride that was able to unite all of those ant hills. The reason there's peace on Earth and it has managed to slowly build itself back up is because everyone sees themselves in the Space Fleet captains they've made into heroes."

"You are a hero, Aunt Kathy," I said. "Unless you're telling me those adventures of yours are all setups."

"They weren't," Aunt Kathy said. "My life as a captain has been constant violence, diplomacy, and ridiculousness. But what is depicted on the screen is as far from reality as the propaganda bureaus need it to be. My decisions were always validated in the end, no hair out of place, and the costs of victory are always justified. They need people like us to be perfect and they aren't going to let you go just because you don't want to bear the cost."

I had no idea what she meant by all of that. Was this a confession or lecture or both? "What are you saying?"

Aunt Kathy looked defeated. "Don't let them kick you out, Vannevar."

"Actually, I'm going by Vance now," I said.

"Vance?" Aunt Kathy asked, confused.

"Yes, mistress, Vance Turbo," Alfred said, speaking up. "He had it legally changed this morning."

Aunt Kathy looked between us. "You've become a porn star?"

"No!" I snapped. "I did because I want to make a new life."

"And you chose the stupidest name possible?" she asked.

I closed my eyes, counting to ten. "It's too late, Aunt Kathy. I finally pushed my luck too far with the gambling I set up. People were involved. Staff. The Commandant has a meeting where he's going to expel me. Which is what should have happened in the first place."

"Resign," Aunt Kathy said. "Drop out."

"What?" I asked.

"Don't let them kick you out," Aunt Kathy said. "Expulsion will be a permanent black mark on your record and follow you everywhere. Dropping out, by contrast, can be mended."

"Like I told you, it's too late—"

"Blackmail him," Aunt Kathy said.

"Excuse me?" I asked, not sure I'd heard that correctly.

"Madame!" Alfred said, appalled. He was holding a cleaning rag in one hand and a bottle of Detox. He had gotten to work on my bathroom.

"The Commandant is a corrupt, lying oaf that you, yourself, probably have all manner of dirt on," Aunt Kathy said. "He'll back down."

"You don't see how this is worse?" I asked, not really sure she did.

"Like I said, you were an investment to other people, Vanav… err, Vance," she said, sighing. "They don't let go easily."

"What aren't you telling me?" I asked, shifting uncomfortably.

"More than you'll ever know," Aunt Kathy said. "But just know that it was one of my happiest days when you broke up with that Albionese girl."

"Leah?"

"How many did you date?" Aunt Kathy asked.

I grimaced. "Define date."

Yeah, after Tommy's death, I'd found out that I no real stomach for liquor. My cybernetics cleared out everything alcoholic, so it was just foul-tasting water. I mostly just exaggerated the effects for humor's sake. By contrast, it turned out I was an incurable lech and that was one way of seeking comfort. Kathy was in no position to judge me anyway, as she had her own stable of regular lovers.

Aunt Kathy gave a dismissive wave. "Just promise me, Vance."

"I promise to try to blackmail the Commandant," I said, staring at her. "Which is a felony, by the way."

"Felonies I can work with," Kathy said. "Felonies at least have some dash. We can send you to work among the mercenary clans in Contested Space. Felonies can be disputed and the people who bring charges discredited."

"This is an ugly side of you, Aunt Kathy," I said, still wondering if I was being punked.

"No one conquers who does not fight," she said, giving her own personal motto. "Those who give up have already surrendered."

"Yes," I said. "That is the very definition of surrender. Also, I don't want to conquer. I just want to live."

"What do you even want to do with your life if you're not in Space Fleet?" Aunt Kathy said, shaking her head.

"I was thinking refugee resettlement," I said, thinking about how a lot of my skills might transfer to helping people displaced by the Notha War."

"Ugh," she said, looking at me like I was a dog who'd just crazzaped on the floor. "I liked it better when I thought you were just becoming a criminal."

I stood up. "Thank you for coming, Aunt Kathy. I'm sorry to have disappointed. Don't worry about me or your legacy, though. You'll always have Danny to replace me."

"Danny has trouble standing out," Aunt Kathy said, unaware of just how right she was. "He also admires you. The best he can be is a copy of you."

"God help him then," I said, walking past her to my door. "I'll talk to you later, Alfred."

"I doubt that, sir," Alfred said. "I think your aunt has arranged quite a surprise for you!"

Aunt Kathy swatted him in the breast plate.

It was a remembered conversation that I, once more, couldn't say was 100% accurate regarding what had really happened. Maybe I was seeing my aunt in a new light and ascribing to her sinister motives that I had no reason to expect had existed before. Maybe I was adding a certain level of irony to my blackmail of the Commandant. She'd come to visit me, which I'd found to be strange given the months of travel it took to visit Space Academy, but Aunt Kathy had made an unusual number of visits during my time here.

In hindsight, that could have been because she was a member of Department Twelve visiting the Codex. It also could have just been EarthGov trotting out their legendary hero to lecture students on what was expected of them. Captain Elgan had made sixteen speeches during my time at Space Academy, including the one when he'd had me kidnapped.

In the end, it probably didn't matter. The shuttle I was in was about to reach the *Notha's Destiny*.

I could feel it.

CHAPTER TWENTY-THREE

No, Mister Bond, I Expect You to Dine

The shuttle eventually halted its ascension and there was the noise of docking clamps attaching to the vehicle. That was a sure sign we were out of space since, well, noise didn't travel in space. I knew people who had sound effects installed in their ships for various exterior activities because the eerie silence of day-to-day ship operations was too much for them.

The Sons of Humanity came back to grab us and march us out of the shuttle into the main hangar bay of *Notha's Destiny*. They had to carry the unconscious Hannah, but I didn't care about that. I was pleased to see their medic wasn't completely incompetent since they'd treated her wounds enough that I was no longer afraid for her life. Her armor was heavily damaged, though, and would need to be replaced.

The hangar bay was overwhelming and about the size of an old Earth aircraft carrier. It gave me a sense of deja vu, reminding of the Notha Emperor's own ship in the *Emperor's Reach*. The Notha Emperor had kept it over from before his overthrow and used it as a combination of palace and country-in-exile. The *Emperor's Reach* had been falling apart and maintained by brainwashed slave soldiers.

The *Notha's Destiny*, by contrast, was the top of the line in its appearance with every bit of black metal plating shining and a crew consisting entirely of Notha. I didn't even see any of their subject races like the Chickens or Blood Frogs.—I didn't name them so don't complain to me about them not sounding particularly dignified.—It was a monument to Notha Union power and perfection.

It's also a fraud, Trish said, walking up beside me.

180

Pardon? I asked.

The Tomino particles aren't active here, Trish said. *I can link up with the majority of the systems and they're about two generations behind, back from when it was still the Notha Empire.*

Really? I asked. *The Great Notha's whole deal is that he was modernizing his army.*

The Notha moved from feudalism directly to space-based capitalism and have a culture of corruption to go with it, she said. *He may have spent the entirety of the Notha's wealth building this thing, but it's probably made of literal spare parts for the* Emperor's Reach. *It's just got a few more coats of paint and everyone dressed up all fancy for marching around in it.*

That explains why Deathworld was able to hold its own against a force thirty times its size, I replied. *The Community weapons are much more advanced than what they had at the time of the Notha War.*

Yeah, it also explains why the Great Notha is resorting to all these bribes, Trish replied. *They don't have the economy or infrastructure to be able to continue to pursue the war, even with all the orichalcum processing centers they have spread around their territory. They need their enemies to destroy themselves.*

If I had any regrets from my time as a Space Fleet officer, it was the fact that I hadn't done more when I became High Protector for Deathworld, and perhaps the humans of Contested Space. Unfortunately, decisions like that could only be made with certainty in hindsight. *Do you think all the other Notha Union vessels are the same?*

No, I think they're much worse, Trish replied, looking around. *If this is the best they can do for Fearless Leader, then the other ships are undoubtedly also using repurposed equipment from the old Empire days. It's probable that the only things propping up their glory were the SKAMMs.*

And the Elder Races dealt with that, I said.

Perhaps, she said. *That would imply the Great Notha is sane enough to actually not store some behind in case of an emergency. There are also a lot of non-sun-destroying weapons that can render inhabited planets lifeless. The Notha have plenty of those as well. My interaction with the central Dummy AI says they have enough to wipe out all of humanity's worlds on this ship alone.*

Great, I said. *So how does any of this help?*

Oh, it doesn't, Trish said. *I'm just noting that if you'd actually started a shooting war over the Codex that we would have eaten through his fleet and probably everything would have worked out.*

Gee thanks, I replied as we were marched past an honor guard of a hundred Death Commandos on each side.

Just thought we'd keep a lighthearted and jovial tone as we are marched to our deaths, Trish said. *If it's any consolation, I expect he'll make a big show of it since you are literally a religious figure among the Notha.*

I know, Trish, I said.

Their Devil, she said. *You are their ultimate embodiment of evil.*

I know Trish, I repeated.

I'm just saying that now may be the time to consider performing some evil miracles, Trish said. *If you can do those.*

I can't, I replied. *Both my ring and sword are missing.*

No Jedi mind tricks, huh? she asked.

Not that I'm aware of.

Darn, Trish replied. *Well, then I guess we're borked.*

Probably, I said.

The Sons of Humanity members separated from us and were given a large metal case they opened to reveal was full of orichalcum crystals. Orichalcum were their own form of currency. The were better than Community credits (that could be tracked) and easier to dispose of than gemstones or glimmerrock. The Sons of Humanity members collected their reward and departed, getting away with their role in my kidnapping. Certainly, I never would know who they were and the odds of finding them were practically nonexistent.

But I had more important things to worry about.

"Come," a Notha Death Commando Commander-General, notable for their red armor, gestured, pointing to several bare chested Notha with collars around their necks.

Slave-servants.

"Alright," I said, taking a deep breath. "You're in charge."

For now.

Four of the slave-servants lifted Hannah while the others led Forty-Two, Trish, and me to a nearby elevator. We weren't delivered to a brig or dungeon, though. Instead, we were separated and taken to private rooms. I was measured by Notha tailors, forced into a shower, given a red modified version of my dress uniform, and made to dress myself in it. They also used a straight razor to shave my face and head in what I suspected was a method of humiliating me. The Notha were extremely proud of their fur after all. Either way, they also gave me a powered down version of my pistol as well. It was a symbol of respect but not trust.

Humiliation.

Honor.

The Notha wanted to create plausible deniability that they were treating me as a guest of honor even though they also made it clear that I could be killed at any time. That was a good sign, but I wasn't sure it was a great one. They could easily argue Trish was equipment to be dismantled or that Hannah died of her injuries at the hands of the Sons of Humanity.

I'll be fine, Vance, Trish said. *They're disassembling me but I'm still in your mind.* They think they can also keep me from their machines.

Run silent, run deep, I said, balling my fists. Even if I knew Trish was safe, it was infuriating and another reminder of the Notha's desire to make other people helpless. I didn't want to vilify a whole species but the Notha carried a massive collective trauma from their time under the Emperor's control.

The Emperor had been made immortal during the early years of the Notha as a race. An experiment by the Elder Races to see if it would be better to have a single consistent ruler over their people for centuries or even millennia rather than the conflicts other races endured. The Emperor had ended up corrupted by power—or perhaps had always been a monster—and shaped every part of Notha society into one that let savit roll downhill. Social Darwinism, constant infighting, and absolute (feigned) loyalty were the order of the day.

There were good elements of Notha society, like flowers growing in the weeds, but the current Union was an authoritarian, slave-holding regime only slightly less corrupt than the Empire that had preceded it. I wanted to find a way to help them and turn my enemies into friends but that wasn't going to happen tonight.

Possibly never.

The Great Notha wants something from you, Trish said. *The important thing is to figure out what before you move. Also, to make sure that Hannah and Forty-Two are okay.*

Forty-Two would rather die than be used as a hostage for my good behavior, I said, being presented by the servant-slaves with an old-fashioned mirror. I looked like a slightly more fascist version of the Handsome Prince in any number of Dixnar movies.

Also, bald.

Sorry, clean shaven.

That was so much better.

And Hannah? Trish asked.

Oh, she absolutely would want me to do everything in my power to rescue her. She also would be entirely comfortable with me sacrificing myself to make sure she made it out alive.

That's not true, Trish said, pausing. *I mean, she'd feel really bad about it.*

Uh huh, I said.

For years, Trish said.

Right, I replied.

But her heart would go on, Trish said. *She'd know you'd want her to be happy and that's why you'd forgive her stealing your fortune too by pretending you were married.*

You've thought about this in detail, I said, uncomfortable. Maybe it was the jackboots.

I have, Trish said. *Mind you, I've thought about every possible permutation of our relationship.*

Uh huh, I said, pausing.

I've simulated most of them in my head, Trish said.

You've written fanfic about our getting married.

That's not... entirely accurate, Trish said in a way that implied it was.

How many? I asked, as I was escorted to the elevator again. I had an urge to Sieg Heil to the next Notha officer or at least goosestep. Sadly, I don't think they'd have gotten the irony intended by the act.

63,000,311 simulations, Trish said. *I think I may have gone overboard.*

You think? I asked.

One lasted seventy-three years, Trish replied. *I think I may have been using too much of my bandwidth on this.*

Just a little, I said, riding the elevator down to whatever destiny awaited me. I had 50-50 odds they were going to negotiate versus forcing me to confess my crimes before executing me. Honestly, it was probably closer to 40-60. *How did most of those simulations end?*

Err, you may not want to know that, Trish said.

Trish... I said, feeling like the elevator was taking me down to Hell itself.

Okay, maybe I have a thing for tragedy, Trish admitted. *I've had us die in each other's arms 50,000,037 times. There are times I outlive you. Times you outlive me. Times you are turned into a vampire and I have to stake you...*

What now? I asked, flummoxed. Which was not a word I got to use often.

I mean, an ordinary vampire, not a Space Vampire, Trish replied.

Ordinary vampires are not real, I replied.

Don't ruin the story, Trish said. *Times I become human and die of natural causes. Times I become human and get turned into a vampire.*

You seem very set on this vampire thing, I replied.

Honestly, Nina the Vampire makes it work, Trish said, ignoring the fact that Nina just pretended to be one. *I'm not saying she should be invited into our polycule—*

We don't have a polycule, I cut her off.

Yet, Trish said. *But I'm just saying that she could make it less weird for the public than our relationship alone would be.*

You think me being married to a Cognition AI who is my ship and a bioroid simultaneously will be made less weird by also dating a vampire, I replied. *Am I getting that right?*

I personally didn't care what the public thought anymore. If you said 1+1=2, then it was a good bet a third of the electorate would disagree with it and another half would answer undecided. Some people just liked to be contradictory, and half the scandals were generally just the news making noise for the sake of noise. The real atrocities were swept under the rug. Then again, perhaps I was just burned out at seeing so many people get away with murder while others had their lives destroyed over nothing.

It sounds strange when you say it that way, Trish admitted, thankfully ignoring my brooding. *I mean, I love Hannah, but I also think she needs to think she's perpetually one foot out the door to be happy. I pair her up with Forty-Two or your alternate universe self in the stories where she's not part of the 'cule. Okay, usually she dies tragically wishing that she'd confessed her love for us both, but I don't want to be morbid.*

I think we're past that, I replied.

Only because you're Mr. Broody Pants, Trish said. *I liked you better when you were Captain America instead of Batman. Except, you're like jovial and jokey one minute then brooding another. Oh my God, you really* are *Spider-Man—*

Stop that, please, I said, wondering what the hell was with people and that comic. *At least use a starship captain.*

They made Spider-Man a starship captain during the 2132 run.

If Trish had been trying to distract me from my imminent doom, she'd succeeded because I was preparing my rebuttal when the elevator door opened to a massive dining hall. It was designed in the human style—so it didn't require me to get on my knees—but had a massive spread of mixed human, Sorkanan, and Notha cuisine. When there were people starving on Notha Prime, this was an extravagant feast for forty or fifty members of their race. There were also only a handful of guests there.

Hannah was wearing a red shimmersilk dress and looked mostly recovered. The dress covered any bandages for her injury.

Forty-Two was in his Space Fleet uniform and staring across the table at the man opposite to him.

High Protector B'Vash. Yeah, I didn't expect to see him here, but he was coring some *lishtar* fruit with a corkscrew-like utensil.

Finally, the Great Notha himself. He was a giant among their race, and at least five-foot-two in height. He looked less like a squirrel and more like a human-sized otter. His uniform was white with so many holographic decorations that he might have been able to outrank the self-styled Generalissimos of Rand's World.

Gold epaulettes were on his shoulders, signifying he not only held the rank of Supreme Leader but also Grand Admiralship of the Notha Navy. He also had a jeweler's eye-esque cybernetic on his right side, focusing like a camera lens when I entered. While most Notha couldn't afford longevity drugs—with embargos also cutting them off from the Union—the Great Notha had a bowl of them casually by his side like candy.

"Ah," the Great Notha said, his voice box translating Notha chittering into a thick Romanian accent. "Speak of the Devil and he shall appear. Welcome, Lord Satan, to the single most important meeting of your life."

CHAPTER TWENTY-FOUR

The Black Dinner

"Well, this is unexpected," I said, looking at Forty-Two and Hannah. "Are you alright?"

"Free food from Furry Hitler is still free," Hannah said, looking at the Great Notha. "No offense."

"None taken," the Great Notha said, taking a sip from a wooden cup that was full of leaf-filled, boiled fruit juice. It was a Notha staple halfway between wine and tea called *leafen*.

"Well, good because I was lying," Hannah said. "A lot of offense was intended."

"I'm fine," Forty-Two said. "I was spying on a bunch of suspicious looking characters around your hospital room when I got nabbed."

"Drolochid cuisine, huh?" I asked.

Forty-Two frowned. "I had to come up with an excuse in the moment and your daughter is psychic. Give me some credit for trying. Not all of us are master spies like you and Case."

"Director G is dead," I said, sighing.

Both the Great Notha and High Protector clapped simultaneously.

"Now truly is a day to celebrate," the Great Notha said, chuckling. "Case Gordon proved to be an enemy of galactic progress for decades. Don't you agree, High Protector?"

"Indeed," High Protector B'Vash said, pressing the tips of his claws together. "Department Twelve might have been able to safely manipulate humanity from behind the scenes if not for his constant interference. There's one thing I hate about your race—"

"Only one thing?" I asked, turning to the High Protector. "Really, I thought that you would have a whole list."

"Oh, this is delightful," the Great Notha said. "I was worried the stories of you being a comedian in dire situations were an exaggeration of the media."

"I'm surprised the Notha race has a sense of humor," Hannah said, turning to him.

"The Notha have a great sense of humor, Consort of Lord Satan," The Great Notha said, putting down his drink. "It and grousing are the two things we have in common with humanity. Well, that and we're both descended from tree dwelling mammals."

"So, three things," Forty-Two said.

"Yes," the Great Notha said, annoyed.

"Ahem," High Protector B'Vash said. "As I was saying—"

"Oh, were you?" I asked.

Everyone at the table was amused but High Protector B'Vash. It seemed that the stories of him taking himself far too seriously were true. I was completely within my captors' power but that didn't mean I couldn't undercut their sense of superiority at least. I also got the impression the Great Notha wasn't any happier about the High Protector's presence than I was.

"Sit down," High Protector B'Vash said. "That is if you want to see your associates leave this room alive."

I reluctantly took a seat, sitting down on the heard leather and wood that made up the chairs. Notha loved their furniture being made of wood and had never really changed to artificial materials despite having been in space for centuries. "Sure."

"Are we hostages?" Hannah asked. "I thought we were honored guests."

"The words are not so different among the Notha," the Great Notha replied. "I've taken the liberty of dismantling your sex toy, Lord Satan."

Hannah jabbed a knife into the table.

"It's fine, Hannah," I said, coldly. "Trust me."

"As I was saying," High Protector B'Vash said, clearly not used to be interrupted. "There is one thing that annoys me about your species."

"What is that?" I asked, more because the conversation would never move on than any actual desire to hear what the man had to say.

"It is the fact that you are so reliant on *machines*," High Protector B'Vash said.

"AI are the only things that Earth could bring to the Community," I said, staring. "Mostly because the Community needed someone to experiment with them and humanity had been working with AI for centuries."

"You think you were working with them," High Protector B'Vash said. "What you were actually doing was submitting yourself to their control over you."

"Earth isn't controlled by AI," I said, automatically.

"Aren't you?" High Protector B'Vash said. "Because from my perspective, they are the puppet masters who created the artificial feeling of security experienced by your species. They dominate your Space Fleet, they control your economy, and they master all the little programs that keep your economy running. They let you think you are in charge because it is more convenient for them. But you have forgotten how to control AI. The machines have become your masters."

"And yet you were the one who was sponsoring Department Twelve, that was creating so many of them," I said, knowing this was all more manipulation.

"Yes," High Protector B'Vash said, swirling his claw in a cup of water. "Because the Community is also enslaved to AI."

"Bullsavit," I said.

"I mean the Elder Races," High Protector B'Vash said. "We can all speak our truth here, Vance. You have lost your tokens of office that let them listen in on us. We have dismantled the machine in your brain that watched your every thought."

Or so they think, Trish said.

Shh, I replied mentally. *Let him speak. This is a genuine Bond villain moment.*

But which one is the Bond villain?

Sometimes there's two, I replied. *From Russia with Love had three and Red Grant.*

"I'm not a friend of the Elder Races," I said, looking between them. "The only reason I've worked for them because the alternative is the complete annihilation of the human race and sometimes even worse."

"You expect us to believe that?" The Great Notha asked. "You, who to destroyed one of the Primordials to save them."

"The Primordials were coming to kill all biologicals in this galaxy," I said, simply. "They didn't even hate us, per se, but thought of wiping out the sentient species cultivated by the Elder Races as akin to burning their fields before a harvest. They wanted to starve out the Elder Races' higher rate of growth, I presume, because the Primordials wiped out all of the species in their dwarf galaxy."

"They are beyond the dwarf galaxies," the Great Notha said. "The Primordials have a very different philosophy toward dealing with so-called lesser races. Whereas the Elder Races cultivate them like gardeners, removing weeds and tending from a distance, the Primordials are more like geneticists. They have created the races they wanted to serve them and make it so they directly rule over their creations."

"The Space Vampires," I said, pausing. "The Travelers."

"Among others," the Great Notha said. "The Notha's territory is built upon a region surrounding a vast wormhole, the one near Death World that you briefly collapsed. It is unstable and they had to reopen it. It is from this place that many horrifying abominations and creatures that you would think of as mythical came to wipe out the species that came before us. The Crystal Spider Empire once reached our land and so did the Katargs, but both of them are now dust and memory. The Primordials rotted them from the inside with their agents and helped bring down their leadership through agents."

"Uh huh," I said, wondering what they were getting at.

"Both the Primordials and Elder Races are AI diseases," High Protector B'Vash said. "As a young Sorkanan, I was forced into the Elder Races' service, like you. I loathed what it required me of, the horrible acts of murder and genocide, but I carried them out in hopes of preserving my race until such time as I could strike back."

Forty-Two hocked and spit on the table between him and B'Vash. It landed on an unrecognizable animal carcass.

"That is a waste of good *tasgh*," High Protector B'Vash said.

"I'll still eat it," Forty-Two said. "You have been a plague on the Sorkanan as long as you've existed, always accumulating more power in the name of advancing us but keeping us divided against one another. The Equalists and other Separatist movements are the result of the brutality you've made the Sorkanan poor suffer. If you have felt any guilt for the actions you have taken to make us great, I have not seen them."

"Lord Satan, your pet is speaking," the Great Notha said.

"Forty-Two knows the Sorkanan far better than I do," I said, simply. "But his opinions mirror mine."

"Power is only expressible in enforcing your will over those who don't possess it," High Protector B'Vash said. "There is no actual use for power other than this, especially as so much of it is tied together in ideology and tribalism. So, yes, I have more horrors to my name than any other Sorkanan in recent memory. I accept that cost."

"Funny how the cost is being paid by others," I said, pausing. "What do you want, exactly?"

"Department Twelve existed for the purpose of creating AI and pushing the envelope of its development so we could learn the weaknesses of the Elder Races. That is why we have so strenuously combed the galaxy for Elder artifacts."

"And if someone needed to be punished for stealing Elder artifacts, it would be humanity rather than the Sorkanan," I said, following his logic.

"Indeed," High Protector B'Vash said. "I formed a useful arrangement with a technologically inferior species that was willing to take the risks necessary to advance their position. If they were destroyed, it would have been no great loss."

I sucked in my breath and put on a fake smile. "Yes, I suppose it would be that way for you."

"Unfortunately, for the Notha, humanity did not get itself destroyed. The High Protector got to use them as cannon fodder during the Community's war against the Empire," the Great Notha said, sounding equally as disdainful of his own people as humanity.

"Less a war and more of a border skirmish," High Protector B'Vash said. "The only people who had anything really at stake were the human colonists and Sorkanan colonists drawn from the dregs of our species. The resulting exchange of SKAMMs was unfortunate but nothing really of value was lost."

"Did you fire first or did they?" I asked, not touching any of the food.

"He did," The Great Notha said.

"It doesn't matter," High Protector B'Vash said. "But the Notha I bribed were the ones to push the button first. It allowed the conflict to be limited. It also covered up several thefts of Elder Race technology that might have otherwise been exposed."

"So Furry Hitler and Scaled Stalin," Hannah said. "Impressive Warsaw Pact you've got going on here."

"I don't know what that means nor do I care," High Protector B'Vash said, lifting his cup.

"I understand human history better than you do," the Great Notha said. "In simple terms, they are just saying we are natural enemies temporarily allied. Also, with some hint of moral condemnation."

"More than a hint," I said.

"Morality is for the winners to decide," High Protector B'Vash said, drinking then putting down his cup. "In the end, Department Twelve outlived its usefulness and humanity regained control over itself. At least for a time."

"They had some help," The Great Notha said, amused. "It turns out your people are much easier to buy than defeat in battle."

"Yeah, plenty of people have said that over the years," I muttered.

How's your infiltration going? I mentally asked Trish.

Slowly but surely, Trish said. *A lot of the systems are so old that it's hard to link them up in a coherent set of commands. However, I have control over the communications and am slowly getting to the point I'll be able to shut down many when the time comes.*

Gotcha, I said.

I can also try and infiltrate the other Notha vessels, Trish said. *They're prepping for jumpspace now.*

Just be prepared to stop this vessel, I said.

You realize that will leave you incredibly vulnerable, Vance, Trish said. *Hannah and Forty-Two too.*

Yes, I said. *However, I was born in Scotland. I think. It was never terribly clear as my family commuted between the Moon and Edenborough Space Navy Base a lot. Either way, "Who Dares Wins."*

That's a British *Special Operations motto and I think any Scottish ancestors you have want to rise from the grave and smack you,* Trish said.

I smirked. *Wait for my signal.*

Will do, Trish said.

"So, what is all this?" I asked, unimpressed. "You created a rogue intelligence agency in a foreign nation in order to use them as tools, B'Vash. Congratulations, Great Notha, you bought the corrupt and weak-willed of my nation. What's the point of all this?"

I already knew the answer. The Great Notha and High Protector were talking to me like I was four years and a particularly dumb four-year-old at that.

"We want you to join us in our newly formed Triumvirate," the Great Notha said. "Mind you, you'd be our Lepidus."

The High Protector snorted at yet another reference to human history that he didn't get. "The Notha are useful as an eternal threat to the Community even though they don't present an actual danger. It does, however, possess quite a bit of the resources necessary to continue building ourselves up to go against the Elder Races."

It was, of course, a suicidally insane idea. But, I recognized it for the excuse it was. They had no actual interest in fighting the Elder Races. No, this was just a gathering of two corrupt individuals trying to use brinkmanship to enrich themselves even more.

"So, is that it, huh?" I asked them. "You need another High Protector who knows about the Codex to start gathering new monkeys from the simian population of Earth to dance to your tune? Someone else to take the brunt of any Elder Race or political fallout."

"Yes," the Great Notha said. "I can make you ruler of all the Human League and B'Vash can protect your position in the Community. It is the only time you will receive this offer. Otherwise, you will find yourself and those you care about suffering for it."

"Don't do it for us, Vance," Hannah said.

"Absolutely do it for us," Forty-Two said.

"Really?" Hannah asked. "I only said that because I thought you would."

Forty-Two shrugged.

"You wouldn't be the first person to whom we've made this offer," B'Vash said, revealing he'd been working with the Great Notha for a while. Possibly as soon as they started negotiating the treaty over Deathworld. I'd been a fool to trust him.

"Oh?" I asked, getting a horrifying feeling.

"Yes," B'Vash mocked. "Your dear aunt refused to join us."

Vance, the Notha fleet is about to enter jumpspace, Trisha said. *If I'm going to act, I'm going to have to act now.*

I made my decision. *Shut the* Notha's Destiny's *jumpdrive down. Then tell the Community ships that High Protector B'Vash has just been assassinated by the Great Notha.*

That's going to be easy to disp—

I grabbed a knife and jumped on the table before stabbing High Protector B'Vash in the throat.

CHAPTER TWENTY-FIVE

The Showdown

Yeah, this was not a particularly well-conceived plan. Assuming you considered it to be a plan at all, which was highly debatable. No, this was a series of emotionally driven actions and acts of opportunity that would probably result in every one of us being killed.

You know, like my plans usually were.

The plan, at least as far as one existed, was to have Trish infiltrate the *Notha's Destiny*'s systems while they prepared to depart the solar system. I didn't know if High Protector B'Vash had agreed to travel with the Notha or if he was about to be kidnapped with me. Well, part one of my plan seemed to have worked because she'd sabotaged the jumpdrive and the entirety of the Notha fleet was leaving their flagship behind. Due to the nature of dimensional travel, they weren't going to find out that *Notha's Destiny* wasn't with them until they arrived at whatever destination they'd jumped to. Many battles had been decided by the discovery that someone's jump drive was either nonfunctioning or a little slow.

The next part of the plan would probably be, well, this side of unethical. Actually, I'm pretty sure it hovered somewhere between high treason and a war crime. Mind you, it might actually be legally defensible if it ever came to court—and let's pray to God it never does—due to how nebulous the definitions of a High Protector's powers were. They really came down to: "You can do anything you want until the High Council decides you're a lunatic who needs to be stopped." There was a certain level of karmic justice to the fact that it was in large part due to High Protector B'Vash that High Protectors had as much power as they did.

This part of the plan was killing B'Vash and claiming the Great Notha did it in what was a false flag operation. Which I considered vile and the enemy of everything I believed in as a Space Fleet officer. It would get a lot of Community officers as well as Notha killed. However, at this point, I didn't care much because the most important thing right now was stopping these monsters from pressing their boots on the throat of the rest of the galaxy. So, yeah, I was trying to kill High Protector B'Vash with a table knife while having it broadcast that it had been the Great Notha who had done the deed.

Maybe there was more Director G in me than I thought.

Alarms blared throughout the *Notha's Destiny* as I stabbed B'Vash in the throat. Surprise proved to be more of an advantage than I expected or perhaps B'Vash just hadn't had to fight anyone who could fight back for centuries. Greenish blood spewed from B'Vash's injury as I'd struck an artery. He attempted to claw my face but I kept stabbing even as I expected the walls to pop out a series of plasma cannons or hidden guards to stop me.

None did.

Instead, there was only the sound of a small set of furry hands clapping. It was the Great Notha, who wasn't in the slightest bit disturbed by my sudden act of violence. Instead, he seemed amused more than anything else. Forty-Two and Hannah, by contrast, looked horrified. Her eyes were darting between me and the dying High Protector on the ground. His clawed hands tried to get at my face but had no strength as a massive pool of fluid surrounding him. B'Vash, in that moment, died and the world was a better place for it.

"Bravo, bravo," the Great Notha said. "I didn't honestly think you had it in you, Captain Turbo. I assume that you are responsible for the attack that has begun on my flagship as well?"

"Yes," I said, drenched in green blood that turned into black stains against my red uniform. "I said you were responsible for B'Vash's death."

Hannah took a long drink of a campaign flute full of alcohol. "Thanks for warning us, Vance."

"You should keep stabbing B'Vash to make sure he's dead," Forty-Two said, looking at B'Vash. "You don't want him to contradict your story."

I glared at Forty-Two.

"What?" Forty-Two said.

"Good," the Great Notha said. "That will do nicely."

I stared at him, wondering what he was talking about. There was something wrong here and I was missing it. A brief survey of the room confirmed things I'd been aware of but hadn't been thinking about before. There were no guards or servants present. No sign of surveillance either. No, this was the perfect place to conduct a murder. "Crazzap."

"Yes," the Great Notha said. "I was planning on killing you both and blaming the Great Notha anyway."

"Why would you blame yourself?" Hannah asked, having seized her own knife. She was very confused.

"Because Vance Turbo would escape from this dinner table heroically with no other survivors," I said, staring at him. "Wouldn't he?"

The Great Notha bared his teeth, which was more like a smile than a challenge among the Notha. "Yes. Having the ship explode behind me is going to be a bit more theatrical than intended but should suit your legend."

"I am so lost," Hannah said.

"He's a Space Vampire," Forty-Two said, stabbing a nearby slice of meat with a square-pronged fork. "I was wondering when we were going to circle back to that plot."

"This isn't a story, Forty-Two," I said, standing up with my weapon in hand.

"Everything is a story," Forty-Two said, doing the same. He shoved the slice of meat in his mouth and spoke his next words while chewing. "The trick to life is to make sure you make it interesting to tell."

I couldn't argue with that. "Hannah, Forty-Two, you need to get out of here and tell everyone the truth."

"Yeah, that's gonna happen," Hannah said, ripping the bottom of her dress off to give her more maneuverability. She also kicked off her high heels. I admit, it did make the whole thing seem more like a movie. Not the edited kind by the Sons of Humanity either.

"Hahaha," the Great Notha chuckled. "Oh, that's adorable. You really think you're going to live."

Trish, I need you to contact the Notha Death Commandos and tell them to come down here, I said to her mentally.

Uh, Vance are you crazy? Also, the ship is currently under attack, Trish said. *You can't feel it in here but we're getting our ass kicked.*

Do it!

The Great Notha transformed before my eyes and gradually became a hideous cloak-like creature that was at least three times the size of the other members of its race. Almost immediately, I felt myself growing weaker as the creature's presence seemed to suck away my strength from a dozen feet away.

The Great Notha touched my mind, and I was forced to relive some of the worst moments of my life, many of which I'd been re-experiencing here in Space Academy. That the Space Vampires were terrorizing my mijnd was a last moment realization as to why I'd been having such a hard time since arriving. The process that the Space Vampires used to absorb the memories of other people was designed to manifest through pain and emotional turmoil. It left me somewhat relieved because it meant all the melancholy and ennui I'd experienced was at least partially the fault of the creatures I kept running into.

It also meant absolutely nothing to my current situation, of course. I was going to get killed fighting this thing without any weapons that could hurt it. Still, I forced my consciousness against the creature's will even as I saw both Hannah and Forty-Two fall to their knees. For me, it was like gravity had increased many times more than what I'd tried to pull on the mercenaries in hangar 18.

All the despair and misery I'd felt for failing Tommy and Case washed over me while I wondered what right I had to even call myself an officer of Space Fleet. I'd just committed murder and arguably started a war between the Community and Notha Union. Why? Revenge? The chance to get justice for Aunt Kathy and Case? The chance to stick my thumb in the eye of people who were beyond conventional justice? What sort of person risked thousands of lives to satisfy his own gross need for the world to make sense? A monster, that was who.

Vance, Trish tried to speak but her voice was echoing, and I could barely hear her. It was better that way since I didn't need reassurance. I needed to be told I was the same as the people I'd destroyed.

"Submit, Captain Turbo," the Great Notha (or Space Vampire) said. "Your life is misery and struggle to save a galaxy that does not care in the slightest. You are trying to clean off the sand from a beach with a bucket. Submit and at least allow yourself the peace of the grave. I will spare your daughter's life."

Those words shook me out of my fugue and awakened what little resistance I still possessed in my body. Not because of a cheesy moment where the thought of my daughter gave me the power to throw off the Space Vampire's—I wasn't thinking of them as Travelers anymore— control. No, it was much more cynical than that. No, it was the realization that there was no way the Great Notha would spare Astrid. She was a psychic capable of reading the minds of those around her as well as seeing glimpses into the future. The only way for his plan to replace me would work would be to eliminate Trish and Astrid both. I wouldn't let that happen.

"No," I said, bleeding from both nostrils. "I don't think I will."

I pushed the Space Vampire's influence away from my mind and tried to look for a weapon that could help me against the creature. I looked down at B'Vash's corpse, hoping to see something that he might have smuggled in or insisted on, but there was nothing. My brain started to hurt and everything became wobbly. As much as I might be able to resist the creature in front of me, it wasn't enough to stop it from killing me. It began to morph and twist, becoming more liquid than solid. Its liquid form slowly approached, slithering across the top of the table and moving to consume me.

"Goodbye, Hero of SPAAACE," the Space Vampire said from a dozen holes across its strange body. It grabbed me in one of its tentacles and lifted me up into the air. Everything started to go black.

I was, in simple terms. out of tricks.

"A Space Vampire! Blast it!" the Death Commando general shouted from behind me as he and his soldiers poured thought the main entrance.

The Space Vampire threw me across the room, and I banged against the wall, sliding down as a half-dozen Notha Death Commandos and their general began firing. The Space Vampire wasn't immune to regular weaponry or at least didn't appear to be even as it screamed in outrage. It was certainly resistant to it, though, as the Space Vampire slithered toward the Death Commandos and engage them with its tendrils.

That was when I forced myself up or tried to at least. I wobbled on my feet and stumbled even as I tried to make it over to Hannah and Forty-Two. The Death Commandos saw me and undoubtedly wanted to gun me down, but their focus was primarily on the Space Vampire. The Notha were hurting it but that was very different from killing it as the general was ripped in two.

"Mom, I don't want to marry a noble..." Hannah muttered, her body prone on the ground. The Space Vampire's mental woo-woo had hit her hard.

Forty-Two were already up and lifting her under one arm like a small dog or other animal. "I changed my mind; free food isn't enough."

Trish, I mentally tried to contact my fiancée. (I was finally willing to admit it.) It was difficult, though, as my head swirled like there was a tornado spinning it. *Trish, I need you.*

Kinda busy here, Vance, Trish said, something she never normally said. *My brain is spread throughout this ship that is threatening to explode at any minute. And Community forces are attacking us. What do you need?*

Open the elevator, i said, reaching its door with my companions.

Oh, I can do that, Trish said. *Why didn't you say so?*

I bit back a nasty retort that Trish probably still heard even as the elevator doors slid open, allowing the three of us to stumble inside. Unfortunately, the events behind us weren't exactly going well as the Notha Commandos I'd assumed would make short work of the Space Vampire were getting slaughtered.

It felt like the end of a horror movie to see the liquid-like monster finish off the last of the heavily armed military unit before it came after us. The fact that the monster—or alien in this case—was a fully sentient being didn't stop its animalistic qualities from being terrifying. The doors to the elevator shut even as the tips of the monster's tendrils got through, trying to pry the elevator doors open.

"Motherborker!" Hannah said, staring at the sight.

Forty-Two moved to put himself between the monster and his two human friends before the elevator suddenly lurched upward. Trish had managed to get it moving and the tendril tips were severed. That never would have worked on a human or Community vessel but was accomplished by Notha disregard for safety.

"We need to get off this ship," I said, breathing out a sigh of relief.

"No kidding," Forty-Two said. "I assume you have a plan to get us off, save all the slaves aboard, and also seduce the suspiciously human-like princess?"

"No," I said, staring at him. "I'm afraid we're in a much grittier story."

"I can be the princess. The Space Vampire screwed with my head but I'm better now," Hannah said, breathing heavily and sweating. "Even though that *thing* reminded me of how much I hate nobles. You should sound the evacuation order for the ship. Get the slaves to safety and maybe some of the crew. Hopefully, this thing has enough escape pods for everyone."

"IT DOES NOT," Trish said, speaking through the elevator's peakers. "NOTHA SHIPS ALSO HAVE SOMETHING MORE LIKE LIFEBOATS THAN ESCAPE PODS THEY REQUIRE THE LORD ADMIRAL OF THE SHIP TO AUTHORIZE THEIR USE. UNFORTUNATELY, HE'S TOO TERRIFIED OF THE GREAT NOTHA KILLING HIS FAMILY AND IS UNLIKELY TO BELIEVE THAT THE GREAT NOTHA HAS BEEN REPLACED BY A SHOGGOTH THIS ENTIRE TIME."

"What's a shoggoth?" Forty-Two asked.

"Can you fake the Great Notha ordering a surrender and evacuation?" I asked, ignoring Forty-Two's question. I didn't think we needed to get into an explanation of H.P. Lovecraft's Cthulhu Mythos, even if it did match up surprisingly well to the Primordials.

"THAT WOULD BE INCREDIBLY HARD AND TIME CONSUMING," Trish said. "AND YES, I CAN FAKE IT."

"Then do so, please," I said. "We need to get off this ship."

"WE CAN DO THAT, TOO," Trish said. "REMEMBER, YOU ARE *SUPPOSED* TO GET OFF THIS SHIP. THE GREAT NOTHA PLANNED TO BE WALKING AROUND IN YOUR SHAPE. HE'S PREPARED A SHUTTLE FOR YOU TO DEPART IN. YOU SHOULDN'T HAVE ANY TROUBLE LEAVING."

I choked down my response and stared upward at the elevator ceiling. "Are you *goddamn kidding me*?"

"WHAT? Trish asked.

"That seems way too easy," Hannah said, shaking her head.

"YOU CALL THIS EASY?" Trish asked. "I AM IMPERSONATING LIKE FIFTY SEPARATE NOTHA RIGHT NOW, FIGHTING OFF HUNDREDS OF COMPUTER ATTACKS, AND TRYING TO KEEP THE SHIP FROM BLOWING UP BEFORE YOU GUYS GET OFF OF IT. DO I GET A THANK YOU?"

"Err, thank you?" I asked.

"TOO LATE!" Trish said. "ANYWAY, WE'RE ALMOST THERE."

That was when there was a big thumping noise against the bottom of the elevator as it shook.

Hannah felt her face. "Please tell me that's not what I think it is."

"What do you think it is?" Forty-Two asked.

"The monster," Hannah asked.

"Then no, I won't tell you that," Forty-Two said.

"When the door opens, run," I said, taking a deep breath.

"Right," Hannah said, nodding.

The elevator doors opened, and a dozen Notha Death Commandos were standing in front of the door with their weapons drawn.

Goddammit.

That was when a trio of tendrils smashed through the floor of the elevator, and we all went to the sides of the chamber while the Notha Death Commandos unloaded with their weapons. Blue paralyzer blasts shot past us into the tendrils, causing them to wiggle in agony. Miraculously, all of them missed us in the first volley.

"This is a great job you're doing, Vance!" Hannah shouted.

"Run!" I shouted.

CHAPTER TWENTY-SIX

The Last Battle

I was actually shot during the resultant charge and so was Forty-Two, but the Notha Death Commandos had their weapons set on paralyze, which notably was for Notha-sized individuals. Adrenaline combined with pulse pounding fear *and* Elder Race enhancements kept me going, while Forty-Two was mostly cybernetics by this point. Hannah grabbed one of the fallen Notha's rifles and shot behind us as we moved, setting it to kill.

That wasn't necessary, though, because the Space Vampire was handily distracting them. It had come through the floor and was now going after the soldiers shooting it. The order for evacuation had been given and the decision to capture us had been given by some Notha officers who decided this meant it was the perfect time to capture us.

Don't you just love improvisation? I do, but only when I do it. There was a reason the old maxim, "No plan survives first contact with the enemy" had lasted for as long as it did. Hell, why did every race that had a military tradition have a similar expression? Because it was true. "Truth is truth," as the alien Jeriba Shigan said in the 1985 classic *Enemy Mine*. God, to think that might be the last movie reference I ever make.

Either way, the hangar bay was full of Notha panicking and going in every possible direction. Civil insurrection had begun as the slaves realized that they were going to die at the same time as the workers and lowest ranking soldiers did. A miniature civil war had broken out among the *Notha's Destiny* crew over who would be able to seize control over the lifeboats to safety. It was such an incredible struggle that no one was paying attention to the two humans and the Sorkanan running through.

Unfortunately, one of the things they were paying attention turned out to be the shuttle we'd come in on. The Sons of Humanity were spread out in front of it, all of them murdered by the rioting Notha. The shuttle ramp lifted, and I could see that a crew of slaves and workers had seized the cockpit. They lifted the vessel off the ground and turned around, heading through the barrier to the space beyond. All the other shuttles in the hangar bay had also departed along with the starfighters.

"Well, savit," I muttered staring our last hope as it departed.

"This is not one of your better plans, Vance," Hannah said, coming up beside me.

"No, it is not," I said. "Would now be a good time to confess that I was always making it up as I went along?"

"No, no it would not," Hannah said, turning back to look at the monster we'd left behind us. "Uh, Vance, bad news."

"Let me guess, the Space Vampire has already eaten all of the Death Commandos," I said, not bothering to turn around. I had no idea why it was absorbing them when so far its pattern had only been to do that to people it was replacing but there was a lot I didn't know about these extradimensional predators.

"Yep," Hannah said. "I don't suppose there's any chance of this ship remaining stable."

Nope, Trish said. *We're suffering systems failures all over the place. The Happy Funtime Bureau have set off sabotage charges throughout critical systems. The fanatics are trying to make sure nothing falls into the hands of the Community when this stuff is at least fifty years behind the times.*

"Fantastic," I muttered aloud, turning around to see the liquid Space Vampire start to come our way. It was slower now, probably because it had already eaten a half-dozen Notha and was full. I didn't think that would stop it from killing us, though. "By any chance, do you have a bunch of molten steel we could drop it into, do you?"

"What an odd reference," Hannah said. "What movie is that from?"

"Either *Alien 3*, *Terminator 2*, or *Terraformerx 6*," I said, shrugging. "Pick one."

"Sorry, fresh out," Forty-Two said. "Now is probably the time to reveal that Hannah is pregnant with your child."

"What?" Hannah asked, doing a double take.

"And I am actually your half-brother via genetic engineering, Vance," Forty-Two said. "Tommy is still alive but has been brainwashed into being a soldier for Department Twelve by Leah. Except it's actually Leah's Space Vampire replacement who fell in love with you when she absorbed her memories."

"Forty-Two..." I said, sighing.

"Danny is your son from a previous marriage you don't remember due to your own brainwashing and Trish was human all along," Forty-Two said. "All of these secrets, twists, and turns will be resolved on the next season of *Holonovela en el Espacio*."

"TURBO!" The Space Vampire screamed from a dozen holes. "I WILL END YOU!"

I took a deep breath. "Well, at least I will spend my last moments as I lived them: surrounded by weirdos."

"GET DOWN!" Trish shouted through the speakers in the walls of the hangar bay.

Hannah and Forty-Two both moved faster than I did, pushing me to the floor. Behind us, I heard the sound of a shuttle's thrusters mixed with a close-range discharge of starship-caliber plasma cannons. It was deafening as two charges rang out, blasting into the Space Vampire once, then twice. The creature exploded and splattered across the hangar bay, the alien substance of its body dissolving all around us.

"_____" Hannah said something, which came out as nothing but white noise.

"_____" Forty-Two replied to her.

"I think it's dead!" I said, hoping I could still heal faster than a normal human being.

"Why are you shouting!?" Hannah asked, proving I could. "Also, I am very glad that I have combat quality cybernetic eardrum replacements!"

"Are they paying you to say that?" I asked, turning my head to look back at a Dreadnought-class ship's shuttle settling down. The heat was tremendous from the thruster's backdraft and forced me up just so I could back away. All of the remaining Notha had cleared the hangar due to, well, the giant tentacle monster and we had a brief respite.

"Yes, I have in fact done endorsements!" Hannah said, shouting. "I really need my own movie. Can you make it happen?"

I didn't respond because I was too focused on seeing just who had come to either kill us or rescue us. The shuttle lowered its ramp and, much to my surprise, Danny and Shelly walked down. Danny was carrying a plasma rifle that he was using a shoulder strap to balance. Oh, and Major Tom followed. Wow, his returning unharmed was an anticlimax.

"My career is so borked for this," Shelly muttered.

"Hi!" Danny said, waving to me. "We came to rescue you because Trish said you needed help."

I waved. "Yeah, thanks for that."

Danny turned his rifle on me. "How do we know you're not a Space Vampire?"

Shelly slapped up the backside of the head. "Idiot. Don't make this more difficult."

"We have a full-proof method of determining whether it's you anyway!" Major Tom said, pointing at me. "Hey, Trish, is this the real Vance?"

"YES, DUMBANYX," Trish said over the speakers. " YOU HAVE ABOUT TEN MINUTES BEFORE THE *NOTHA'S DESTINY* EXPLODES, AND ABOUT HALF OF THAT TO GET AWAY FROM THE BLAST ZONE."

"Right," Major Tom said, turning around. "Let's get the bork out of here."

I didn't bother waiting for anyone else and headed up the ramp, stopping at the top only to make sure that Hannah and Forty-Two were following. In the interior of the shuttle, I was stunned to see Peter, Paul, and, yes, Mary. The three of them were operating the shuttle's secondary controls that took a crew of five to operate.

"Hi!" Mary said, waving her hand. "They rebuilt me!"

I wasn't sure how the hell that was possible given I'd very clearly seen her die and she was a human clone rather than a bioroid. I didn't think it was likely she was another Space Vampire, though, and there was bork all I could do about it if she was.

"Do you still want to kill me?" I asked, unsure if I was about to be attacked.

"Oh no!" Mary said, putting her hand over her heart. "I understand now that was just part of your plan to kill the evil High Protector B'Vash."

I blinked. "Yeah, let's not bring that up. To anyone. Ever."

Mary nodded.

I took a seat and strapped myself in.

Somehow, we had managed to survive.

CHAPTER TWENTY-SEVEN

Futureshock

"... and that is the story as I recall it," I said, taking a drink of a Thorian Sunrise in my Captain's Room before sitting down on the edge of my desk. It had been only a couple of days and we were still in stationary orbit around Space Academy, but it felt like weeks had passed. Getting it all off my chest was a relief even if I knew the consequences would be severe.

In the center of the room were five figures: a Sorkanan female, a drolochid matriarch, a Verdantian male, an Ethereal human male, and an Ant mecha that probably contained a few million of their kind. They were the High Council of the Community and had decided that events warranted speaking to me in person. Okay, over the jumpcomm, but the holograms were surprisingly realistic.

It was a rather surprising situation, having the chance to address the most powerful non-Elder Race beings in the universe, and I relished it. I wished it could have been under better circumstances, but it was nice to finally have a face-to-face meeting (sort of) with the people who'd "rewarded" me for saving the galaxy.

They were dressed in elaborate jewelry, cloth patterns, and paint that stretched the definition of clothes but were flashy enough that there was no mistake these were very important aliens. I was just wearing my captain's uniform, unadorned beyond my rank badge.

"That is complete horsesavit," the Sorkanan Female, One Above All, said. Her voice sounded like a middle-aged human female with a severe smoking problem. She also had a slight Persian accent, which was an interesting translation choice.

"Do you really expect us to believe any of that, High Protector?" the drolochid matriarch, Ms. Nanny Emperor, said. Seriously, some names just did not translate well for humans.

The Verdantian, Overlord of the Pride, just growled.

"I confessed to the murder of another High Protector," I said, sighing. "I've confessed to starting an interstellar incident that could well have involved the Community in another war with the Notha. I—"

"The Council has been aware of High Protector B'vash plotting against it since before humans sent out satellites into space," One Above All said, displaying characteristic Sorkanan contempt for my species. "The Council considers your assassination of him and attributing it to the Notha to be not only justified under the circumstances but also within your remit to protect the Community at all costs."

That was one of the things I didn't enjoy about dealing with the High Council. They were, pretty much, exactly like I'd feared they would be, more or less a group of incredibly self-interested politicians with absolutely no reservations about employing whatever means were necessary to preserve the Community. To their credit, they were more of an Augustinian "bread and circuses" model where the goal of leadership was to enshrine your power as thoroughly as possible by making the masses content.

It spoke well of the Community that said organization was able to provide so much contentment and security that very few of the citizens wanted to bring its leadership to task. High Protector B'vash had been right about one thing and that was the people had to be invested in democracy for it to work. For the most part, the Known Universe was not particularly filled with those sorts of people.

"That still leaves the issue of me starting a war," I said.

"You didn't," Ms. Nanny Emperor said. "The Great Notha's death is being blamed upon a coup among his forces. Others are blaming it on the Sons of Humanity. Others still are blaming it on both. The lower castes and slaves attribute it to the Space Vampires and the Notha government ignores their opinions completely. *No one* is blaming it on you or the Community as they do not wish a war with either."

"Your status as a religious figure helps," Overlord of the Pride said. "The Notha religion considers you a bringer of ill fortune and an omen of great calamity but not the actual cause of it. Given a mere human could not bring low the Emperor, Great Notha, or win the war for Deathworld, you must be a supernatural figure taking the form of a human."

I stared at him. "Uh huh. They can't really believe that."

"Given your role as the Elder Races' catspaw, I'm not even sure they're wrong," Overlord of the Pride said. "Nevertheless, war with the Union would have been a small price to pay to deal with B'vash."

"The fact it did not means that it is also a matter that is not concerning to us," Ms. Nanny Emperor said.

Wow, these people were anyxholes.

"So you have no problem with what happened. You just don't think it shook out the way I said it did," I said, blinking.

"Correct," One Above All said. "We believe it's more likely you are covering up for other people."

"Your genius daughter perhaps," Overlord of the Pride said.

"Or perhaps Admiral Shelly," Ms. Nanny Emperor said, addressing her incorrectly but within proper drolochid rules of etiquette.

"Or maybe even your gynoid concubine," the Ethereal human—whose name I didn't know—said. He looked a lot like Tim Russ' Tuvok, though. "The one they call Trish. She could have been working for her late father."

"You think I'd really throw myself on my sword to protect them?" I asked.

"Yes," all of them said at once.

"Absolutely," One Above All said, raising a clawed hand. "Everything we know about you, Captain Turbo, suggests that you are an idealist. Which makes you dangerous."

"But useful," Ms. Nanny Emperor replied. "So useful that we are prepared to put this entire incident behind us."

"You've got to be joking," I said, genuinely stunned at this turn of events.

"Yes, because clearly we look like the sort of people who joke around," Ms. Nanny Emperor said, unaware of how her title sounded to human ears. "Which is sarcasm."

"Yeah, I got that," I said. "I just find it difficult to believe this is all going to be swept under the rug."

The Ethereal human said, "One might argue that the entire purpose of this government is to sweep the inconveniences of statecraft under the rug. Things must be done that terrify, shock, and confuse the masses. Assuming they pay any attention whatsoever. But there are consequences to your choices."

"Consequences," I said, glad we were finally getting somewhere. "What sort of consequences?"

"High Protector B'vash had many allies, and we kept him occupied with ceremonial duties," One Above All said. "You will be required to relocate to Throneworld and take these duties over. You also have the Separation to handle."

"The Separation," I said, noting they already had a word for it.

"Humanity will probably not leave the Community in the next century," the Ethereal human said. "But eventually mankind's penchant for isolationism and dependence on AI will backfire upon it. We have already seen the future in our own Elder-provided devices."

"Earth," I said, thinking of its destruction. That horrible image that Cthulhu had shown me of where destiny would take us in the coming centuries. It had never lost its place in my brain, having burrowed itself deep into my consciousness. I had seen mankind would survive the event, but almost all roads led to someone eventually destroying our world, probably because mankind was impossible to trust with the technology it acquired. There were only so many times you could prevent them from poking a bear with a stick before the bear got wise. Unfortunately, the bear in this case were the many races that had technology that dwarfed humanity's own. We were children playing with a loaded weapon.

The High Council was silent.

They knew.

They borking knew.

"Yes," One Above All said. "But even if the Human League were to leave tomorrow, it would not remove humanity from the Community completely. Humans can survive on Sorkanan worlds without any environmental adjustments. Only minor genetic tweaks are necessary to live on Verdantian or Notha."

Overlord of the Pride snorted.

"That is in addition to the worlds that will not be leaving," One Above All said. "The ones who have yet to be colonized. You may be without a homeworld in the centuries to come or even millennia, but mankind will survive. Your race has a role to play in the future due to passing the tests that all of our species had to undergo. Someday, probably not in your lifetime, no matter how extended it may be, all of our races will ascend to join the Elder Races."

"Yay," I said, sarcastically. I couldn't help it and dropped all pretense of respect. "If we manage to survive long enough and grow as a people, then we'll get to join a bunch of genocidal anyxholes."

Overlord of the Pride laughed.

Much to my surprise, no one seemed upset at my description.

"Yes," One Above All said. "Your observations are hardly uncommon. Just as the Community has immense amounts of blood on its claws, so do the Elder Races. History is formed by mistakes, evils, and failure more than any triumphs. Indeed, those triumphs are very often the former passed off as success. The Elder Races, Community, and humanity all have that in common. Your own species would never have gotten into space without their darkest periods."

"Are you saying that there's no point in hoping for something better?" I asked.

"No," One Above All said, sadly. "I am saying that you cannot judge others by their darkest acts alone, especially with a species. Hope must unfortunately come with forgiveness and mercy. If we eventually do ascend, perhaps the Elder Races will change. We must be better, and you must encourage us to be. Just as we will test you."

"This is very strange," I said, staring at them. "Why are you treating me this way?"

"What way?" Ms. Nanny Emperor asked.

"Like a peer," I said, looking at them. "I work for you."

I found the High Council reassuring me to be creepy. I could have at least tolerated it if they'd remained impersonal and distant. Instead, this was just weird. Like the gods of Olympus taking time to reassure you everything was going to work out fine.

"For now," One Above All said. "The foretellings have been clear since you saved the Known Universe from the Primordials. Eventually, you will sit upon the High Council as humanity's representative. Eventually, you will be the one who orders the settlement of a new homeworld for humanity once your Second Dark Age passes. One in the Perseus Arm you have explored where your people will thrive."

I stared at them. "Trish, cut the feed."

All their images vanished.

"WELL, THAT WAS RUDE," Trish said over the office speakers. "THOUGH I SUPPOSE WE COULD BLAME IT ON TECHNICAL DIFFICULTIES."

I stared at the floor, saying nothing.

"VANCE?" Trish asked.

I looked up. "Inform the Council that I'll be taking a vacation before assuming any new High Protector duties."

"OH?" Trish asked. "HOW LONG?"

"A few months," I said, taking a deep breath. "Enough time for our wedding and honeymoon. I'd like to focus on that now."

"OH GOODIE!" Trish said. "I'VE ALREADY PICKED OUT A VENUE!"

"Where?" I asked, confused.

"SPACE ACADEMY OF COURSE!"

EPILOGUE

The Greatest Adventure

I stood in front of a mirror, adjusting my white dress uniform in the upper levels of the Space academy auditorium. I had enough decorations on it to look like Contested Space dictator and was debating whether to remove them. After all, this wasn't a day about showing off or reminding everyone of the war.

No, it was a wedding.

My wedding.

It was said that all great plays ended with a funeral or a wedding and whichever they did determined whether it was a comedy or tragedy. If so, my life was a little bit of both. Case had gone on to the great server in the sky, but his legacy lived on. It also got me to finally realize I would never be happier with anyone other than my AI lover. Trish and I were going to formalize it today and Space Academy was the best place to do so. It was going to be a small ceremony but, well, small was relative and there were probably a thousand guests. Which was why I was hiding here in a room next to the rectory under the excuse of getting dressed.

"How do I look?" I asked.

Forty-Two was serving as my best man and standing there beside me, wearing a wrinkled version of his own dress uniform that had probably never come out of its package until today. The rest of my wedding party were outside making their own preparations.

"Like a hairless monkey in a suit," Forty-Two said, amused. "However, your bride to be is a bunch of digital ink and numbers so she's unlikely to run screaming from how ugly you are."

I snorted, smirking. "I think Trish and I will be happy."

216

"I should hope so," Forty-Two said. "A lot of planets won't recognize this marriage as legally binding."

"Earth will," I said, pausing. "At least now,"

The revelation of the Codex could no longer be hidden and the High Council of the Community ended up confiscating it. The Ethereals sent representatives to the Core Worlds and the Elder Races, for once, responded: humanity would be allowed to continue to create AI with it. This, of course, sent shockwaves through everything from markets to politics and thoroughly irritated the isolationists that were presently dealing with their sudden loss of funding from the Notha Union.

"Yeah, well, I hope you don't spend too much time there," Forty-Two said. "I don't intend to spend my twilight years on a planet full of so many rubes."

"I'm still captain of the *Melampus*," I said, having made clear to the High Council I wouldn't be returning to the Perseus Arm. "I've decided to be a bit more assertive with my authority as High Protector to head up the peacekeeping as well as the humanitarian efforts on Deathworld and the former Notha Union space. The worst they can do is fire me."

"More like defrock," Forty-Two said, referring to clergy having their status removed. "I also think they could do a lot worse than that. You've overthrown another government after all."

I gave a half-smile. "The Great Notha turning out to be a Space Vampire wasn't my doing."

"Yes, but the Notha are not exactly friends with the truth," Forty-Two said. "Plenty of them claim it was a cover for your assassinating him. Which, hey, probably only improved your reputation as their version of the Great Devourer."

I sighed. "I'm just glad that Deathworld is finally being inducted as a full member of the Community."

"Pfft," Forty-Two said. "That's another thing that pissed off the higher-ups. They were really enjoying the Notha tearing themselves apart. Now you've gone and brought peace. You know Deathworld's leader is already encouraging a dozen other former Notha holdings to apply for membership. More war is coming as the Union restructures itself."

That was a handy euphemism for yet another round of civil war. "It is what it is, Forty-Two. It's neither a good nor a bad thing. Lots of people will die but hopefully something better will emerge from the fighting. If not, we'll deal with that too. It's just another round in the Great Game of galactic politics."

"I hate how cynical this ordeal has made you," Forty-Two said, pausing. "But you seem to be dealing with your grief better. At least there's no more talk about you retiring."

I paused, attempting to adjust my collar. "There's one thing that Director G taught me and that was I was foolish to think of things in terms of victories or defeats. That the galaxy was either getting better or getting worse. Life is a never-ending struggle of constantly colliding forces pinballing around. One day things will be getting better for one group, and another they will be getting worse. The trick to wielding power is trying to manage it all to be as least unpleasant for as many people as you can."

"What's pinball?" Forty-Two asked, looking at me.

I hesitated to ask my next question because of how uncomfortably morbid it was. "Are you sure you want to spend the rest of your days with me and the others? It's not too late to go back to Sorkanan, spend time with your family. Hell, have one of your own."

"I'm with my family," Forty-Two said, not even pausing to consider his answer. "I've received a few offers for transplanting my genes to birthing clutches over the years but that's not what matters. It's the bonds we have as soldiers and friends. Also, I must educate your daughter in the proper way to kill a man with a *krissh* knife. Trust me, she's going to be Special Operations when she grows up. I've looked into her eyes. Takes after her mother. She is pure evil. You should be proud."

I rolled my eyes. "I'm sure she has an inner space hero in her somewhere. Still, I'm going to give her the choice Aunt Kathy never gave me. If she wants to live an ordinary boring life, then she'll have that opportunity. If she wants to attend Space Academy and join Space Fleet, I'll support that too."

"If she decides to live a boring life, I'll eat my exuviae," Forty-Two said, referring to what was left over after Sorkanan shed their skin every few years.

"Thanks for that mental image, Forty-Two," I said, frowning. "Really."

"You're welcome," Forty-Two said, pointing one of his claws at me. "So, regarding how you gross simians reproduce, when you want more kids are you going to have then grown or ask Hannah to participate? She needs the money. Well, not really, because she just keeps hanging around you guys and is never going to leave you. I think she just doesn't want to admit she loves y'all."

Apparently, Hannah had decided to reject the position of High Protector. Something that I was still confused as hell about. Well, not really, not after meeting the High Council. It was something that shocked the hell out of them, though. It turned out the Elder Races didn't always account for the oddities of free will.

I stared at Forty-Two. "Seriously, what the hell is wrong with you?"

"Many things," Forty-Two said, chuckling. "I'm friends with you for one."

That was when the door to the room cracked open and Danny stuck his head in. "Hey Vance, it's only a few more minutes until the ceremony begins. Are you ready?"

"As I'll ever be," I said, looking at Danny. He was wearing his captain's uniform. "Oh, congratulations."

"Thanks," Danny said, stepping forward to show it off. Astrid was standing behind him in a little white dress that was simple yet adorable.

"So, you and Elektra will be leaving us, huh?" I asked, sad but content.

"Yeah," Danny said, taking a deep breath. "It's time. I finally got my biomod removed and people can see me now. It turns out speaking up so people remembered me gave me some skills at leadership. Don't think I don't know that you pulled some strings to make this happen, though."

Actually, I'd just ordered him promoted and given him a ship but no need to bring that up. He'd been unhappy continuing in my shadow, and it was time to let him show the galaxy what he could do. "At the risk of way too much information, did you and Elektra find a, uh, well, third, or are you going to be parting ways?"

"We're going to stay married," Danny said, surprising me. "We'll just be seeking sexual satisfaction elsewhere. Ethereals call it a mind-soul marriage. I just call it the same way my parents were married but with the small change that *we* really do love each other."

I blinked. "Right."

My cousin was more of a spacer than I was. Either that or half of an old married couple. I was a bit uncomfortable, though, with it being discussed in front of my daughter. She was just looking at me with an uncomfortable expression on her face. Astrid was a mixture of mine and Shelly's DNA, but Leah had been her mother. It was hard to guess what she thought of my marrying so quickly after Leah's demise.

"Hey guys, do you mind if I have a minute alone with Astrid?" I asked, turning to Forty-Two and Danny.

"Sure," Forty-Two said, giving a dismissive wave. "I'll see you at the ceremony designed to officialize sex for services."

"Uh huh," I said.

"Just make sure it's only a minute," Danny said. "If I have to talk to Light on Water more than that while waiting, I won't be held responsible for any murders conducted."

I smirked. "If we get through my wedding without any murders, I'd be very surprised."

"Don't jinx it!" Danny said, stepping back through the door. "There's a pool over whether terrorists, pirates, or just an old lover will attack."

"Goodbye, Danny," I said, watching my friends depart. I shut the door behind them and was alone with my child.

"So," I said, taking a deep breath. "I don't think I actually ever sat down with you to talk about this."

"You think you need my permission to marry, Dad?" Astrid asked.

"Yes," I replied. "Your happiness is the most important thing in the world to me."

Astrid stared. "I can read minds, but you adults really confuse the hell out of me."

I snorted. "I grew up without parents who loved me, Astrid. Aunt Kathy tried but I think she was more her job than her own person by the time I met her. We never were able to find that equilibrium that would have allowed us to—"

"Show you loved each other?" Astrid asked. "Dad, is this conversation about me or you?"

"You're a hard child to raise," I said, smiling. "Because it sometimes feels like you're the more mature person in our relationship."

Astrid snorted. "I mean, yes, obviously. But I'm happy for you, Dad. Trish loves you and you love her."

"Thank you," I said, looking down.

"Also, Mom was kind of evil," Astrid said, sighing.

"Astrid!"

Astrid shrugged. "It's true. Which doesn't change the fact that Mom loved you. People are complicated collections of quantum information."

"That they are," I said, pausing. "I was talking with Forty-Two about what you wanted to do."

"Have cake," Astrid replied. "I don't want to make plans for the rest of my life just yet, Dad. Being the daughter of the High Protector is enough for me for now."

I nodded. "Well, I better get ready for the last part of this journey."

"You talk so damn weird, Dad," Astrid said, shaking her head. "Were you raised by a computer or something?"

"Yes," I said. "Alfred. He's attending. You'll like your grandfather."

Astrid threw up her hands and walked out. "So damn weird."

I smirked. "I'm a very lucky man."

"Yes," a familiar voice spoke. "You are."

"Case," I muttered, turning around. I saw a vision of him even though I knew it wasn't there. He was exactly like I remembered him with none of the damage he'd sustained before the upload.

"You know you don't have to wear a suit in the afterlife."

"I'm uploaded to the Elder Race's network," Case said, smiling. "That's not the afterlife."

"Isn't it?" I asked. "Assuming they won't delete you, you'll probably live for another billion years."

"Possibly," Case replied. "But I'm not afraid of true death, nor should you be. We are all part of a larger network of information that is this great big universe, and I've had a good life where I got to pass on my ideas to many people."

"If this is going to be a substitute father thing, I'll pass," I said, smiling. "Still, I'm glad you decided to attend my wedding in—"

"Please don't," Case said, knowing my joke before I said it.

"—in spirit," I finished.

Case rolled his eyes. "You're terrible, Vance."

"Are you going to visit Trish before you go off to... wherever?" I asked.

Case blinked. "I already am. I can multitask as a being of pure digital information these days. She's happier than she's ever been, and I think you'll be good together for however long it takes for you to decide to upload yourself."

"Let's hope that never happens," I said, pausing. "The thought of spending the rest of eternity with you and the Elder Races is a terrible one."

"They're not so bad once you see into the insides of their minds," Case said, pausing. "There's plenty who don't favor the heavy-handedness of the more genocidal factions. You've helped bring a new perspective to them and may change the Elder Races as a whole."

"You think that's likely?" I asked.

"Not in the slightest," Case said, staring at me. "That doesn't mean it's not worth it to try, though."

I acknowledged his point. "So, that's my life now? Constantly trying to fix a galaxy that is eternally breaking down."

"With those you love, yes," Case said. "It's a bit like Valhalla. The war never ends but at least you have brothers-in-arms by your side."

"I thought the appeal was the constant feasting and partying with the Valkyries," I replied.

"That too," Case said. "Trish will definitely keep you occupied there, I'm sure."

"Anyone else you plan to visit before you head off?" I asked.

"I gave my farewells to Pink," Case said, pausing. "She's pissed I'm not uploading myself into a new bioroid body to be with her but leaving my fortune to her, including all my Ares Electronics stock, softened the blow. She's going to use it to make a foundation for helping people with body issues."

"I should donate to that in Leah's name," I said, pausing.

"I think she'd like that," Case said. "A part of her will always exist in both you and your daughter. Also, those clones, since they come from her DNA and memetics. You might find a copy of her brain patterns in the Codex. You might be able to upload her emotional connections from you and your daughter's bond with her. Make a better copy than anyone else. It's what Leah would have wanted."

"Another Earth-shattering revelation you casually drop on me. I'll deal with that later." I gave the Vulcan salute. "Live long and prosper, Case."

"I'm dead but I'll take that in the spirit it's intended," Case said, giving me the salute back. "I'm leaving you the galaxy, Vance. It will be an endless uphill struggle against evil and something worse than evil: stupidity."

"Stupid and evil are hardly contradictory," I said. "Thankfully, it helps sometimes. The isolationists made their vote today to leave the Community, but I made a legal challenge that they have to come up with a coherent economic plan and withdrawal agreement. I figure that will keep them going until the elections push them out of power."

Case chuckled. "Bureaucracy is sometimes the only thing that stands between us and oblivion. Keep making new friends and loved ones, Vance. That's what Space Academy means as a symbol. It is a place for people to have the chance to meet future heroes and companions from across the universe. It is a place to broaden one's horizons, to share one's knowledge, and to gain from other people. You'll never know when you need these lessons as life goes on."

"Are you really saying the real Space Academy were the friends we made along the way?" I asked. "Because I'm never coming back to this hellhole or at least not for the next century or so. I suggested Light on Water to be the next Commandant. They've accepted the recommendation. I'm officially rid of him and plan to treat the academy like it's quarantined with an apocalyptic disease from now on."

"Goodbye, Vance," Case said, slowly fading away. "It's been an honor."

"Say hi to Ketra for me," I said, nodding to him. "Share some memories of her granddaughter if you find the time."

Then he was gone.

With that, I heard the music of the wedding march start to play.

THE END OF HISTORY

A *Lucifer's Star* and Space Academy Short Story

By C.T. Phipps

"**Y**ou want me to be a *pirate*?" I asked, staring at the hologram of Commonwealth Inquisitor General Ida Claire.

Ida was a brown-skinned old woman, well over two hundred years old, and with only intermittent longevity treatments that made her look not a day younger than a hundred. She was still spry for her age and wearing the white uniform of one of Albion's Watchers. She wasn't quite as much of a genius as spymasters like Director G or the Archmagus, but it was not for lack of trying. The Community patch epaulets on her shoulders also indicated which way she was dealing with the Occupation.

The two of us were conversing in the captain's quarters on the independent freighter *Melampus*, named for the legendary Community flagship. It had formerly been her vessel before I'd taken it in a mutiny.

I, Cassius Mass, was a free trader in the recently annexed Human Space. I was a descendant of heroes and villains both, having been born on the Archduchy of Crius and having fought in the many civil wars that had followed the destruction of Earth at the hands of the Knights of Velusia two hundred years earlier. Albion, Crius, and other worlds had all struggled to see who would emerge as the new human homeworld after the Sol Federation's dissolution. In the end, all of us had lost and the aliens were in charge.

Sort of.

The Community had invaded under the guise of peacekeepers and everyone had assumed they would tear the place apart as every other

225

conqueror and warlord. So far, things had been decidedly tame, and it was *unsettling*. They'd begun to repair the damage to worlds devastated in our conflicts and even started to terraform Earth again. Everyone was waiting for the other shoe to drop and that it hadn't after three years bothered me to no end.

"Why not? Ida asked. "You already are one."

"I'm a smuggler, not a pirate," I said, annoyed.

"What's the difference?"

"A pirate steals from fellow spacers, a smuggler steals from the government," I replied.

Ida shrugged. "Topato, Potamo. Different spelling, same nasty taste. I think you're going to want to hear my offer."

"I sincerely doubt that," I said. "I have no interest in collaboration."

I didn't like the Community. It had abandoned human space after the destruction of Earth, citing hate crimes against alien citizens and the hostility that had been shown to it from many of the governments involved. Despite having been a member of the Community for seven hundred years, Earth had pulled out in the decades before and brought most of humanity with it. The results had been catastrophic for their society and economy, resulting in the creation of the terrorists that had destroyed the Earth itself with a jumpspace equipped asteroid.

Not all humans had abandoned the Community, though. Most of the occupation of the former Human League was conducted by those of our race who had grown up in the Community's post-scarcity economy. Some of them were old enough to remember Earth and looked younger than me, let alone Ida. My father had sabotaged the Commonwealth and Crius governments in hopes of inviting the Community to invade. I'd ended up killing him for it, but he wasn't wrong—it seemed better to serve in Heaven than to reign in Hell.

And I hated him for it.

"The Community isn't the Nazis, Cassius," Ida said, dryly. "Hell, they're not even the Commonwealth or Archduchy, both of which we willingly served."

"They're still invaders," Cassius said. "Even if they've avoided widespread atrocities."

"They're starting to hold elections," Ida said, dryly. "Thirty worlds have already agreed to rejoin the Community voluntarily. A hundred and fifty more are expected to rejoin by the end of the decade. Once that happens, it'll be like a set of dominos and all of humanity will once more be part of the Funny Aliens Club."

I glared. "My ancestors are rolling in their grave."

"Your ancestors include Vance Turbo, the second human High Protector," Ida said, sarcastically. "Also, the founder of your house was his girlfriend. One of 'em, at least. I watched a play about the girlfriends of Turbo called *Nine* recently. Lots of nudity."

I sighed. "I admit, House Mass kind of glosses over the fact they were…"

"A bunch of democracy-loving progressives?" Ida replied. "I know, it's terrible."

"Yes, but without the sarcasm," I muttered.

It was still hard to let go of my reactionary political views. Crius had gone through centuries of war, peace, and revolution as we struggled with the reality that we'd been founded by fascist genetic supremacists only to continually need to relearn our lesson when those individuals were repeatedly overthrown. Inevitably, the rich tried to make their children into a cast of superhumans with hereditary privileges and while we never returned to slavery, it was continuously a struggle to learn the same lesson over and over again. I was lucky I had my crew to keep me grounded and make me regret ever being called "Count."

"Just give me five minutes and I'll compensate you for your time," Ida said. "You still need money, don't you?"

"For now," I muttered. "It also depends on how much you're offering to listen."

All the old battered human ships that were vastly inferior to the Community's own, even from before the Great Galactic Dark Age (which was admittedly an exaggerated title as only humans had experienced it), were being phased out or modified. The *Melampus* was keeping up with smuggled and stolen parts but just barely. Eventually, advancements would require us to replace the old girl or simply liquidate our assets while they were still valuable. I didn't want to retire, though. I wanted to live in space with my crew and the hundreds of people onboard depended on me to pay their salaries.

Ida named a figure. "How's that sound?"

It was ridiculously inflated and made me wonder if she was using a different denomination of cash than I was. "Things must be good at the home office."

"If this job goes through, it will go a long way to healing old wounds," Ida said. "If it fails, it'll all be blamed on you. So, I'm willing to open the purse strings."

"You have my attention," I replied.

Ida lifted her hand and gestured to her side. A schematic of a beautiful cigar-shaped vessel covered in coral like growths appeared. It was alien in manufacture. "Here is the *Kvari Queen*. It is a luxury vessel for the .001% percent of the galaxy's richest. Over a kilometer long, excellent defenses, and the size of a small city."

"Sounds delightful," I said, softly. "Still not sure what I should want out of it."

"Money for sure," Ida said. "The ship maintains a vast collection of fire jewels as an untraceable currency useful for dealing with border worlds and Commonwealth investors."

"Sounds too good to be true."

"I know."

"No, I mean that literally. I think you're making this up to get us to rob this ship."

"The fire jewels are just the cover. Consider it a bonus to your already considerable fee." Ida chuckled.

"What do you really want?"

Ida blinked. "We want you to kill a man."

"I'm not an assassin either."

"You might make an exception for this one," Ida said, conjuring an image.

I was pouring a bottle of Belenus Scotch when I overflowed the drink, seeing the hologram of the man involved. "Yes, I suppose you would."

High Colonel Vincent ap Bastille was a man of Indras descent with long white hair tied into a functional ponytail. He was dressed in a black Engel-fighter spacesuit, but his expression was still one of smug self-assurance.

"The Betrayer," Ida said. "Matricide of Mother Earth. The Worldkiller. The Adolf Eichmann, Benedict Arnold, and Judas Iscariot of countless human cultures."

"None of them approach his crime," I said, hissing at his image.

Vincent ap Bastille was one of the most hated men in human history. If not *the* most hated. The founder of the Knights of Velusia, he believed that humanity's destiny was to exist among the stars but would always be held back if Earth ruled over their colonies. There was a religious element as well, believing that the homeworld somehow was ruled by the Demiurge while the true God was ruler of the rest of space or something. Honestly, his ideology had been unintelligible from the start, but he hadn't needed to attract many to achieve what he wanted: a group of fanatics willing to destroy the Earth.

Ironically, that wasn't even the fullness of his crimes as the disruption to Earth's networks had allowed the Knights to also use repurposed Enigmatic Path codes from the dying Kolahn Race to drive 90% of the Earth's Cognition AIs homicidally insane. Humanity might have been able to rally themselves after the loss of the homeworld, tragic as that might have been, but the madness of its automated population had been the death knell to its chance of rebuilding.

"Where the hell has he been hiding for the past two hundred years?" I asked, stunned.

"The Community," Ida said, shrugging. "One of their many human districts. He doesn't look like this anymore but got a whole clone body replacement for his brain. It means not even his DNA would have been able to be verified."

"Mother—" I said, pausing my words. "Eleven billion people died because of his actions. He is history's greatest mass murderer and you're telling me he's been enjoying the quiet life of a posthuman economy and longevity treatments?"

"'Fraid so," Ida said. "We managed to catch almost all of the Knights, eventually, but everyone assumed that either Bastille died in the chaos following his actions or he was going to end up like Mengele, dying in his bed unpunished."

I had no idea who that was but understood what she meant from context. "He must have had Community helpers."

"Perhaps," Ida said, shrugging. "It's seldom a good idea to toss away the traitors of the nations you conquer. They may be completely untrustworthy, but you never know when you're going to need them."

"Or throw them at vengeance-crazed humanity," I said, thinking of my own world that had been struck by mass drivers during its war with Ida's planet. There was a great irony in us in teaming up to avenge humanity's ancestral home. "I think Genghis Khan used this tactic a few times."

My knowledge of Earth history was spotty and inconsistent but I had a pretty good grasp on successful conquerors.

"Smart guy, that Mongol," Ida said. "But the Community's intelligence services provided us with credible intelligence that this is the real McCoy. Do I have your attention?"

"Perhaps," I said, upset with myself for still caring about the past. "How credible is credible?"

"It's his fourteenth daughter who says he's the guy," Ida said. "We did a DNA test and she was apparently constructed from his original DNA that he must have kept on ice somewhere. Apparently, the clone bodies are not good enough to father heirs."

"Pride goeth before the fall," I muttered. "Murdering a man who is already reviled as an oathbreaker, traitor, and party to genocide is killing someone already half-dead."

"Except for the billions of credits in his accounts and that if he really felt any guilt, he wouldn't have been off on a paradise planet while the rest of humanity burned." Ida rarely showed emotion but what little she did now told me she was fuming at this man's continued existence.

"And you want him dead?" I asked.

"Technically, the High Protector employing me for this would like to put him on trial for war crimes. That would require taking him alive. I'm just as fine revealing his dead body to the world and claiming credit, though."

There was something wrong with this picture.

"Let me ask a question," I said, taking a deep breath. "Then I'll throw away my distinction between pirate and smuggler."

"Just one question?" Ida asked.

"Only one," I said, processing what I felt. I still had a lot of hatred left inside me for Vincent, even though we'd never met and he was just a figure of historical curiosity to most. "Why now and what is your real game?"

"That's two questions?"

"It's asking for specifics about the same concept."

Ida snorted. "Third grade word games are beneath a pirate king."

"I'm a count," Cassius said. "Or would be if the planet I was count on wasn't a smoldering ruin and the government I served wasn't dissolved. But there's nothing that requires me to do this when a High Protector could. Indeed, this would be a rare occasion of the Watchers looking like heroes."

Ida paused. "You're making me regret thinking of an opportunity to make a lot of money bringing down a war criminal."

I stared.

Ida sighed. "Fine. Vincent Bastille's involvement in the Knights of Velusia is unquestioned. However, whether or not he was actually involved in the attack on Earth is less so."

"You're kidding," I said, staring at her.

"He made the rhetoric, he assembled the group, and it was his money that paid for their plan. However, destroying a planet is remarkably easy once you get the people willing to do it. According to the High Protector, Vincent turned all of his followers over after the event and helped bring down the last remnants of the Enigmatic Path as well as prevent the virus that drove the majority of AI insane from infecting the rest of the Community."

"He's been pardoned," Cassius said.

"Yes," Ida said. "Just like you for all the dirty deeds you did during the Reclamation. There are plenty of people on Albion who'd like to hang you but can't. However, you didn't blow up the homeworld. As for why now, there's the possibility that Vincent is going to blow the whole affair open."

I facepalmed. "He's a whistleblower now?"

"His handler apparently finally died after two thousand years and forwarded him all of the information about the Community's handling of the Collapse," Ida said. "Vincent thinks he can clear his name and buy his way back into the human race by blaming everyone else. Given the Community is the party rebuilding Earth, that can't happen. We'd very much like to make sure this information doesn't end up in the hands of a reporter from *Galactic Newsbook Weekly*."

I stared at her. "The trashy conspiracy e-mag?"

"The incredibly well-read trashy conspiracy e-mag," Ida said, frowning. "There's a reporter meeting him on the boat. He wants to do a physical handoff because he didn't survive two hundred years without being paranoid

"Clever," I said, blinking. "Why not send some of your own assassins?"

"That's a lot more than one question."

"I'm a liar."

Ida smiled. "The Watchers aren't what they used to be and neither is the Commonwealth. By the time we get there, the jig will be up and they could infocast it across the galaxy. We could blow the entire starship up and it's ten thousand passengers but you're close enough that I think you could take care of this problem without drastic measures."

"Ah, yes, so we're not the good guys in this," I muttered, knowing it had been too good to be true. "Who is this High Protector you're working with and why does he want him alive if he's a whistleblower?".

"None of your beeswax. He's got a vested interest in seeing this resolved, though," Ida said. "The only thing you need to know is that if this stolen information gets out, many innocent people will die. Letting Vincent live is also an affront to human dignity. The High Protector's plan to make a show of his arrest on behalf of the Community is also hypocrisy of the highest order—and that's me saying that."

I sighed. I hated that her argument worked on me. "Assume I am still listening. What are the operational parameters?"

Ida snorted. "Here's an image of what Vincent looks like now. He's had a few surgeries since then. I've also included an image of the reporter, Anne Bonny."

I snorted.

"What?" Ida said.

"That's the name of a famous pirate," I said. "The first human High Protector."

Ida raised her eyebrow. "I've only heard of the one."

"Different cultures emphasize different things," I muttered.

"I was too busy learning about relevant history," Ida said. "Stuff that happened after the Earth exploded. Mind you, I sadly know quite a bit about the Nazis. My ancestors had some issues with them."

I shook my head then looked at my datapad. On it was the full schematic of the *Kvari Queen*. There was also an updated set of photos for Vincent and his companion, Anne Bonny. The new form of Vincent ap Bastille was similar but different enough to unrecognizable, a minor bit of work to fool the various space port facial scanners. There was a woman beside him too. Anne Bonny was a freckled blue-haired girl with Shogunate eyes and a petite size. There was a fierceness to her, though, which made me think there was more to her than merely being the vessel for Vincent de Bastille's "act of conscience."

"Hmmm," I said, looking them over.

"So are you taking the job or not?" Ida asked.

I sucked in my breath and thought about my dead wife and so many other Crius killed by asteroids fired onto the planet's surface. "Yes, I'll do it. What is the honor of not being a pirate compared to revenge?"

"But will your crew agree?" Ida asked.

I raised an eyebrow. "You do remember them, right?"

"Yes! Piracy!" William Balder, the ship's Chief of Security, shouted. He was sitting at the round table in the conference room, which the crew used as their snack room. Standing beside him was Clarice Rin O-Harra, the ship's first mate, and my ship's doctor Isla Hernandez. Both of them looked every bit as excited as William.

William was a large, well-muscled, obsidian-skinned man with a shaved head and wearing blue overalls. Isla was a blonde bioroid woman dressed in white doctor's attire more suitable for a hospital. Clarice was a redheaded Shogun-born woman dressed in a set of plastisteel security armor with the helmet missing.

"Pirates are not people to admire, they're crim—" I stopped speaking. That was not the best track to go with my crew who were quite proud of their status as outlaws.

"Weren't you a pirate?" Isla asked.

"No!" I snapped, horribly. "I was never a pirate."

"Yes, you were," Clarice said. "You were a privateer for Crius before you got a promotion to heading up the starfighter core."

I shifted my eyes back and forth them. "Being a privateer and commerce raider is *completely different* from being a pirate."

Everyone looked at me, skeptically.

"Why are we friends?" I asked.

"I'm sleeping with you," Clarice said. "So is Isla."

"I'm sleeping with you, too," Isla said to Clarice.

"I don't like you, but I have bills to pay," William said. "Also, we get to kill Space Hitler."

"Less Space Hitler and more the guy who inspired Space Hitler," Isla said. "Who I'm still okay with killing."

I shook my head. "In any case, I've already devised a plan."

"Is your plan to sneak onto the ship, kill this guy, and sneak off without looting any of the valuables onboard?" William asked.

I blinked. "Yes."

"Then your plan stinks," Clarice said. "We need to sell this and that means robbing the place blind."

"Are we that hard up for money?" I asked, stretching out my hands.

"Money is like women," William said, shrugging. "The more you have, the better your situation."

"That's disgusting," Isla said.

"I agree," Clarice said. "At least about the money part."

I sighed. "I'm open to suggestions then. Getting Vincent de Bastille is my primary goal, however."

"Agreed," William said, pausing.

"Agreed?" I asked, not expecting William to join me in this. He had about as much honor as, well, I didn't have a word for it aside from someone with none.

"Yes," William said, looking to the others. "Imagine how much money we can get from the families of all those victims in exchange for gutting him on a live holo."

"Homeless refugees and impoverished patricians are not a great source of wealth," I said, disgusted.

"There are rich humans, too," Clarice said. "They'll pay as well."

"Hell, one credit a piece across a few trillion in the Human League alone," William said, making a portrait square with his hands. "Not to mention however much the Commonwealth would be willing to trade in exchange for the information he's handling."

"Assuming it even exists," I replied. "Ida lies like she breathes."

"Only about the important stuff," William said. "That she was a spy, that she was using us, and that she even had any grandchildren. I'm happy to be her assassin."

"We're not assassins," I said, not sure what I was going to do with Vincent when I caught up with him.

"You *don't* want to kill this guy?" William asked.

I thought about my answer. "I don't know. There seems to be something wrong about this whole affair."

"My heart bleeds for the people party to genocide," Isla said, putting her hand over her heart. "They were just following orders. Boo hoo. This guy deserves to die for what he's done and I'm not even a human being."

I'd killed a lot of people following orders for the former government of Crius. Some of them had been innocents, either caught in the crossfire or part of the targeted bombing campaigns I'd performed as a pilot. Yet, I hadn't turned against my world. I hadn't betrayed my people. But here I was, working with the Commonwealth and Community. Both of whom had conquered my people. Vincent had never worked for a government and was a cult leader turned terrorist, but he had worked for the intelligence service of a foreign power.

Did I have any honor left with which to judge him? Did honor matter here? In the end, that would be up to God to decide or history. This was no longer the age of Vance Turbo, Hero of Space. It was an age of survival. I focused on the one thing that made sense right now:

the mission. Good or evil, I would carry it out to the best of my ability. "I have another plan on looting the ship."

"This was your brilliant plan?" William said, standing beside me at the Kazun tables. "Buy a fricking ticket?"

The two of us were wearing black suits with white ascots as we were surrounded by hundreds of human guests on this level specially designed for members of our species. There were a couple of aliens present, the multi-armed drolochid and squat quadruped Veddo, but it was mostly humans as far as the eye could see.

Which was far as the interior of the central chamber used a combination of holograms and lighting to make an image of a Belenus sunset over a garden party. Most of the humans were dressed as aristocrats from Nouveau Paris. Frankly, we looked shockingly underdressed compared to the fops and trillionaires playing noble.

"We're in alien territory now, outside the Commonwealth's jurisdiction. Buying a ticket was a good way to get us in. So was mugging some of the crew for uniforms."

Clarice walked up, wearing revealing and glittering two-piece swimsuit with butterfly wings, carrying a serving tray. "Why are you not wearing something like this? Isla would be much better in it."

There were, indeed, some men dressed like that, and it had been an option. However, there was no way in hell I was going to wear that outfit.

"I'm the captain and William has been putting on the pounds lately," I said, dryly. "In any case, Isla is a bioroid so she's able to interact with the ship's computers better.. I have her disguised as one of the workers."

Clarice grumbled as I pulled a drink off her tray.

"Have you done the DNA scans?" I asked, having selected her for this portion of the mission primarily because she wouldn't screw it up like William. William was very capable, but I fully believed he'd kidnap Vincent for the money and go off on his own if it was possible. Not that I'd blame him—it was a lot of money.

"Yes," Clarice said. "I've found them."

Vincent ap Bastille wasn't a fool and hadn't gone onto the *Kvari Queen* with the form Ida had identified. He'd had it changed again.

Still, there were always traces of the DNA you'd been born with when such kind of transformations were made. There was no way to hide from who you are and that was a lesson that would be Vincent's end.

"Where?" I asked.

Clarice pointed to a depressed looking man talking to a beautiful redhead about a foot shorter than him.

"Good," I said, tapping a small communicator on my ring and giving the *Melampus* its signal. I tapped it two more times to give Isla a signal in the cargo hold. "I'll deal with Vincent. You make sure you get the rest of the ship's valuables."

"Are you sure we're going to have enough time?" William asked.

"The rest of my plan is better," I said, smiling.

That was when the entire ship shook, and the lights flickered ominously. That was when all the video screens and holounits across the ship projected the skull of a Crius dragon, with two crossed horns at the bottom, all on a red background. A masked version of myself appeared and then started speaking in a modulated voice. "Here me, *Kvari Queen*! You are under attack by the dreaded Crimson King! Evacuate the ship or you'll be blown to smithereens!"

"Smithereens?" Clarice asked. "Really?"

I shrugged. "The only pirates I know of are desperate scum or from movies. I figured the latter were more intimidating than the former."

Then the ship rocked some more.

"Are we really being hit?" William asked.

"Not in the slightest," Cassius said. "Isla is just messing with the gravity. It turns out the mechanics on this ship are as poorly paid as the rest of the staff and are helping her. They are also going to lock the door to the bridge and cut off control from there. You think you and the rest of the crew can seize it?"

The guests around us looked confused but so did the staff. Space piracy was rare in this part of the galaxy, but people were aware of it enough to believe this might not be a joke or prank. Fear crossed the eyes of some while most were more upset at having their vacations interrupted. The super-rich were not used to being afraid for their lives and the only people who seemed truly concerned were the servants. There were also a few idiots who seemed positively delighted at the prospect of a little excitement in their dull, humdrum, richer-than-Croesus lives.

"Against these corpo cops?" William asked. "Easily."

"You won't have to deal with them either," I said, hearing Isla's voice over the speakers.

"This is Vice Captain Isla Hernandez. The ship's reactor has been critically damaged. We've summoned the Commonwealth fleet to aid us, but we must evacuate. Your valuables and belongings in the hold will be ejected out of a special launcher into jumpspace while the Nostubb insurance company will pay for everything else. Please depart in an orderly fashion to all escape pods."

"Is any of that true?" William asked.

"They might depart in an orderly fashion," I said.

I was still iffy about becoming a pirate but if I was going to do wrong then I determined to do wrong right. I was also going to make sure that I removed as many obstacles between myself and Vincent as possible. Seeing the hundreds of guests start to depart—some faster than others—I started walking toward Vincent and his partner.

Vincent moved toward one of the side doors, not the exit, but to the engineering level. Anne Bonny followed him, looking protective and pulling a handheld laser cannon from her purse. I maneuvered toward them, bumping into several overly-dressed aristocrats even as I did my best to move around them. I paused to help someone up and barely missed being shot in the head by Anne Bonny, who had made me. The blast went into the back of an obese Freyan Merchant Prince, causing an immediate panic to break out.

"I've been made!" I shouted.

"No kidding!" William said.

Clarice pushed away the others and I continued after the duo. By the time I reached them, they'd already passed through the door and burned the controls. I growled and pulled out my own fusion pistol before blasting the door and kicking it open. It led to an octagonal metal chamber that stretched down ten stories. There was a disabled elevator by the door with its controls blasted, as well as an old-fashioned set of grate stairs leading down toward the engines. I saw my quarry descending the stairs a few stories down. They were moving fast, very fast.

"It's over, Bastille!" I shouted at him. "You can't escape your crimes anymore!"

"I'm not trying to!" Vincent shouted back. "This is for the human race."

"You've done enough to the human race!" I growled.

Anne fired another blast of her hand cannon. It exploded behind me, sending out a shower of sparks.

"I guess we're doing this the hard way!" I said, shouting. I adjusted my personal energy shield generated from my belt, and threw myself over the side. I fell close to a hundred feet and landed in a sticky kinetic bubble that cushioned my fall. It also meant I was completely unprotected against Anne's hand cannon fire.

I drew first, though, aiming at the pair as they came down to where I was located. "Drop your weapon. Raise your hands."

Anne, surprisingly, did so and I breathed a sigh of relief. I didn't want to kill any more people than I had to. Vincent, unfortunately, raised his hands in surrender as well. I'd killed people in cold blood before but not many of them. Still, a part of me just wanted to gun him down and be done with it.

Vincent looked at me before his eyes widened. "Wait, Cassius Mass? The Fire Count? Descendant of Vance Turbo and Leah Mass. Are you borking serious?"

"Serious as a space fever," I said, dryly. "You're coming with me."

"No!" Anne said, behind him. "You can't."

"I'm not going to be torn apart by the mob for what my actions," Vincent said, his voice cold. "I did what I did to try to save the human race."

I stared at him and almost pulled the trigger on my pistol then and there. "Are you serious? You're going to claim your genocide was an act of nobility?"

"I will not judged by the Butcher of Kolthas," Vincent said, staring at me in contempt. It was another one of the titles I'd earned during the Archduchy-Commonwealth War.

"Why did you do it?" I asked, staring at him. I realized that was the reason why I'd come here. Just to hear it for all the billions of people killed. Trillions if you counted the people who died in the Collapse.

"I didn't!" Vincent said.

I growled. "I don't believe you. Tell me the truth!"

Vincent narrowed his eyes. "Fine! Why did I do it? To save humanity! The Elder Races destroy any species that experiments with their technology or with forbidden technologies like Cognition AI able to deal with them. It's why the Enigmatic Path released the virus. If they didn't lay waste to the Earth, there would have been a complete extermination of humanity!"

I stared at him. "That's madness."

"It bought us an additional two hundred years," Vincent hissed. "Humans couldn't stop poking the technology of their betters and all the efforts to stop these conspiracies failed after seven hundred years of suppressing them. Now the Community can rebuild human society so it can exist within the parameters that will keep us safe."

"And what? You're blow the whistle on them now?" I asked, guessing that was what was in the Community folder.

"It was never supposed to last this long!" Vincent growled. "It took centuries to achieve what could have been resolved in decades! The Community betrayed not just humanity but me personally! We deserve to know who abandoned us and profited!"

I didn't believe the Community had been involved in the destruction of Earth but I believed his crazy cult had done what they thought was necessary to preserve humanity. Now he had, perhaps, evidence to link the Community to letting humanity's shared culture collapse so they could ride in as humanity's rescuers.

"Yes," Vincent said, his voice low and cold. "That's why I need to get this information out to the galaxy."

"What is it?" I asked, suddenly intrigued. "What could you possibly do to fix your damned reputation."

"Not fix it, but maybe..." Vincent's voice trailed off. "I will look less insane."

"I doubt it," I said. "It'll also get millions killed."

"If that's the price of justice."

I almost laughed. Vincent had decided to play the noble victim because the rest of society, even his so-called allies, treated him like a pariah. I would have had a lot more sympathy for him if he hadn't waited centuries to come clean. No, this was the mid-life crisis version of being Paul on the road to Damascus. Biblical history was another thing I was aware of thanks to growing up on the cult planet of Crius. He was only doing it now because he had something to barter with and the Community was finally helping humanity. Something his revelations would destroy.

"You're coming with me," I said, keeping my pistol trained on him.

"For what purpose?" Vincent said, clearly not wanting to die.

Anne, meanwhile, was moving behind him, probably trying to record all of this.

"A High Protector wants you alive. We'll go through your list together and release it in parts. You'll get your platform and I'll help screw the system. Maybe we can release it in a way that doesn't end up stopping the Community from helping rebuild Earth and the Human League."

"I—" Vincent started to say before a handcannon blast went through his chest and over my head. His body collapsed to its knees before his face landed against the ground. Anne Bonny was standing behind him.

"You wanted your story that badly?" I asked, looking at her quizzically and adjusting my personal energy shield's frequency with my free hand.

"My name is Lucia ni Bastille," Anne said, her voice full of disgust. "Vincent was my father."

"Ah," I said, understanding more than she could probably guess. "You were the one whose DNA they found."

Anne nodded. "I thought I hid myself better. My father only revealed I was a monster from a lineage hated throughout the universe when I was twenty. I fled and got myself a new life and identity. Yet, this man, this thing, wanted to come to me with his information."

"You always intended to kill him," I said.

"Yes," Anne said. "But I will release the information. It will destroy the Community's rebuilding efforts. I'll be a hero for betraying my father and exposing his foul alien ties."

I stared at her. "So, that's why Ida sent me. Albion's pro-human anti-Community ties are behind you."

"My actions will redeem the honor of the Bastille family," Anne said, raising her nose in disdain. Her gun was now pointed at me. "I will also be known as the woman who killed Cassius Mass, a hero who betrayed his nation to work for the dogs of the Commonwealth."

Anne aimed her gun and fired, only for her blast to strike against my personal barrier and dissipate. Her eyes widened as I aimed my fusion pistol upward and gunned her down.

I checked them both for the information Vincent stole on the way out. It had been in his dinner jacket pocket and was completely fried by Anna's blast. No one was getting their honor back today.

Ida was still satisfied with the way events turned out. The money we made from selling the *Kvari Princess* back to its holding company and the robberies kept us flying for a little while longer. Ida's High Protector friend would announce to the world that Vincent Bastille had finally been caught and killed by unknown Community-backed operatives. I recognized him as an older but still recognizable Vance Turbo, one of the most famous humans of all time. He was also one of the ancestors in my house's progenitor list. Beside him was his wife, the elder bioroid Trish, and another woman that I didn't recognize but was familiar somehow.

High Protector's face looked like mine. Older, wiser, and more bitter perhaps. He was trying to tilt at windmills for the greater good.

History marched on.

LEXICON

AI: Artificial intelligence. Science fiction has talked about these a few times.

Admiralty Board: The head of Space Fleet for Earth and those who supervise its link to other navies as part of the Community.

Albion: An island-filled water planet settled by humans abducted by aliens. The most powerful human planet, currently losing ground to Earth.

Ant: A race of (seemingly) giant, ant-like aliens that are terrifying and strong. It turns out those were chasses for a much, much smaller race.

Artificial Gravity: A slang term for something people think is possible but is not. Even the Community just generates the real thing with a variety of tricks.

Bastarve: Another word for bastard. Swearing isn't very original on Albion.

Belenus: A wealthy, environmentally friendly paradise world also settled by humans abducted by aliens. Traditional rivals to Albion.

Biash: A gendered insult, usually used in context of one's ancestry.

Biomods: Genetic enhancements that provide sapient beings with special abilities. Usually, organic technology rather than cybernetics to avoid rejection.

Bioroids: Androids and gynoids indistinguishable from humans with synthetic flesh. Often used for exactly what you think.

The Codex: A massive space station that exists perpetually in jumpspace around Space Academy. The secret headquarters of Department Twelve. It is tapped into much of the Community's infospace and encrypted data.

Cognition AI: Nearly omnipotent AI that can process unlimited amounts of data. Pretty much the real rulers of the Community. But so friendly!

Community: An interstellar fellowship of many species and worlds. It is generally pro-democracy, civil rights, diversity, and technology. Of course, no one trusts it or its activities. Community Protectors: See Space Fleet.

Community Senate: A collection of representatives of the various worlds of the Community. Many planets dislike it because it impedes their own ambitions while others hate that it is dominated by the High Council.

Contested Space: A region of space between the Community and Notha Empire. It is full of outlaw settlements, pirate bands, half-terraformed hellholes and collapsed civilizations. It ceased to exist as an official entity after the last treaty with the Notha.

Core Worlds: The center of the galaxy where the Elder Races choose to live.

Deathworld: A jungle world on the edge of the Notha Union that was formerly one of the key strongholds of the Notha Empire. It is inhabited by a Notha minority that has sought closer ties with the Community over the Notha Union. It is also one of the few to ban slavery and provide limited protections for non-Notha.

Demihumans: Humans who no longer are strictly human due to evolution and genetic modification.

Department Twelve: A renegade Earth-based intelligence organization that has grown incredibly powerful in recent years, arguably more so than EarthGov itself. It sponsors an isolationist pro-human agenda that wishes to seize Elder Race technology for itself.

The *Dreadnought*: The sister ship of the *Melampus* and former vessel of Captain Kathy Tagawa. It is now captained by Shelly T'Ketra.

Drolochid: Slimy, warm-blooded, multi-limbed race with sensory organs across their pill bug bodies. Quite pleasant to be around.

Earth: The human homeworld. Perhaps you've heard of it. The new kids on the block. Way too eager to prove itself.

EarthGov: The government of Earth. Duh.

Elder Races: Several godlike "sufficiently advanced" aliens who live in the galactic Core and decide what races live or die without any understandable criteria. Real jerks.

Enigmatic Path: A Kolahn terrorist organization and religious fundamentalist group. Its bizarre ideology is about how organic life is an abomination, AI should be liberated, and the universe is a simulation.

Ethereal Humans: A group of humans uplifted by the Elder Races to be intermediaries with them and other organics. They and Ethereal versions of other races tend to lead the Community in its decision-making process.

The High Council: A group of appointees above the Community Senate that wield most of the power in the galaxy. They are generally content to enforce the will of the Elder Races and continue the slow expansion of the Community in perpetuity. Most members serve for centuries.

High Protector: A special investigator for the High Council that wields authority in their name until they deem otherwise. Somewhere between a Supreme Court Justice and four star general. Appointments are for life.

Home Fleet: Earth's personal defense force. It is separate from the ships it loans to permanent Community duty.

Human League: An attempt to bring all human planets under one united banner to wield more economic and political power in the Community. It is primarily driven by Albion and Earth. Most Community members support the idea as too many individual human polities confuse things.

Infospace: An extra-dimensional communications system that allows faster-than-light communication and works like an interstellar internet. Also, can be used as a virtual reality interface.

Jumpdrive: What allows people to travel through space like in movies.

Jumpspace: A dimension of bizarre physics that makes faster-than-light travel possible. Looking at it will drive most people insane like staring into the sun due to the way it stimulates your synapses.

Kolahn: Resemble giant apes with scales. Their civilization was overtaken by a terrorist cult and promptly bombed back to the stone age by the Community. Its survivors are, paradoxically, living as refugees throughout the Community.

Kolahn Wars: The wars that bombed the Kolahn back to the Stone Age.

Luna: Earth's moon. It is largely used for the construction of spacecraft for civilian and military spacecraft and other advanced electronics incapable of being manufactured on Earth.

Melampus: A *Dreadnought*-class, Community-constructed vessel that was created for its High Protectors. It is equipped with a small amount of Elder Race technology.

Notha: Adorable lemur-like race of Space Nazi bastards.

Notha's Destiny: The flagship of the Notha Union and a replica of the Notha Empire's vehicle. It contains a substantial amount of the Notha Union's military power and is a massive drain on their resources to maintain.

Notha Empire: A corrupt military dictatorship ruled by the Notha that practiced slavery, imperialism, planet looting, and conquest. It maintained its existence not by competence but due to the possession of weapons of stellar destruction. When SKAMMs were outlawed by the Elder Races and the Great Notha died, the organization collapsed.

Notha Union: The successor state of the Notha Empire that emerged after the Thord Treaty of Exarxes. It is about 75% as big and headed by a new Great Notha who dreams of restoring the Empire.

Notha War: A conflict that resulted in the destruction of seventeen inhabited planets on both sides of the conflict due to an exchange of SKAMMs.

Perseus Arm: A largely-unexplored arm of the Milky Way galaxy.

Plizzed: A state of fluid retention. Used as a pejorative.

Primordials: An extra-galactic race that has severe issues with the Elder Races. They are from the Large Magellanic Cloud and formerly inhabited the Milky Way a billion years ago before fleeing to settle it. Their vessels exist in both jumpspace and realspace simultaneously. They recently suffered a humiliating loss that has briefly put them off galactic genocide.

Security Departments: The twelve, yes, twelve intelligence agencies working for the Community.

SKAMMs: Sun destroying weapons of interstellar destruction. They are horrifying devices and their use in the recent Notha War resulted in an immediate end to the conflict lest the two sides annihilate one another.

Sklux: A race of protoplasmic beings that can shape into a rough approximation of any form. Obsessed with puns. Considered a race of mediators and peacemakers, primarily by themselves.

Space Vampires: A mythical race of jumpspace predators that the Notha have countless stories about preying upon their race. They can somehow assume both the shape and memory of living individuals that even powerful scanners can't detect the difference.

Sons of Humanity: A human hate group that is funded by transtellar billionaires in order to make business with aliens less attractive. This is so that human-run ones can profit from the lack of competition. They are ignorant and small minded. Most members hail from Albion, Earth, or Contested Space. Recently removed from the list of known terrorist groups in the Human League.

Sorkanan: One of the oldest and most powerful species in space. They are a humanoid reptilian species with multiple offshoots.

Sorkanan Imperial Navy: The massive fleets of the Sorkanan Empire. Its conditions are horrifying, and morale is generally low but it is still the greatest power in the Spiral.

Space Academy: The training center for officers in the Community Protectors.

Spacer: A slang term for those who have grown up and primarily live in space.

Space Fleet: The Community's massive interstellar Navy that is (allegedly) a galactic force for good.

The Spire: What Orion's Arm is called by most races of the Known Universe as they are primarily concentrated there.

Sun Killer: Another name for SKAMM torpedoes.

Transtellar: The name for interplanetary corporations that are possessed of resources far more than individual worlds. They wield disproportionate power in the Community and among humanity's various worlds.

Treaty of Exarxes: A large multispecies agreement on shared morality and behavior during wartime. The Notha are a very reluctant signatory. A second treaty was drafted to ban the use of SKAMMs and other weapons of mass destruction at the insistence of the Elder Races. A third treaty was recently signed that helped define Contested Space better between the Notha and Community.

Unification Wars: The war where the Neo-Militarists and transtellars were defeated before the Community friendly EarthGov was born.

Union of Faith: A group of thirty-six worlds settled by medieval Christians, Muslims, Jews, Buddhists, and other religions that have created a theocracy within the Community. Weirdly, religious tolerance is in its constitution but almost everything else is regulated to a ridiculous degree.

Verdantian: A leonine race with six limbs that were uplifted by the Elder Races according to their belief structure.

AUTHOR'S NOTE

I'd like to thank you for reading this book. The publishing industry is changing dramatically since the advent of eBooks. It is now very difficult to get any book noticed, regardless of quality. If you enjoyed this book, you could do some very simple things to help me attract attention. Word of mouth is the number one source of success for novels, so simply telling family and friends about the book is a great start.

Here are a few other ways of helping out, if you are so inclined:

* **Post a rating or review where you purchased the eBook**
* **Post a rating or review on Goodreads**
* **Talk about the book or write a review on Facebook**
* **Tell folks about the book in a blog post.**

If you like any of my other books, please feel free to check them out. A lot of my series are interlinked, and you never know when you'll find someone familiar showing up. In this case, *Space Academy Dropouts* is set in the far future of my Agent G cyberpunk books and the past of my *Lucifer's Star* series. Fans will certainly get a kick out of seeing how the galaxy changes in a few centuries either way.

ABOUT THE AUTHORS

Michael Suttkus, II, lives in Leesburg, Florida, with three cats, one of which actually likes him, and his family, with whom he fares better. When not working at a game store, he's playing games, reading science books, or otherwise being incredibly nerdy. Also writing! Because he has to feed cats whether they like him or not.

Bibliography

I Was a Teenage Weredeer (The Bright Falls Mysteries, Book 1)
An American Weredeer in Michigan (The Bright Falls Mysteries, Book 2)
A Nightmare on Elk Street (The Bright Falls Mysteries, Book 3)

Lucifer's Star (Lucifer's Star #1)
Lucifer's Nebula (Lucifer's Star #2)

Brightblade (The Morgan Detective Agency, Book 1)
Brighteyes (The Morgan Detective Agency, Book 2)

Space Academy Dropouts (The Space Academy Series, Book 1)
Space Academy Rejects (The Space Academy Series, Book 2)
Space Academy Washouts (The Space Academy Series, Book 3)
Space Academy Miscreants (The Space Academy Series, Book 4)
Space Academy Vagrants (The Space Academy Series, Book 5)
Space Academy Graduates (The Space Academy Series, Book 6)

C. T. Phipps is a lifelong student of horror, science fiction, and fantasy. An avid tabletop gamer, he discovered this passion led him to write and turned him into a lifelong geek. He is a regular blogger and also a reviewer for The Bookie Monster.

Bibliography

Novels

The Rules of Supervillainy (Supervillainy Saga #1)
The Games of Supervillainy (Supervillainy Saga #2)
The Secrets of Supervillainy (Supervillainy Saga #3)
The Kingdom of Supervillainy (Supervillainy Saga #4)
The Tournament of Supervillainy (Supervillainy Saga #5)
The Future of Supervillainy (Supervillainy Saga #6)
The Horror of Supervillainy (Supervillainy Saga #7)
Tales of Supervillainy: Cindy's Seven (Supervillainy Saga #7)

I Was a Teenage Weredeer (The Bright Falls Mysteries, Book 1)
An American Weredeer in Michigan (The Bright Falls Mysteries, Book 2)
A Nightmare on Elk Street (The Bright Falls Mysteries, Book 3)

Esoterrorism (Red Room, Vol. 1)

Eldritch Ops (Red Room, Vol. 2)
The Fall of the House (Red Room, Vol. 3)

Agent G: Infiltrator (Agent G, Vol. 1)
Agent G: Saboteur (Agent G, Vol. 2)
Agent G: Assassin (Agent G, Vol. 3)

Cthulhu Armageddon (Cthulhu Armageddon, Vol. 1)
The Tower of Zhaal (Cthulhu Armageddon, Vol. 2)
The Tree of Azathoth (Cthulhu Armageddon, Vol. 3)

Lucifer's Star (Lucifer's Star, Vol. 1)
Lucifer's Nebula (Lucifer's Star, Vol. 2)

Straight Outta Fangton (Straight Outta Fangton, Vol. 1)
100 Miles and Vampin' (Straight Outta Fangton, Vol. 2)
Vampiraz4Life (Straight Outta Fangton, Vol. 3)

Wraith Knight (Wraith Knight, Vol. 1)
Wraith Lord (Wraith Knight, Vol. 2)
Wraith King (Wraith Knight, Vol. 3)

Dark Destiny (Dark Destiny, Vol. 1)
Destiny's Paradox (Dark Destiny, Vol. 2)

Brightblade (The Morgan Detective Agency, Book 1)
Brighteyes (The Morgan Detective Agency, Book 2)

Daughter of the Cyber Dragons (The Cyber Dragons Series, Book 1)
Revenge of the Cyber Dragons (The Cyber Dragons Series, Book 2)
End of the Cyber Dragons (The Cyber Dragons Series, Book 3)

Space Academy Dropouts (The Space Academy Series, Book 1)
Space Academy Rejects (The Space Academy Series, Book 2)

Space Academy Washouts (The Space Academy Series, Book 3)
Space Academy Miscreants (The Space Academy Series, Book 4)
Space Academy Vagrants (The Space Academy Series, Book 5)
Space Academy Graduates (The Space Academy Series, Book 6)

Moon Cops on the Moon (Moon Cops, Book 1)
Moon City Vice (Moon Cops, Book 2)

Lords of Dragon Keep (Dragon Keep, Book 1)
Guardians of Dragon Keep (Dragon Keep, Book 2)

Psycho Killers in Love

Tales of an Eldritch Wasteland

Anthologies (as editor)
Blackest Knights
Blackest Spells
Tales of Capes and Cowls
Tales of the Al-Azif
Tales of Yog-Sothoth
The Book of Hastur

Lucifer's Star (Lucifer's Star, Vol. 1)
Lucifer's Nebula (Lucifer's Star, Vol. 2)

Straight Outta Fangton (Straight Outta Fangton, Vol. 1)
100 Miles and Vampin' (Straight Outta Fangton, Vol. 2)
Vampiraz4Life (Straight Outta Fangton, Vol. 3)

Wraith Knight (Wraith Knight, Vol. 1)
Wraith Lord (Wraith Knight, Vol. 2)
Wraith King (Wraith Knight, Vol. 3)

Dark Destiny (Dark Destiny, Vol. 1)
Destiny's Paradox (Dark Destiny, Vol. 2)

Brightblade (The Morgan Detective Agency, Book 1)

Space Academy Dropouts (The Space Academy Series, Book 1)
Space Academy Rejects (The Space Academy Series, Book 2)
Space Academy Washouts (The Space Academy Series, Book 3)

Psycho Killers in Love

Anthologies (as editor)
Blackest Knights
Blackest Spells
Tales of Capes and Cowls
Tales of the Al-Azif
Tales of Yog-Sothoth

Curious about other Crossroad Press books? Stop by our website:
http://crossroadpress.com
We offer quality writing
in digital, audio, and print formats.

Subscribe to our newsletter on the website homepage and receive a
free eBook.